Lady Tregowan's Will

Three penniless half sisters.
An unexpected inheritance. A year to wed.

When Lady Tregowan dies, she leaves an
unexpected will. Her estate is to be divided
between the three illegitimate daughters of her
late husband—complete strangers until now.
The terms? They must live together in London
for a year and find themselves husbands or
forfeit their inheritance!

The Rags-to-Riches Governess

When Leah Thame kisses her enigmatic boss,
the Earl of Dolphinstone, she must choose
between a marriage without love or life
as an independent woman.

The Cinderella Heiress

Beatrice Foth
a marriage of co
she doesn't e
y

The Penniless Debutante

Left destitute when her parents die,
Aurelia Croome doesn't trust men—especially
aristocratic ones. Until she meets Maximilian,
Lord Tregowan...

Author Note

I do hope you've enjoyed reading about Leah, Beatrice and Aurelia and their happily-ever-afters. I know I've thoroughly enjoyed writing these stories, even if Aurelia in particular didn't behave quite in the way I originally planned!

It's hard to say goodbye to the couples I've invested so much time in, especially as I wrote these three stories during lockdown at a time when all of our worlds were upended and none of us knew what the future would bring. It helped me to lose myself in my fictional world, where I could be sure that, no matter what else was going on, there would definitely be a happy ending. I hope reading romance has given you some sort of escape from reality, as well!

But—me being me—we might not have to say goodbye to the Tregowan heiresses forever because the stories are set within my wider Regency world and, if you've read all three, you might have noticed some old friends making a brief appearance! So, in the future, who knows? We may meet Leah and Dolph, Beatrice and Jack or Aurelia and Max again. So it's not really goodbye, but *au revoir*.

Until then, please stay safe, and do stay in touch via my website or on social media.

JANICE PRESTON

The Penniless Debutante

ISBN-13: 978-1-335-40746-7

The Penniless Debutante

Copyright © 2021 by Janice Preston

This edition published by arrangement with Harlequin Books S.A.

For questions and comments about the quality of this book, please contact us at CustomerService@Harlequin.com.

Harlequin Enterprises ULC
22 Adelaide St. West, 40th Floor
Toronto, Ontario M5H 4E3, Canada
www.Harlequin.com

Printed in U.S.A.

Recycling programs
for this product may
not exist in your area.

ISBN-13: 978-1-335-40746-7

The Penniless Debutante

Copyright © 2021 by Janice Preston

Harlequin Enterprises ULC
22 Adelaide St. West, 40th Floor
Toronto, Ontario M5H 4E3, Canada
www.Harlequin.com

Printed in U.S.A.

Janice Preston grew up in Wembley, North London, with a love of reading, writing stories and animals. In the past she has worked as a farmer, a police call handler and a university administrator. She now lives in the West Midlands with her husband and two cats and has a part-time job with a weight-management counselor—vainly trying to control her own weight despite her love of chocolate!

Books by Janice Preston

Harlequin Historical

Regency Christmas Wishes
"Awakening His Sleeping Beauty"
The Earl with the Secret Past

Lady Tregowan's Will

The Rags-to-Riches Governess
The Cinderella Heiress
The Penniless Debutante

The Lochmore Legacy

His Convenient Highland Wedding

The Beauchamp Heirs

Lady Olivia and the Infamous Rake
Daring to Love the Duke's Heir
Christmas with His Wallflower Wife

The Beauchamp Betrothals

Cinderella and the Duke
Scandal and Miss Markham
Lady Cecily and the Mysterious Mr. Gray

Visit the Author Profile page
at Harlequin.com for more titles.

For my wonderful editor, Julia Williams,
who has never failed to improve my stories
with her insights and suggestions.
Thank you x

Chapter One

Miss Aurelia Croome had become so accustomed to the nausea that came with hunger she now barely noticed it. As she stood on the kerb watching the post-chaise carrying the second of her newly acquired half-sisters away from her, however, the mixture of feelings that churned her stomach was more complex, even though the hunger—that dreaded hunger—still lurked. A reminder of the dangers of life for a woman alone.

Not for much longer, though.

She hugged the knowledge to herself, barely able to believe the change in her fortunes since she had arrived at the offices of Messrs Henshaw and Dent, solicitors, for a noon meeting that day—a meeting during which Henshaw had informed her and the other two attendees that not only were they half-sisters, but they were also joint beneficiaries under the will of Lady Tregowan, widow of their natural father, the late Lord Tregowan.

An heiress! Her! After so many years of struggle for her and Mama, both before and after the death of Augustus Croome, the man who had raised her, when she was eleven. Thirteen years ago now. He had left them penniless, and Mama had worked tirelessly to provide for them both until her own untimely death last year.

Aurelia shook the memories of her more recent past from her head. She would not dwell on them, or on the hunger. Or the fear. They were history. She had a future now and family—the two half-sisters she had met for the first time today, when they had all learned that the men they had believed to be their fathers had been bribed to wed all three of their mothers after the late Lord Tregowan—clearly as entitled and selfish as all aristocratic men—had got them with child.

A biting breeze darted down the Bristol street, sneaking through her threadbare coat. Aurelia shivered, wrapping her arms around her waist and tucking her chin into her chest. It was time to return to the shelter of the general office of Henshaw and Dent, where Mr Henshaw had told her she might wait for his clerk to return with her ticket for that afternoon's mail coach to London. She turned from the roadside and was almost sent flying as she cannoned into a tall, greatcoat-clad figure. As she teetered on the edge of the kerbstone, two hands gripped her shoulders—hard—and she found herself hauled against a broad, solid chest.

'Watch where you're going!'

At that barked reprimand, Aurelia's gaze moved up from the large, bone button mere inches from the tip of her nose, the mingled scents of soap, dust, sandalwood and musky male wreathing through her senses. Her dazed vision travelled up past a pair of wide shoulders and a tired-looking neckcloth, to a jutting chin complete with a deep cleft and shadowed with stubble and then to a mouth, currently pursed with displeasure and yet somehow giving the impression of mobility, with lips so beautifully sculpted her fingers twitched with the urge to *touch*.

Her own gasp rattled Aurelia back to reality, and she tore her gaze from that fascinating mouth to find herself the subject of a scowling glare from a pair of the darkest brown eyes, shaded beneath the brim of a beaver hat and surrounded by unexpectedly long, thick lashes any woman would envy. As their eyes locked, however, his glare softened, his eyes widening and, astonishingly, darkening still further. She got the sense he actually *saw* her, his eyes boring into hers with unbearable intensity, causing a strange fluttering response deep in her belly.

Aurelia tore her gaze from his, breaking that spell, and she scanned him once again. This time, with her all her faculties on the alert. A gentleman. Her hackles rose. A gentleman like Augustus Croome, impecunious younger son of an earl, who she had just learned had accepted a bribe to marry Mama when she was with child and who had subsequently made both their lives hell. No wonder he had despised his young daughter, openly mocking her if she tried to gain his attention or approval.

It was her turn to scowl as she met his eyes again, this time with her guard well and truly up.

'I could say the same to you. *Sir.*'

The man stilled momentarily, his eyebrows flicking up as he held her gaze. A muscle twitched at the corner of his mouth; he stepped back and raised his hat to reveal a shock of dark brown hair. His gaze swept over Aurelia, from head to foot and back again, provoking firstly the regret she looked so very shabby and careworn and, secondly, igniting a flash of annoyance at that misplaced regret and for even *noticing* his handsome features. Augustus had been handsome, and her mother had worshipped him despite him treating her like dirt. Poor, poor Mama.

'I beg your pardon, ma'am. My fault entirely. Good day.'

He bowed, sidestepped Aurelia, and continued on his

way…straight to the door of Messrs Henshaw and Dent. He rapped loudly. Impatiently. Every rigid line of his body screamed suppressed anger. Aurelia remained where she was as her racing heart steadied, loath to reveal the office was also her own destination. The door opened and the stoop-shouldered clerk who had earlier shown her up to Henshaw's office appeared. His sallow skin paled, leaving a spot of colour on each cheek.

'Lord Tregowan!' He bowed low. 'Is…is Mr Henshaw expecting you, my lord?'

Tregowan? Oh, dear God! Her pulse raced once again, this time at the implications of his arrival at the solicitor's office. *No wonder he's enraged.*

'He is now,' growled Tregowan and stalked into the building.

Henshaw had earlier revealed the current Lord Tregowan had been the beneficiary of Lady Tregowan's will until she had unexpectedly, and without Mr Henshaw's knowledge, made a new will leaving her entire estate between Aurelia and her two new half-sisters, Leah Thame and Beatrice Fothergill.

Surely I owe it to Leah and Beatrice to find out more about Lord Tregowan before we have to face him?

Having justified to herself her desire to learn more, Aurelia hurried across the pavement before the clerk closed the door. She put her finger to her lips and he nodded, allowing her inside before chasing after the fast-disappearing Lord Tregowan, who was already halfway up the steep, narrow stairs.

The general office where Aurelia was supposed to wait was through a door to the left. Aurelia ignored it. She wanted to hear what Tregowan had to say when he tackled Henshaw about missing out on the inheritance. The solicitor's earlier words echoed through her head.

'*Lord Tregowan—the current Lord Tregowan—will be unhappy, you may be sure of that. I have written to him again, to clarify matters. Bad tidings for him, but I did not draw up this will, you understand. I thought I had her latest will and testament—drawn up by me and signed and witnessed three years ago in this very office.*'

She hurried up the stairs, back to Henshaw's office. The door was ajar, the clerk blocking the opening. The irate Lord Tregowan was inside, his exasperated words clearly audible. Aurelia darted up the first few steps of the staircase to the upper storeys, to hide from the clerk as he exited the room and shut the door. As he went downstairs, she flitted across the landing and pressed her ear to Henshaw's office door.

'What the devil was the meaning of that first letter, Henshaw? You explicitly informed me I was Sarah's heir... I have secured a loan on the strength of that letter. Do you have any idea of the trouble you have caused?'

Yet another entitled aristocrat running up debt and borrowing money to clear it.

Memories of Augustus strong, Aurelia determinedly suppressed any notion of sympathy for the man and told herself she enjoyed hearing him squirm.

'I can only humbly apologise, my lord. Indeed, it was not my intention to mislead you. No, not at all. But you will recall the precise wording in my first letter was that *to my knowledge* Lady Tregowan had no more recent will than the one we discussed last year. If you made financial decisions based on an unconfirmed matter mentioned in correspondence, I can hardly be held accountable. Lady Tregowan's recent will was drafted by another firm of solicitors. But there is no doubt as to its authenticity.'

'And who the hell are these imposters who turned Sarah against me and purloined what should by rights be mine?'

Imposters? Purloined? The utter gall of the man.

'They are three young women, but I regret I can divulge no further information. Client confidentiality, you know.'

The sound of a chink of glass reached Aurelia and her stomach rumbled in response, reminding her to eat before getting on the mail coach which, according to Henshaw, left the Bush Tavern in Corn Street at four o'clock. Aurelia was the only one of the three half-sisters to travel straight to London. The other two were to return to their homes first to put their affairs in order before—in accordance with one of the conditions of the will—living in London for the entirety of the upcoming Season at the now jointly owned Tregowan House under the chaperonage of a Mrs Butterby, Lady Tregowan's erstwhile companion.

They were lucky to have homes to return to, she thought glumly. Although—recalling Beatrice's timidity and her seeming fear of her brother—maybe not so fortunate in her case. Aurelia had no reason to return to Bath, where she had been living in squalid lodgings for the past month, frantic with the worry of how she could earn enough to live without turning to that traditional, age-old occupation for destitute females.

She shivered at how very close she had come to succumbing to prostitution, driven to desperation by the debts that had built up relentlessly during Mama's final illness despite Aurelia working as hard as she could in their milliner's shop while also caring for her mother. When Mama died, Aurelia had had no choice but to overcome her wariness of others, especially men. Distrust she had learned at Augustus's hands. She had confided in the landlord of the shop, begging him to rent her the premises on the same terms as her mother, promising to work night and day until she could pay what they owed. Rather than help her, he had taken full advantage of her desperate situation by doubling the rent, before offering to lower it on condition Aurelia allowed him to visit her in the rooms above whenever he chose.

She shuddered at the memory. He had thrown her out the same day she declined his offer, keeping all Mama's stock to clear their rent arrears. Aurelia had then turned to their neighbours—fellow milliners and dressmakers and, she thought, their friends—for employment. But the moment they smelled her desperation for a job they had exploited her desperate need by offering her a wretched pittance—not even sufficient to live on. She'd had no option but to accept, but she often went hungry.

'What are their plans for Falconfield?'

Falconfield Hall was the estate in Somersetshire that had been left to Aurelia and her half-sisters, along with Tregowan House and a considerable sum of money invested in funds.

Five thousand pounds a year each. Exhilaration spiralled through Aurelia. She need never go hungry again.

'I cannot say, my lord. No...' Henshaw's voice contained a note of alarm and Aurelia pictured the furious Earl, towering over the solicitor. 'Truly I cannot say. This was all news to them, too. They had no idea about the inheritance, nor about the conditions attached to it.'

'Conditions?' Tregowan's eagerness was almost painful to hear. Almost. 'What conditions? If they fail to meet them, might I still have a chance of inheriting *something* at least?'

How Aurelia wished it could have been Augustus having his hopes dashed like this. That would have been a joy to hear. He had learned nothing by being disowned by his family even before he married Mama, just as Tregowan would likely learn nothing from this. He would still doubtless run up debts without a care in the world, leaving tradesmen and other good, honest folk unpaid—men and women who worked hard for every penny, just like Mama had been forced to do after Augustus died, leaving her and Aurelia with nothing.

'I'm afraid I really cannot divulge any more than I already have, my lord,' Henshaw replied.

'If I could just know where to find them, though, Henshaw...you said they are young. I could marry one. An heiress would suit my purpose very well.'

Aurelia choked back a laugh, crossing her fingers Henshaw would not tell Tregowan about the other conditions of the will—one of which would utterly scupper that cynical plan of his. For not only had Henshaw told the three of them they must each marry within a year, or forfeit their share of the estate—a dreadful condition from Aurelia's point of view, as she loathed the thought of any man wielding such control over her—but the final condition concerned Lord Tregowan himself. They were forbidden from marrying the current Lord Tregowan—a distant cousin of the previous Earl—on pain of, once again, forfeiting their share. Aurelia held back her snort of derision. As if any of them were stupid enough to fall for the lies and sweet talk of a man such as this.

Henshaw had been unable to tell the half-sisters why those conditions were attached to their inheritance but Aurelia hoped Mrs Butterby could shed some light on those when she reached London, as well as what had caused Lady Tregowan to change her will not long before she died.

'All I will reveal is they are likely to be in London for the Season, my lord. And, I am afraid, my lips are totally sealed as to any further information.'

The sound of a chair scraping against the wooden floor reached Aurelia's ears and she eased away from the door.

'You do have my sympathy, my lord. I understand this

has come as a bitter blow. But I can do no more. The matter is entirely out of my hands. I apologise for the misunderstanding when I first wrote to inform you of Her Ladyship's passing but, as I said, I did emphasise it was the latest will of which I was aware. As soon as the second will came into my possession, I wrote to you immediately.'

'Very well. I can see my journey to Bristol was futile and there is nothing you can do. I shall bid you good day, Henshaw.'

Aurelia ran on tiptoes to the stairs and reached the bottom before the sound of the door opening above reached her. In the general office, the stooped clerk looked up and frowned when he saw her. Two younger clerks kept their heads down, pens scratching as they transcribed legal-looking documents.

'I wondered where you had gone, miss,' the chief clerk said.

'I—'

She snapped her mouth shut at the heavy tread of Tregowan descending the stairs and sent a silent plea for help to the clerk. He responded with a cynical smile and a jerk of his thumb to indicate she should go to the back of the room. There was no need to hide, however, for the door opened and banged shut without Tregowan showing his face in the office.

'Thank you,' Aurelia said.

'I doubt he'd be overjoyed to meet you, miss. Not at the moment. Now... Mr Smith—' the clerk indicated one of the younger clerks '—purchased a ticket on the mail on your behalf.' He held out a slip of paper. 'They have your name on the passenger list, but it will leave promptly at four whether or not you are aboard.'

Aurelia took the slip and put it safely in her reticule along with the sealed note Henshaw had written for Mrs

Butterby, the copy of Lady Tregowan's will and the leather pouch of money that Henshaw had given each of the half-sisters, not to mention all of her belongings that had any value to her—either practical, such as her brush and comb, or sentimental, such as the pincushion Mama had given to her. She had learned over the past weeks not to leave anything unattended in her lodgings, as they were likely to vanish.

She removed the leather pouch and opened it. A glance inside showed a variety of coins, including guineas. It was certainly heavy…just holding it made Aurelia feel safe and, again, she blessed her good fortune.

'Thank you,' she said, feeling humble. 'How much do I owe you for the ticket?'

The clerk waved in a dismissive motion. 'No need to repay now, miss. Mr Henshaw said it was to be put down as a disbursement against your share of the inheritance.'

An unaccustomed lump formed in Aurelia's throat. How long had it been since she felt safe? That's what this inheritance meant to her. Safety and security. Never again would she feel as though she were teetering along on a knife edge with the deep, dark chasm of the unknown gaping beneath her. One stumble…she had been just one stumble away from disaster, and she would never, ever forget it.

'Thank you,' she said again. She poked around in the pouch to find three sixpences and she gave one to each of the clerks. 'Thank you and goodbye.'

She headed out on to the street and turned in the direction of Corn Street, her heart lighter than it had been since Mama's death. She knew the way, having travelled to Bristol on the stagecoach with Mama a few times—it was not far, and she was looking forward to eating and drinking her fill at the Bush Tavern before the mail coach left for London.

Chapter Two

Max Penrose, Fourth Earl of Tregowan, strode away from the solicitor's office, blind to the direction he took. What did it matter? Deep in his heart, he'd known this impulsive dash to Bristol was a waste of time but… Angrily, he shook his head.

Damned fool! What the devil did I expect? That Henshaw would turn round and say there'd been a mistake?

He laughed out loud, causing a passing woman to eye him suspiciously and move to put the width of the pavement between them.

What in Hades am I to do now?

Henshaw was right…he should never have taken out a loan on anything less than a cast-iron guarantee the Tregowan inheritance was his. But he'd *trusted* Sarah—his predecessor's widow—when she had assured him she would see him right eventually, after the Third Earl had bequeathed his entire unentailed estate to his widow eight years ago. That had left Max—as his rightful heir—with only the title and the entailed property, consisting of the dilapidated, debt-ridden Tregowan estate in Cornwall. Any profits produced by the estate during his predecessor's tenure had been siphoned off and poured into Falconfield

Hall and its lands to provide old Tregowan and Sarah with a sumptuous home in Somerset.

Max thrust open the door of the first alehouse he passed. The interior was dim and there were no other customers, which suited him perfectly. He marched to a table in the corner, sitting out of habit with his back to the wall. A serving wench approached.

'Ale and a plate of your ordinary, please.'

He tossed a coin on the table, not even glancing at her, not in the mood for any sort of flirtatious exchange.

Where on earth can we all live? If only Mama had not taken it into her head to come back to England.

If only he had been honest about the state of Tregowan from the first…but Mama, who needed a wheelchair to get around most of the time, and Max's sister, Leticia, had lived in Italy for almost ten years now. Max had never expected them to return, even after his Italian grandparents died, and so he had seen little point in worrying them over the shaky state of his finances.

But Mama had been fretting that Letty was wasting her life caring for her and had decided the answer was to find her twenty-five-year-old daughter a husband. And where better to do that than in London during the Season? With few funds of her own, however, Mama had written to Max that the least a fond brother—now a peer of the realm—could do for his little sister was to sponsor her for a Season.

It would help that Mama and Letty would stay with Lady Langbrook—Mama's old school friend and Max's godmother—while they were in London, but Max would be expected to pick up the tab for all their expenses and, once the Season was over, Mama had been clear she saw her future home as being at Tregowan. And Letty's, too, if she failed to find a husband.

The serving maid returned, carrying a tray bearing a

steaming bowl, a plate with hunks of bread on it and a tankard and, as she set the tray on Max's table, she leaned over, displaying her deep cleavage. Max averted his eyes and, with an audible huff, the maid flounced away.

Max half drained the tankard, barely tasting the beer he swallowed, and set it down with a bang. He scrubbed his hand through his hair, then tore off a piece of bread and dipped it into the bowl of stew...mutton, by the smell of it.

The letter from Henshaw announcing Sarah, Lady Tregowan's death had reached him at Tregowan shortly after Mama's letter announcing their imminent return to London and Max had grabbed that lifeline with both hands. He'd lost no time in raising a loan against his expectations at the East Cornwall Bank in Liskeard, although Mr Robins, the senior partner, had needed some persuasion. Max had immediately engaged a team of builders and labourers to make a start on the work desperately needed to transform Tregowan Place into a fit home for the Earl of Tregowan and his descendants.

He ate a spoonful or two of the stew, with its chewy chunks of mutton and variety of root vegetables floating in a greasy broth, and grimaced before pushing the bowl away and draining his tankard. He signalled for a refill.

He'd had it all planned. After the Season ended, Mama and Letty would live at Falconfield Hall until the renovation of the Place was complete. It was uninhabitable as it stood: the smell of rot and decay pervaded the entire place, the roof leaked like a sieve and one entire wing would need to be demolished and rebuilt. Max's current residence was the old gatekeeper's lodge, which at least boasted a weatherproof roof and it was not big enough to house Mama and Letty, too. He would have to rent them a house in Liskeard. Or Launceston. He rubbed his forehead.

More expense! Damned, damned fool! Why the devil did I spend that inheritance before it was mine?

By the time Henshaw's second letter had reached him, he was irrevocably committed to at least the first stage of the renovation, with the entire roof already half removed. There could not be a worse time for Mama to take it into her head to return to England, even though he understood her concern about Letty's future. How on earth could he explain? He rubbed his forehead again. He was the head of the family and he had let them down just like his father had always let them down, with his gambling and his philandering.

The maid poured him another measure of ale and Max nodded his thanks. He swigged a mouthful, then stared down into the tankard as ideas and possible solutions ricocheted around inside his head. He had no idea how long he sat there, thinking and getting nowhere, but he was eventually dragged from his thoughts as someone slid on to the bench seat on the opposite side of his table.

'You look like a man who enjoys a game, sir.' The newcomer grinned, revealing long, yellowing teeth in a thin face, as he placed a deck of cards on the table between them. 'D'you fancy a hand or two?'

'I don't gamble,' Max growled.

Except on a foolish impulse, the minute I heard of Sarah's demise. I deserve everything I get.

He'd liked Sarah. *Trusted* her. She'd seemed fond of him, too, in that she didn't share her late husband's prejudice against Max's father—an inveterate gambler—and, hence, against Max himself. She had no other family and she had *told* him the last time he visited her that she had left him everything. Why would he doubt Henshaw's first missive? It seemed Sarah had duped him. Very successfully. Although he couldn't fathom why she would play such a cruel trick. He felt again the sick hammer blow to his chest that he had experienced on reading Henshaw's second letter. The words that told him he was no longer Sarah's heir…that he had been cut out of her will entirely. Nausea gripped his throat, choking him as he contemplated once again the disaster staring him in the face.

He shoved back his chair and stood up, draining his tankard of ale.

'Gambling is a fool's game,' he added to his fellow customer. He looked at a clock on the mantelshelf over the hearth where a sullen fire burned. Quarter to four! Where had the time gone? 'And I have somewhere to be.'

'Please yerself.' The man shrugged. 'Never said nothing 'bout money changing hands, now, did I?'

Max contented himself with a glare and strode from the inn, leaving the rest of his food uneaten. Glancing back before he pulled the door shut, he saw the man pulling the plate of cold stew towards him. Any guilt Max felt for his unfriendliness was assuaged…at least the fellow would have something for his belly. He had the look of a hungry man.

That thought reminded him of the woman he had seen outside Henshaw and Dent earlier. She, too, had looked gaunt. Her fierce blue eyes—the colour of the ocean on a sunny day and framed by strong golden eyebrows and long, spiky lashes—had been altogether too dominant in a pretty, heart-shaped face marred by a dull complexion and unhealthily hollowed cheeks. He recalled that tug of awareness, deep in his gut, as their eyes had met and clung. The kick of his pulse. The heating of his blood. The ridiculous impulse to press his mouth to hers…to claim her.

He thrust her from his thoughts with a silent curse as he hesitated on the pavement outside the alehouse. He had no time to waste, but he realised he had no idea which way to turn.

'Which way is Corn Street, if you please?' he asked a passer-by.

The man sucked air in through his teeth and peered up and down the road. 'Corn Street...' he repeated, frowning.

'The Bush Tavern.' Max took care not to reveal his impatience. The mail coach left at four and he knew it would not wait if he wasn't there. 'I have a seat reserved on the London mail coach.'

It was bad enough he'd wasted money he didn't have on the diversion to Bristol rather than going straight to London where his family's arrival was imminent, but he had then compounded his stupidity by impulsively purchasing a ticket on the more expensive mail coach to complete his journey to London. Had he, in his initial panic—a panic he now recalled with a sense of shame—somehow, ridiculously, believed he could change reality by coming to Bristol to confront Henshaw? There was no logic in his doing so and he damned himself for allowing his troubles to obliterate his good sense. So many impulsive, inexplicable decisions and, facing him, a quandary of gargantuan proportions.

'Ah! *Corn* Street.' The passer-by nodded sagely. 'It's that way, sir. First left and then left again.'

Max touched the brim of his hat. 'My thanks.'

As he hurried in the direction the man had indicated, the face of the woman Max had bumped into materialised again in his mind's eye. He felt once again that jolt of pure energy that had seized him as he had gripped her shoulders to steady her, recalling their boniness, and wondered what her story might be and how she had ended up on a Bristol street on the last day of January in a threadbare black coat and shabby chip-straw bonnet, looking as though she had not eaten a decent meal in days.

Her lack of a Bristolian accent had declared her education and gentle birth when she had, quite rightly, snapped straight back at him given his own gruff reaction to their collision. Surely only a female of his own class would have dared to answer him back as she did. *'I could say the same to you.* Sir.' The pure sarcasm contained in that single, final word brought forth a grin now although, at the time, he had been in no mood for grinning…far too intent on tackling Henshaw about that fateful second letter—the letter that had dashed all his hopes and sent his mood spiralling downwards at dizzying speed.

Max broke into a trot and grinned again, this time mirthlessly. Two penniless waifs, down on their luck, whose paths had crossed and were destined never to cross again.

He turned into Corn Street, recognising the four-storey outline of the Bush Tavern up ahead. The Royal Mail coach stood at the front ready to go and Max now sprinted, holding his hat to his head. The guard—distinctive in his gold-braided red coat and cocked hat—stood by the coach.

'How long before you leave?' Max puffed.

The guard consulted his fob watch. 'Four minutes, sir.'

'I'll be back.'

Max knew better than to ask them to wait for him. The Royal Mail would leave on time whether or not a paying passenger was on board. The Bush Tavern porter was by the door and he touched his hat as he recognised Max from earlier.

'I'll stow your bag aboard, sir.'

'Thank you.'

Max flipped him a penny and rushed to the privy, knowing he would get little to no time to relieve himself on the overnight journey and already regretting that second tankard of ale. He ran back outside and clambered into the coach just as the guard sounded his horn to signal their departure. The coach rocked into motion and Max collapsed into the only available seat—a backward-facing one, of course. They were always the least popular. He fished in the pocket of his greatcoat for his handkerchief, removed his hat and mopped his forehead, castigating himself bitterly for cutting it so fine when there had been no need. He replaced his handkerchief and his hat and then stared out of the window as they sped through Bristol.

No wonder my life is such an abominable mess. I can't even be trusted to keep track of the time.

'Nearly missed it, sir,' said a cheery voice. 'They'd not have waited, you know.'

'I am aware of that.'

Max dragged his attention from the passing streets. The owner of the voice sat opposite him…an older gentleman with a substantial girth, a ruddy complexion and the look of a prosperous farmer.

The man grinned at Max, his eyes twinkling as he held up his hands, palms forward. 'Nay, sir. Don't poker up on me. No insult intended, merely a friendly observation.'

Max pursed his lips. He deserved that reprimand, for he had been unintentionally brusque. 'My apologies, sir.' He thrust his hand out. 'Tregowan.'

Max's hand was pumped energetically. 'Ah… Cornwall… God's own country. Haven't I always said so, Mother?'

The plump woman seated beside the gentleman smiled contentedly. 'You have indeed, Father.'

'William Austerly, at your service, my lord. And this is my good lady wife, Mrs Austerly. We hail from near Redruth—Gwenhaven. You might have heard of it?'

Max felt his eyebrows climb. Gwenhaven was one of the largest, most prosperous estates in Cornwall—far further west than Tregowan—and its lands included several high-yielding tin and copper mines.

'I have indeed. It boasts an enviable reputation.' Max raised his hat. 'Delighted to meet you, sir. And you, Mrs Austerly.'

The thought of Austerly's successful mines dealt another blow to his self-esteem with yet another reminder of his own abject failure. On acceding to the Tregowan title and estate, he had reopened the tin mine, Wheal Rowenna—named for a previous Lady Tregowan—eager to provide much needed jobs for his tenants and neighbours, many of whom were poverty-stricken. He had done so knowing the risk but, as was his wont, he'd allowed his heart to rule his head because he so wanted to make a difference to those people's lives.

Since then, the mine had limped along at a loss, but Max could not bring himself to admit defeat and close it, causing the loss of so many livelihoods. Then, last year, he had taken a gamble and raised a loan to invest in the mine after a newly discovered seam of copper had shown promise. That gamble had ended in failure. The loan had simply not been enough and they'd had to give up the attempt to expand the mine. The recent bank loan he had secured against his inheritance—his non-existent inheritance—had not only been to start the refurbishment of Tregowan, but also to further invest in the mine.

'And allow me to introduce the fourth member of our merry travelling band,' said Mr Austerly. 'This is Miss Croome.'

Max shifted slightly in his seat in order to see the woman seated by his side. Those bright blue eyes pierced straight to his core...it was her! His fellow waif. His lips began to stretch into a smile of recognition, but the movement slowed at the wariness in her gaze and then reversed, his brows twitching into a frown as he recalled his brusqueness. Much as, he realised, with a touch of shame, his initial exchange with Austerly had been unnecessarily curt.

This must serve as a wake-up call for him. His predicament was no fault of these strangers and it was unfair of him to inflict his bad mood and his worries on them. He relaxed his brow and completed that smile, again raising his hat.

'I am delighted to make your acquaintance, Miss Croome.'

Chapter Three

Aurelia had pushed down the fear that gripped her the instant Lord Tregowan jumped into the coach and collapsed on to the seat beside her. Her teeth, quite without volition, had clenched so tightly a bolt of pain shot through her jaw. Logically, she knew he could not know who she was—Henshaw had not disclosed the names of the three new beneficiaries of Lady Tregowan's will—but still those old fears rose up, almost paralysing her in those first few moments.

As he settled, and during his exchange with Mr and Mrs Austerly, she concentrated on controlling her breathing and willing her pulse rate under control. Just the thought of being in a confined space with a man who had every reason to be angry with her—and who had already demonstrated his quickness to rouse to temper—made her insides quake, but she reached deep inside herself for the defiance that had stood her in good stead for so many years against Augustus Croome, the scoundrel who had pretended, even on his death bed, to be her father.

He, too, had been quick to anger and often lashed out when frustrated about his lack of funds and what he viewed as the burden of Mama and Aurelia. After his death—a blessing as far as she was concerned—Aurelia had promised herself that never would she allow *any* man to conduct a reign of terror over her, as Augustus had terrorised Mama.

While the men introduced themselves to one another, Mrs Austerly—kindly, motherly—caught Aurelia's eye and mouthed *Are you all right?* Aurelia nodded and unclenched the fists lying in her lap. It was the shock. That was all. She would survive this, as she had survived so much. After all, what could Tregowan do to her?

He could hurt you.

She cast an involuntarily glance at his large hands and flinched at the remembered force behind Augustus's blows.

But he won't, whispered the voice of reason she had cultivated over the years. *You are safe here and he does not know you.*

'This is Miss Croome.'

Her name, spoken by Mr Austerly, jerked her from her thoughts and the last vestiges of panic drained away, to be replaced by the defiance that was now an intrinsic part of her and with which she faced the world. She turned her head to acknowledge the introduction as Tregowan swivelled slightly to look at her. Aurelia elevated her chin and held his gaze.

His dark brown eyes were as beautiful as she remembered from their earlier encounter…but alluring eyes did not equal a good person. Or a trustworthy one. Although her eyes remained glued to his, she was aware his budding smile faltered as his brow darkened in a frown. The frown soon cleared, however, and his smile—revealing even, white teeth—widened as he raised his hat.

'I am delighted to make your acquaintance, Miss Croome.'

Aurelia, despite shame at her own shabby appearance, inclined her head graciously, in unconscious imitation of the many ladies who had frequented her mother's hat shop.

'My lord.'

His smile faded, but his lips twitched as though he found something amusing about her response and she felt again that strange fluttering sensation deep inside her. She pointedly looked away at Mrs Austerly.

'You were telling me about your daughters, ma'am?'

'Oh, yes.' Mrs Austerly's shoulders lifted as she smiled her delight at Aurelia's question. 'It is a rare treat for us, isn't it, Father?'

Her husband nodded, smiling benignly.

'We have been staying with our eldest, Mary, and her family. She is married to a most respected banker here in Bristol. Thomas Bell...do you know of him?'

Aurelia shook her head, but Mrs Austerly happily went on to tell her all about Mary's five children and how much they had enjoyed their stay.

'And now—' Mrs Austerly glanced sideways at her husband, her eyes alight with excitement '—*now*, we are off to London to stay with our *youngest* daughter, Emma. *She* married Lord Pewsey last year...a *baron*, don't you know? And we have been invited to stay in London with them for the Season...no high-and-mighty airs for dear Pewsey, you can be sure of that. He is not ashamed to ac-knowledge the likes of us as his family.'

She paused for breath and, feeling that some response was required from her, Aurelia said, 'Goodness. How ex-citing for you. But I do not see why anyone would be ashamed of having you and Mr Austerly as part of their family, dear ma'am.'

Mrs Austerly glowed at the compliment, then turned pink. 'I am sorry if I have run on a bit. I have never been to London, you know… I am so looking forward to it. I can hardly contain myself.'

Mr Austerly patted her hand. 'I can promise you will have a splendid time, Mother. Now then, enough about our lives. We don't want to bore His Lordship…let me see… Tregowan…that's the south-eastern edge of Bodmin Moor. Am I right?'

'It is.'

Tregowan's clipped response failed to deter Mr Austerly.

'You have a mine, if I remember rightly?'

'Yes. Wheal Rowenna. We mine tin and a small amount of copper.'

'Ah. Yes. A good area for copper.'

Aurelia closed her eyes as the two men discussed mining and farming matters. She didn't even try to understand all they talked about—lodes and shafts and ore and soil and crops and roofs and repairs—but she heard enough to fathom that Tregowan was in a bad state of repair. No wonder the man was so angry to miss out on Lady Tregowan's bequest.

Still… Sleep began to claim her as the coach swayed and the men's voices rumbled on. *That is his problem. I am off on the adventure of my life.*

Aurelia woke with a start at a blast from the guard's horn. She cranked open one eyelid. The interior of the coach was dark and the only sound from within the vehicle was a duet of snores from the opposite seat. Gradually, she became aware she was tilting to her left and that her cheek rested against fabric of some sort. She opened her other eye as the coach slowed. The darkness faded as light from outside fingered around the edges of the wooden shutters they had pegged up to cover the windows as night fell. She was reassured by the familiar sounds of the team being changed for fresh horses and of post bags being exchanged. This was one of the regular stops for the Royal Mail and they would soon be on their way again.

A movement of that fabric beneath her cheek roused her further, however, and, as realisation hit her, she sat bolt upright, her cheeks burning.

'Don't move on my account.' The low-voiced comment held more than a hint of amusement. 'I rather enjoyed being used as a pillow. Besides, you were keeping me warm and now I am like to catch a chill.'

Aurelia peeped sideways at Tregowan. His eyes glinted, reflecting a stray finger of light. He smelled rather nice—she identified the remembered notes of sandalwood and muskiness from their first encounter, now joined by the sweet, almost fruity scent of ale. The dimness of the coach interior and the lateness of the hour induced a sense of intimacy—she felt no threat now from being in a confined space with him…it was as though the surly responses when they first met and when he first climbed into the coach, and his rage when talking to Mr Henshaw, had come from a different man than the one who had chatted so amiably with Mr Austerly.

'I am certain your coat will provide adequate insulation.' Her instinctive snippy retort was ruined when an involuntary shiver racked her.

'But yours is entirely *in*adequate.'

He lifted his right arm sideways, but made no move to touch her. Just left it suspended in mid-air, with an inviting space beneath where she would fit perfectly, were she bold enough. She hesitated, torn.

'Please believe me when I say I have no ulterior motive,' he said. 'There is no one here to see or disapprove. We shall be on our way again soon. The Austerlys are

sound asleep and I shall make sure to release you before
we arrive in London.'

Aurelia stared up at him, her eyes now more accustomed to the gloom inside the coach—the dark eyebrows
that framed his eyes; his lean cheeks and slightly crooked
nose; his well-shaped, sensitive mouth; the strong jaw
shaded with stubble; the dark cleft in his chin. She ought
not to trust him. He was everything she despised. A gentleman. Even worse, a nobleman—and she knew all too well
the sense of entitlement that permeated such men. Men like
Augustus. But she always tried to be honest with herself
and she had to admit her instinct was telling her she *could*
trust him. Not that she would ever admit that out loud.

'Thank you.'

She shuffled closer. His arm came around her shoulders, pulling her close to his side, the heat of his body
warming her. The mail coach rocked into motion again
and Aurelia breathed in Tregowan's scent, luxuriating in
his warmth as well as the reassurance of his steady heartbeat in her ear as she closed her eyes, relaxing in a cocoon
of safety and security. Those feelings were an illusion, of
course, for she was aware if he knew her true identity he
would not be so quick to offer comfort. Idly, she pictured
his reaction if…when…they met again in London and he
discovered the truth, inwardly flinching at the scorn she
imagined would harden those beautiful dark-lashed eyes.

But hopefully he would not stay long, for London at
this time of year must be an expensive place to be and
it certainly sounded as though he would more usefully
spend his time on his Cornish estate. That thought raised
new doubts about his true character—maybe that belief
in their own superiority and sense of privilege she so
loathed in most aristocrats had persuaded him he was

entitled to enjoy himself in London despite his obvious financial problems.

Eager to regain her former relaxed state, Aurelia wrenched her thoughts away from Tregowan and on to her newfound inheritance and her new half-sisters, Leah and Beatrice. Her heart swelled with joy as she relived her meeting with the two women.

Reserved and ladylike Leah, a governess, was tall and slender with fiery red hair, the most amazing blue-green eyes and a dusting of freckles across her high cheekbones and straight nose. She might be reserved, but she hadn't been cowed by Henshaw's poorly disguised contempt—she had been as ready as Aurelia to stand up to the solicitor, who had at times appeared to sneer at the three girls, making clear his disapproval of their status as by-blows of the late Lord Tregowan.

Beatrice—petite, pleasantly plump and pretty, with golden-brown hair and the same eyes as Aurelia's, albeit of a softer greyish-blue—had been very different in character to either of the others. Shy and clearly nervous, she had barely said a word but, when she did, it was obvious her timidity stemmed from how she was treated at home. Aurelia had found herself hoping Beatrice would soon get away from her brother, with whom she lived, to join her in London.

Leah, like Aurelia, was alone in the world, with no family, and Aurelia recalled their brief conversation on the pavement outside Henshaw and Dent, before the post-chaises had carried her half-sisters away from her.

'I am happy to meet you both,' she had said. 'I always wanted a sister.'

To which Leah had responded, 'As have I.'

And Beatrice, her voice choking with emotion, had said, 'And I. And now I have two.'

A glow of contentment spread through Aurelia. Family. They were family now. And she could not wait for the time they would all be together in London.

Chapter Four

Max tightened his arm around Miss Croome and closed his eyes, breathing in her clean scent of soap and woman. No perfumes for her...hardly surprising when her clothes were so shabby and she was so thin. He frowned at the contradiction—she gave every indication of being poverty-stricken, yet she was travelling on the mail to London. Hardly the cheapest form of transport. Indeed, any form of long-distance travel was expensive and, although the Austerlys had been full of their reasons for travelling to London, Miss Croome had been less than forthcoming, revealing only that she'd been living in Bath where her late mother had been a milliner.

He pushed his conjecture from his thoughts. Even if he knew every little thing about her life, he could not help her, much as he might want to. He could barely help himself, for God's sake, and soon he would have Mama and Letty to worry about, too. He could see no way of keeping his true circumstances from them...he could already picture their disappointment in him. He was the man. He was supposed to provide for his womenfolk and he had let them down, and made everything worse by borrowing that money. Although he had not yet spent all of it, he was already committed to replacing the roof of Tregowan Place. How on earth would he service that debt, let alone ever repay it?

Miss Croome stirred, murmuring inaudibly, and then snuggled closer into him. His arm around her tightened instinctively. She felt so right, tucked in by his side. Less than a minute later, however, she pushed herself upright.

'What is wrong?' she whispered. 'Why did you suddenly go tense?'

He could feel the weight of her blue gaze on his face even though he could not see her eyes. What to say without sounding like a pitiful failure?

'Did I?'

'You did.'

'It is nothing. I was trying to sleep.'

'Well...' her voice was warm with laughter '... I can tell you for free that you will not sleep when you are so tense. It is like lying against a tree.'

'I shall try to relax. How could I forgive myself if I keep you from your rest?'

She chuckled and the sound rippled through him, warming him. He did try to relax, but his mind continued to fret over what the future might hold. When he propped his cheek on his hand, it reminded him he needed a shave, and then that thought led to the question of whether he ought to appoint a valet while he was in London for the Season, for the sake of appearances, and then *that* thought led to him wondering how he could even think of justifying that expense when he was already struggling to keep Wheal Rowenna open. The mine's closure would spell penury for the men and women who would have to be laid off—surely of more importance than his sartorial elegance. Every penny would have to count from now on if he was to complete the refurbishment of the house, let alone sponsor Letty through the Season… His stomach dipped at the enormity of what faced him. Letty had given up so much to care for Mama, remaining in Italy with her all these years where the climate was more favourable for Mama's lung condition. How could he let his sister down? She deserved to find a husband, happiness and security.

'My lord?' The whisper penetrated the haze of hopelessness that held him in thrall. 'It is dark in here. If it will help to talk about your troubles, I can be a good listener.'

Oh, God. He was so tempted. But…she could do nothing for him and his pride would not allow him to parade the full extent of his failures in front of anyone. Especially in front of a woman such as her, when it was clear she had led a hard life and when he—inexplicably—felt the urge to be worthy of her good opinion.

'It is nothing. I am hungry, that is all.'

'Oh.' He heard a rustle. Something was placed in his hand. 'Here. It is a wrapped slice of pie. I bought ample provisions at the Bush before boarding the coach. Please. Eat up. I have plenty more. Fruit. Bread. Cheese. You are welcome to it.'

He was struck yet again by the inconsistencies of this woman who gave the impression of having not eaten well in some time and yet appeared to have sufficient funds to travel to London on the mail coach and to buy ample provisions for the journey. But he did not ask the questions he longed to, he was too hungry for that, and removed his gloves to remove the wrapping before he bit into the cold meat pie with relish.

'I hope I did not hurt you when I bumped into you earlier?'

'No. Not at all. And I should thank you for stopping me from falling into the road.'

'Are you heading to London to look for work?' Even

though she was no longer resting against him, he sensed the tension that seized her. 'You need not speak of it if you do not wish to.'

'I…my plans are uncertain. But I should imagine there is more opportunity for work in London than there is in Bath. Or Bristol.'

'I should imagine so.'

Was that what she was doing in Bristol? Seeking work? Max ate the last mouthful of pie, wishing there was some way he could help her. 'You said your mother was a milliner. Is that your trade, too?'

'I have not her flair for design, but I am skilled with a needle. Here…would you care for some bread and cheese? I have a flagon of small beer here to wash it down.'

'I cannot eat all your provisions!'

'You will not. I have enough here to feed all four of us. Look…' he heard the crunch of teeth biting into an apple '…or, rather, listen,' she said, a gurgle of laughter in her voice. 'Sorry…that was rather noisy, was it not?'

He laughed. 'I do not mind. In fact, have you another apple? I am rather partial to cheese and apple together. Have you ever tried it?'

'No, I never have. Wait a minute…' He soon felt a smooth round apple pressed into his hand and the tip of his middle finger tingled as it inadvertently brushed the inner surface of her wrist. 'There is an apple for you.' Her voice sounded a touch strained as though she, too, had felt that spark of connection. She cleared her throat. 'And I shall eat some cheese with mine and tell you my verdict.'

After several minutes, she declared, 'Well! That is astonishing. I have never tasted them together and yet they are perfect—sweet and salty and crunchy and smooth. Who would have thought they would complement each other so perfectly?' She laughed. 'Opposites attract, as my mother used to say.'

'Ah. Your mother, too? It appears to be a trait of mothers…all manner of traditional proverbs to pass on the wisdom of the ages. My mother is full of them although, as she is Italian, she often gets them muddled. Her favourites are *That is the whole kettle of fish in a nutshell* and *Do not count your chickens while they are still in the bushes*. She always said that last one to me when I was a boy if I was cocksure about something.' His heart brimmed with joy at the memory. So good to think of happy memories, even if they were only a temporary respite from his problems.

Miss Croome laughed. 'I like them! I might use them myself. But… I did not realise you had a mother.'

Max frowned. What an odd comment to make to a complete stranger. 'Well, I was not delivered by a stork,' he said drily.

'Oh! I apologise. I… It is only I overheard your conversation with Mr Austerly and it did not seem…but then, of course, there is no reason why your mother would be living with you…that is…' Her voice dwindled into silence. He heard her suck in a breath. 'I apologise. I did not mean to pry.'

'My mother has lived in Italy for the past decade.' There was no need to go into the whole saga of her return. That would lead him perilously close to confessing his failings. 'Do you not miss her?'

'At times, yes.' And, with hindsight, if she had never gone to Italy he would not be facing this dilemma now. She would have known the truth about Tregowan from the first. 'You must miss yours. I think you mentioned she passed away last year?'

'She did.'

He felt rather than saw her withdrawal, and he stifled

the urge to probe further. He had enjoyed their quiet companionship, here in this dark, rocking mail coach in the dead of night. He pictured her face—those stunning blue eyes and the golden glow of the few tresses visible under her bonnet—and idly wondered how she might look, properly nourished and dressed in the latest fashions. Stunning, was the verdict and he wondered, too, how a clearly gently-born woman had ended up in her predicament.

She interrupted his conjectures. 'Would you care for a drink before I go back to sleep?'

Max accepted her offer and then, respecting her clear desire for no more talk, he pulled his gloves back on, saying, 'Would you care to use me as a pillow again?'

He expected her to refuse and was delighted when she accepted. She shuffled closer to him, tucking herself beneath his arm and rested her head below his shoulder. His hand lay against her upper arm and he forced it to remain slack and not to squeeze or caress her.

'Thank you for the refreshments,' he said. 'I feel better.'

And it was true. He did feel better. Something inside him shifted and settled. Contentment. However fleeting that state might prove, it felt good for now, with her close by his side, warming him. And knowing he was warming her, too…taking care of her. He was ready to sleep now. All he needed to do was to keep his constantly pecking thoughts away from his predicament. But as soon as that thought entered his head, the one solution that had been tiptoeing around the periphery of his deliberations, ever since his interview with Henshaw, burst into the forefront of his mind.

Marriage. It had to be the most sensible solution. He must find a wealthy bride, and find her quickly. He closed his mind to his instinctual objections to such a union, knowing he could no longer afford the luxury of wishing for love in his marriage. He could no longer afford pride.

Having finally acknowledged to himself there was at least one solution to the disaster his life had become, he relaxed back into the squabs and closed his eyes.

The mail coach arrived on schedule at the Swan with Two Necks in Lad Lane, Cheapside. True to his word, Max had eased Miss Croome from within his embrace as the mail approached the Hyde Park Corner tollgate and gently manoeuvred her to lean into the corner of the coach, away from him. Mr and Mrs Austerly were still sound asleep and Max lowered the shutter covering the window nearest to him so he could look out on the passing streets. It was not long before they reached their destination and his travelling companions stirred from their slumber. Miss Croome, he noted, was as beautiful as he had pictured in the night—even more so, as the greyish tinge to her skin had already receded a little. He thrust down his disappointment that their paths would probably never cross again, reminding himself of his new, practical approach to his troubles. That is, marriage to a woman with a generous dowry.

'Well, now.' Mr Austerly rubbed his hands over his face and then through his greying hair. 'Here we are, safe and sound.' He stretched, yawning vigorously, forcing Mrs Austerly to duck her head to avoid her hat being knocked askew. 'The miracle of modern travel, eh? You fall asleep in Bristol and wake up in London the next morning. Who would even have thought we could travel such distances at such speed, eh, Mother?'

'Who would have thought it?' echoed Mrs Austerly as they all began to stir and gather their belongings ready to alight from the coach. 'Now then, what about you two young people? Dear Pewsey is sending his carriage for us. May we offer either of you a lift?'

'If it will not inconvenience you, I will happily accept,' said Max as he stepped from the coach and turned to hand the ladies down. 'Pewsey resides in Mayfair, if memory serves me right. I am staying nearby, so I shall walk from there.'

He was fortunate his friend, Simon Effingham, had offered to put Max up for the Season at his house in Portman Square, saving him from having to stay with Mama and Letty at Lady Langbrook's house.

'He does,' said Mr Austerly, pride evident in his tone. 'South Audley Street.'

Miss Croome appeared somewhat flustered by Mrs Austerly's offer, her gaze darting around her. 'Thank you, ma'am, but I…it is so kind of you…but I was given money for a hackney carriage.' She glanced at Max, then stared around again, a frown creasing her brow. 'I shall make my own way.'

Max bit back a smile as he guessed she had no clue how or where to find said hackney carriage. He hailed a passing porter. 'This lady is in need of a hackney, if you will direct her to one, my good man.'

'Of course, sir. I'll show you the way, miss—shall I take your luggage?' He looked at the bags that had been unloaded from the mail coach.

'Um… I do not have any luggage.'

Max frowned. 'Why not? What—?'

'There is no need for concern, my lord,' she said quickly. 'I shall manage.' She turned to the Austerlys and clasped Mrs Austerly's outstretched hands while including them both in her smile. 'Thank you both for your company. I do hope you will enjoy your stay in London.'

'But…my dear…' Concern etched Mr Austerly's face,

mirroring Max's own unease. 'Are you sure...it does seem odd...no luggage...do you have somewhere to go? I am sure Pewsey will be able to find you a post if you seek work. It will be no trouble.'

'No!' Miss Croome's cheeks bloomed pink. 'No. I shall be all right, I promise you, sir. I... I must go. Goodbye and thank you again.'

She flashed an unfathomable look at Max, then hurried after the porter, out of the inn's yard, and had vanished from sight by the time Max and the Austerlys emerged on to Lad Lane to find Pewsey's town carriage awaiting them. But Miss Croome's behaviour had once again stirred Max's curiosity about those strange contradictions he had noticed before and when he spied the same porter hurrying back to the coachyard, he couldn't resist the urge to discover more.

'I won't be a minute,' he said to the Austerlys. 'I've just remembered something.'

He followed the porter and soon located him within the bustling yard.

'Did you overhear the address that young lady gave to the driver? She left something behind in the mail coach.'

'It was South Street, milord.'

Chapter Five

South Street? Understanding struck Max with the force of a fist to the solar plexus, for South Street was the location of Tregowan House. The coincidences—bumping into her outside Henshaw and Dent; her travelling to London on that day's mail coach—and those contradictions—her shabby, inadequate clothing and her general air of poverty and hunger such a striking counterpoint to the food she had purchased and the cost of a ticket on the mail… could it be? Could it *really* be?

A volatile mix of emotions spiralled through him as he headed back to Pewsey's carriage and the Austerlys. Why had it not occurred to him before? And she…*she* knew who he was, of course, by his name and she must know—surely—that the inheritance should have been his. No wonder she had been so cagey about…well, about everything. Could there be any other explanation?

He thanked God he hadn't confided in her about his financial woes in the intimacy of the dark coach while their travelling companions had slept. And then, from within that tumult of emotions emerged a glimmer of hope. He had liked her, even though she'd been deceitful and secretive. He was attracted to her, undoubtedly. What if…?

If marriage to an heiress is the answer to my problems, then why not Miss Croome? She is attractive. And justice would be served. I deserve that inheritance. Sarah promised it to me.

But he must make certain of his facts first. It would be useless to court Miss Croome if she had inherited only a minor portion of Lady Tregowan's estate for, if he were to solve his current dilemma, he must marry sufficient wealth. He had always rejected the idea of marrying for money—his romantic Italian side longed for love and passion, and in his parents' disastrous union he'd seen the unhappy consequences of a match based on financial considerations alone. And, of course, his conjecture could be entirely wrong. There might be an entirely unconnected reason for those coincidences and contradictions, and Miss Croome might have no connection with Lady Tregowan whatsoever. He could easily find himself in a bigger tangle than he was now.

'Are you sickening for something, my lord? You look exceedingly pale.' Mrs Austerly eyed him as he climbed into the carriage, her forehead wrinkled with concern.

'I am fine, I thank you, ma'am. Simply tired. I did not sleep well.'

'Ah, that'll be it, then,' she said comfortably.

'If you tell the coachman your address, he can drive you right to your door,' said Mr Austerly.

'No, thank you. I rather think a walk in the fresh air will help clear my head. Mr Effingham's house is in Portman Square, which is not so very far from South Audley Street.'

And South Street is just around the corner. I could go there. Just to look. Just to see.

Although he wasn't certain quite what he expected to see other than the exterior of Tregowan House. Still...it would not hurt.

* * *

They soon arrived in South Audley Street and, as luck would have it, Pewsey's residence was at the southern end meaning Max's route to Portman Square would take him past the end of South Street.

'You must come and dine with us one day, my lord,' said Mr Austerly, vigorously shaking Max's hand after they had all alighted from the carriage. 'I would welcome the chance to talk more about that mine of yours.'

'Father!' Mrs Austerly shook her head at her husband. 'It is not our place to hand out invitations to dine in some-one else's house.'

'Ah. Well. Yes. Of course. Well, we shall find our feet directly, I dare say.' Mr Austerly eyed the footmen who had emerged from the house to carry in their luggage, and the butler standing erect by the open door. He shook Max's hand again. 'We shall see you again, I am sure.'

Max inclined his head. 'I hope so.' He had liked the couple with their unpretentious enthusiasm and their down-to-earth ways. 'I should also welcome the oppor-tunity to further discuss mining with you.' He was cer-tain he could learn a great deal from Austerly with all his experience. 'Goodbye, Mrs Austerly.' He bowed. 'It was a pleasure to share my journey with you both.'

Mrs Austerly beamed, her plump cheeks pink with plea-sure. Max smiled at the couple, picked up his bag, and walked away. He soon reached the corner of South Street and paused to look back. The Austerlys had already dis-appeared inside Pewsey's house.

As the hackney carriage drove away, Aurelia halted at the kerb and contemplated the neat, four-storey Georgian terrace that was Tregowan House. Until this moment, her good fortune and what it would *actually* mean to her and her future had taken root in her mind as a relatively simple: *I need never go hungry again. I am safe.* Now, though, standing on a strange street in a strange city—this huge, bustling metropolis, as different to Bath as a poke bonnet to a lace cap—and with the reality of her future staring her in the face, she let her thoughts whir into motion, like the cogs inside a newly wound clock, bringing new doubts to the surface.

The truth was, her future would be anything but simple. Somehow, she—a gentleman's daughter in the eyes of the world, but also a former milliner—must find acceptance in the *ton,* that group of high-born, wealthy and closely connected people who judged themselves superior in every way to the rest of the population.

Augustus Croome's scornful view of people such as her sounded inside her head. *Such pathetic pretensions to gentility,* he would say, sneeringly, of people he judged below his own class. *He* would not have lowered himself to converse with folk such as the Austerlys but would have dismissed the couple as unworthy of his attention, despite their wealth and connections. Aurelia herself—and her half-sisters—would have been viewed with contempt, as upstarts.

Well, she would show him and anyone else who might think the same! She would have wealth such as Augustus could never have imagined and she would enjoy every minute of the freedom that went with it.

She wasn't sure how long she lingered there, her mind full of memories and of conjecture about her future, but eventually movement at an upper window captured her attention. A woman had come into view and now stood there, staring across the street, directly at Aurelia. Not a servant, by her appearance—could that be Mrs Butterby, Lady Tregowan's former companion and the three half-sisters' chaperon? The very notion of requiring a chaperon was ridiculous when she remembered all she had gone through since Mama's death. No one had thought her in need of respectability when she had been down to her last few pennies, scraping around for food. Chaperons, it seemed, were only required to protect the reputations of wealthy young ladies. The rest could be left to get by as best they could, responsible for shielding themselves from unwanted male attention.

Holding the watching woman's gaze, Aurelia raised her chin and marched across the street to rap on the door of Tregowan House. She happened to glance along the street as she waited for the door to open and her stomach dropped as she glimpsed a gentleman standing at the corner of the street. Tregowan! Her heart thumped against her ribcage. He was too distant for her to distinguish his expression, but she felt sure he had seen her and she could just imagine what he must think of her. She felt sad, because she had liked him and, when they met again, he would no doubt view her as the imposter he had denounced her as to Mr Henshaw.

She snapped her gaze back to the door as it was opened, but uneasiness curled through her as she imagined Tregowan striding along the street behind her, intent upon confrontation.

'Yes?' A pale man with mousy hair eyed her with suspicion as he peered down his long nose at her.

Aurelia fought to wipe any hint of nerves from her features as she reassured herself Tregowan would never challenge her on the doorstep in front of a witness.

'I am Miss Croome. I have...' She hesitated as she fumbled open her reticule and felt inside with clumsy fingers. Why, oh, why had she not extracted Henshaw's note before she knocked at the door? The rasp of a clearing throat reached her ears. 'I have a note here for Mrs Butterby,' she went on, still searching her bag. 'I am not expected... not yet...'

'The staff entrance is down there.' The man indicated a flight of steps leading down into an area where there was a door into the basement. 'Although Mrs Burnham said nothing about taking on another girl. We have sufficient staff for the time being.'

The note still eluded her, although it must be in there somewhere. But, at the man's words, Aurelia stopped searching. She straightened her shoulders and narrowed her eyes at his condescending expression.

'Are you the butler?'

'And if I am?'

'I clearly have not explained myself well enough for you to grasp the fact that I am *Miss Croome* and, if you are indeed the butler, *I* pay your wages.'

She raised her brows, taking some satisfaction from the worry that now wrinkled the man's forehead.

'Miss Croome? I am afraid... I do not...you had better come in and I will speak to Mrs Butterby. I only started here yesterday. My name is Vardy. I did not mean to—'

Aurelia took pity on him and interrupted him. 'Let us forget it.' He might need this job desperately, and she was not about to cause difficulties for a man new to his post. 'Yes, indeed,' she added. 'Please do summon Mrs Butterby.'

She stepped past Vardy into the entrance hall and gazed around her in awe at the luxury of her surroundings. A white staircase—surely that could not be marble?—curved up around the open stairwell over which a huge chandelier hung from a carved ceiling rose in the centre of a magnificent painted ceiling.

'Take a seat, Miss Croome, if you please. I shall inform Mrs Butterby of your arrival.'

The butler bowed and set off up the staircase, leaving Aurelia to perch on a chair against the wall. Even the dread that Tregowan might at any minute rap on the door demanding to know what she was doing there couldn't prevent a thrill of sheer excitement rippling up and down her spine. Was this her life from here on in? Servants bowing and curtsying? Marble staircases? She scanned her surroundings once more. Clean, spacious living accommodation?

'Miss Croome?' The clatter of heels sounded on those marble treads. 'Gracious me! So soon?'

The woman from the window came into view—slim and elegant, with grey hair scraped back into a bun and neatly dressed in dark blue. She stopped at the sight of Aurelia and frowned. 'You are the person I spotted from the window.' She continued her descent. 'Miss Croome, you say?'

Aurelia stood up. She felt herself cringe inside under the weight of the older woman's scrutiny, only too aware of her shabby, unkempt appearance.

'I have been travelling all night.' How she loathed the compulsion to excuse herself. She must explain, though. The quicker they understood she really was entitled to be here, the better. It wouldn't hurt to be conciliatory for now even though her pride prodded at her to stand up for herself, as she had with Vardy. 'Mr Henshaw said I might come immediately after he told us—my sisters and I—about our inheritance. I had nothing to keep me in Bath, so I came straight away. He gave me a letter for you, but I couldn't find it just now.'

She picked up her reticule and opened it again.

'Wait!' Mrs Butterby had reached the hallway. She

stood erect, her hands clasped before her, looking severe. 'We shall go to the morning room—you will find it easier to search your bag in there. Vardy,' she addressed the butler, who had followed her downstairs, 'send someone to light the fire in the morning room immediately. And request Mrs Burnham to attend us there at her earliest convenience. Mrs Burnham is the housekeeper,' she added to Aurelia.

She led the way towards the back of the house, her back poker straight. Aurelia followed, feeling like a schoolgirl caught out in some misdemeanour, but determined to hide how intimidated she felt. The years of penury caused by Augustus's gambling and careless extravagance—followed by the struggle to remain polite, but never subservient, to the well-heeled clientele of her mother's milliner's shop—had taught her the knack of presenting a care-nothing face to the world.

'Never reveal your true feelings until you know your trust will not be betrayed,' Mama had used to say and, following her death, Aurelia had learned the hard way that to show weakness merely encouraged others to take advantage. Her experiences had only strengthened her determination to hide her true feelings behind a nonchalance she did not always feel.

As the distance between herself and the front door lengthened, so her fear that Tregowan would batter it down and confront her faded. He was not a stupid man—that much she had gleaned during the journey. He would soon work out the truth for himself and, all in all, she was pleased she had glanced along the street before entering the house because it meant that when they met again, as they surely must, Aurelia would at least be prepared. Forewarned...forearmed. Another of Mama's favourite sayings.

That is the whole kettle of fish in a nutshell.

She bit back a grin at Tregowan's mother's saying…it seemed, somehow, apt.

Her grin soon faded, however, at the thought of their next meeting as sorrow washed through her. But that was surely only sorrow at having misled a kind man, was it not? It had nothing to do with his handsome face and fine figure, or those captivating lips, or those fascinating dark brown eyes that sparked a flicker of hidden desire deep in her belly every time their gazes collided. And it had nothing to do with the knowledge that any attraction between them was futile.

Did it?

The pleasant morning room, with its floral wallpaper, was chilly as no fire was lit. The table was laid, although only one setting was in place.

'I only took up residence here last week,' said Mrs Butterby. 'The house is being readied, but things are not running as smoothly as I should like just yet. Now…' she indicated a chair '…perhaps you would like to sit down and find Mr Henshaw's note.'

Aurelia sat with her bag on her knee and opened it. There was no need to turn out the contents, however, as having two hands with which to search made all the difference. She found the sealed note almost immediately and handed it to Mrs Butterby, wondering as she did so what the solicitor had written about her. The chaperon's expression gave nothing away as she read. She folded the note and raised her grey gaze to Aurelia's face.

'Thank you, and welcome to Tregowan House, Miss Croome. I can only apologise for your initial reception but, as I said, we have been caught entirely unawares. I hope you will appreciate that your staff exercise caution over whom to trust when it comes to such a sizeable inheritance.'

'I do indeed.' Now she had been accepted, Aurelia could admit to being impressed with such prudence. 'My sisters—half-sisters, that is—will not be joining us for a few weeks. They both had to return home to put their affairs in order before moving to London.'

'Yes. So Mr Henshaw wrote. Now...' Mrs Butterby tilted her head in enquiry. 'What would you like first? A bath to warm you up or breakfast?'

'Breakfast, if you please.'

Her shared meal with Lord Tregowan was many hours ago and she was now ravenous again. The memory of the journey and their shared snacks made her wonder if she should mention her meeting with His Lordship and, hence, his presence in London but she decided to say nothing. Mrs Butterby might be more inclined to talk openly about the reason Lady Tregowan changed her will if she was unaware Aurelia had already met the Earl.

What would happen when they met again? Was he furious that she hadn't told him she was one of the beneficiaries of Lady Tregowan's will? Her insides quivered at the thought of facing him, but with guilt, not with fear. Guilt that she had misled him. And she wondered—the very notion intriguing—if he might actually be hurt she had not told him the truth? Her silence had been undeniably deliberate. That guilt spurred her to vow to tell him about the condition in the will that prevented any of the three heiresses marrying him. That overheard hope uttered to the solicitor—about wedding one of them—no longer roused scorn within her, but sympathy. It would be too cruel to allow him to continue to believe that marriage to one of them might be a solution to his financial woes.

She thrust down her regret that such a union was an impossibility. She might dislike and distrust the aristocracy—courtesy of Augustus Croome and the dismissive superiority of so many of Mama's customers—but Tregowan had proved himself a decent man and, after all, she must marry someone… The thought of a man like Tregowan as her husband elicited that strange flutter in her stomach once again and she unconsciously pressed her hand to her belly as her heart skipped a beat.

Really, Aurelia! This will not do!

She heaved an inner sigh. It would be so much easier to forget him had his handsome face and manly figure concealed a rotten core but, despite that overheard fury in Henshaw's office, she did not believe he was a violent man. A man of high passions, maybe, but not violent and he had been nothing but kind and gentlemanly to both her and to the Austerlys, talking to them with no hint of condescension.

He seemed a true gentleman, although… Lady Tregowan *had* cut him from her will for a reason and Aurelia had heard with her own ears that he was in debt. He might not be so very different from Augustus in that respect and, even if a match between them were possible, could she really countenance a match with a man who was unable to control his spending? Maybe that clause was for the best and would stop her making a huge mistake. She vowed to forget all about him.

A maid bustled in at that moment and set about lighting the fire. Aurelia, realising she was *home* and had no need to wait for anyone to give her permission to remove her coat, did exactly that.

'I shall require new clothes,' she said, pre-empting any comment Mrs Butterby might make about her appearance.

That lady smiled, revealing a sweetness in her expression missing until that moment. 'Indeed you shall! And a lady's maid.' She clapped her hands together briskly. 'There is much to be done but, first, something to eat and a warm bath for you. And then, I think, a rest. I shall contact the employment agency and ask them to send a selection of candidates over as soon as possible. And I shall request the modiste to call upon us with a selection of fabrics and to take your measurements. We have a busy few weeks ahead of us.'

A woman, clad in a grey gown, entered the room. The chatelaine at her waist led Aurelia to deduce this was the housekeeper.

'Ah, Mrs Burnham. This is Miss Croome, one of the young ladies we are expecting. Will you arrange for one of the front bedchambers to be readied and the bed aired, please? And water to be heated for a bath?'

'Of course.' Mrs Burnham smiled at Aurelia. 'Welcome, Miss Croome. Breakfast is about to be served.'

At her words, a maid came in, carrying a laden tray from which the tantalising smell of freshly baked bread arose. She laid a second place and Mrs Butterby and Aurelia sat at the table as the servants left the room.

'Tea or hot chocolate, Miss Croome?' Mrs Butterby raised her brows as well as the teapot.

'Please, call me Aurelia. And tea, I think.'

Mrs Butterby poured a cup of tea and added a splash of milk before handing it to Aurelia and then pouring her own. She did not, Aurelia noted, suggest that Aurelia might address her by her Christian name. 'Now,' she went on as Aurelia reached for a slice of bread which she proceeded to spread thickly with butter, 'do tell me all about your meeting with Mr Henshaw and your two half-sisters, for I confess I burn to know every detail.'

Chapter Six

Max strode along South Audley Street towards Oxford Street, the fury pumping through his veins lending speed to his pace. He'd suspected the truth—eventually—but to see her with his own eyes…brazen…walking into Tregowan House as if she owned the place!

He halted abruptly as the absurdity of that last thought hit him and a startled laugh burst from his lips.

She does own the place!

'What ho, Maximilian!' A heavy hand landed between his shoulder blades. 'Why the devil are you standing on the street with your mouth gaping in that—quite frankly—deeply disturbing manner?'

Max looked at Simon Effingham and blinked as, to his horror, he felt tears prickle behind his eyes. *Pull yourself together, man.* He cleared his throat.

'A thought struck me. Made me laugh.' He eyed his friend as his spinning emotions steadied, taking in Simon's somewhat dishevelled appearance. 'And what are you doing out and about so early? No! Don't tell me. You are on your way home to bed?'

It felt good to think about something other than his own troubles. His fury had subsided, to be replaced by resignation, for what was the use of railing against reality? It would only make him bitter and he'd seen that emotion ruin many a good man as it drove them to drink and to gambling.

A satisfied grin spread across Simon's face. 'That I am, my dear fellow. That I am. I am in dire need of rest and recuperation although I am not too weary to notice you're heading in the direction of Portman Square.' He indicated Max's bag. 'Are you coming to stay?'

'Yes, if it is no bother. Did you not receive my letter? It should have arrived yesterday.'

'Oh, I haven't been home for a day or two. Or is it three?' He winked. 'I dare say it is there waiting for me. And you know damned well it is no bother,' he added as they began to walk again. 'I'm always delighted to have your company even though—and please do forgive my curiosity—I am somewhat surprised you are not staying at Tregowan House now Lady T. has finally shuffled off this mortal coil and solved the problem of your mother and sister returning to England. They are due shortly, are they not?'

'Ah.' Where to start? 'They are due next week, but they are to stay with Lady Langbrook. There has been a setback with regard to the will, however.'

They had arrived at Simon's sumptuous Portman Square mansion and Max fell silent as the butler, Parkinson, opened the door. The last thing he needed was for the servants' gossip network to get hold of what had happened. Everyone would know eventually, he knew. But he wasn't ready yet. It was too raw.

Simon frowned at Max as they handed their coats and hats to Parkinson and a footman who had hurried from the nether regions of the huge house to help. 'We'll break our fast before a well-earned rest for us both, Parkinson, if you will see to it.'

'Certainly, sir.' Parkinson bowed. 'Shall you wish to bathe before you retire?'

Simon smiled the gentle smile that never failed to charm people. 'You know me too well! Yes. Baths for us both, I think?'

Max nodded in response to the question in Simon's voice. 'That would be most welcome.'

They headed for the drawing room to await the summons to breakfast.

'Might I offer you a glass of Madeira?' Simon waved at a decanter on a walnut cabinet.

'Thank you, but, no. It is rather early for me.'

'Wise man.' Simon crossed to stand before the fire that was already alight. 'Now. Tell me about this setback, my friend.'

Max paced the room. 'The solicitor's letter was a mistake.'

'Mistake?' Simon's brow furrowed. 'How can you be mistaken over whether or not someone is dead?'

'Not over that. There was another will. A *later* will.'

'Ahh.' The sympathy in Simon's tone told Max he had already guessed. '*Do* sit down, dear boy. You are making me dizzy with all this pacing. Sit.' He pointed at a sofa. 'And tell me all.'

Max told Simon about borrowing money against his inheritance and about the new will, omitting only that he suspected he had already met one of the three heiresses. 'And now I have dug myself deeper into a financial hole,' he confessed. 'I had thought to invest further in Wheal Rowenna, as well as refurbish Tregowan Place.'

'You should close that mine. I have told you before.

What is the point in getting into debt over something that ought to be *making* money for you?'

'I have a duty to the men and women who work there. There is no alternative work available. I will not see them—or their children—starve.'

Simon sighed. 'You're a good man, Max, but you are inclined to allow your heart to rule your head.' He flashed a smile. 'But do not change, for it is one of the many reasons I value our friendship. And do not worry yourself unduly over that loan, my friend. If you find yourself short, I will happily pay it off for you.'

'You will *not*,' Max growled. 'It is bad enough I am still beholden to you for somewhere to stay when I come up to town.'

'Pride, my dear, is for those who can afford it.'

'I appreciate the offer, but no.'

'Well, if you are determined not to accept financial help, you stubborn ox, then I shall appoint myself your official matchmaker. For marriage, my dear Maximilian, is the answer to your woes and there, at least, I can help. I shall set about discovering which of this year's crop of debutantes come with the most generous dowries. Or, you never know but one of these Tregowan heiresses might prove the answer to your prayers.'

Max's pulse kicked. Courting Miss Croome, if she *was* one of the Tregowan heiresses, would be no hardship at all, for any courtship would be more about the woman than the money. But, if she were not... The thought of marrying solely for the sake of money left a sour taste in Max's mouth.

'I know marriage is a practical solution, but—'

'It is your *only* solution,' interrupted Simon. 'You can no longer afford to delay.'

Max sighed. 'I always hoped to remedy my financial

position before looking for a wife,' he confessed. 'I dare say you think that is a foolish notion, to want to marry for love?'

'Naive, perhaps. Especially in your case, although I know you Italians—sorry, *half*-Italians—have a romantic streak we less passionate Englishmen lack. But sometimes, my dear chap, we men must make decisions with our brains and harden our hearts. You have the future of the earldom to consider. Do you want your son to have to face the same dilemma that faces you, or would you rather he is financially secure?'

Max leant forward and propped his elbows on his thighs, staring down at his loosely clasped hands. He sighed again, feeling the inevitability of his situation settle like a lead mantle around his shoulders. His father had married Mama for her dowry. They had neither of them been happy and had spent the later years of their marriage estranged. He had no wish to repeat their mistakes. But...

What choice do I have?

There must be nice women out there with decent dowries and what if Miss Croome did turn out to be one of the Tregowan heiresses? He'd felt instantly drawn to her, seeing beyond her drawn, hungry appearance and, when they'd met again on the mail coach, he'd enjoyed her company. She'd been interesting, making intelligent conversation, and she'd made him smile, taking him out of his troubles when he most needed it.

But...he must learn the lesson of that over-hasty loan and not count his chickens while they were in the bushes, as Mama would say. He must not allow himself to even consider Miss Croome as a possibility until he knew the truth of her circumstances. What if she had gone to Tregowan House for a job? Besides...he could not dismiss the fact that *he* might not have known who *she* was, but *she* had chosen to conceal the truth. What did that say about her trustworthiness?

'I will think about it,' he said to Simon.

Simon clapped his hands together. 'I do love a project,' he said. 'First things first, we need to discover who these Tregowan heiresses are. Do you agree?'

Max nodded.

'Breakfast is served, sir.'

'Thank you, Parkinson.'

The butler left the room as discreetly as he had entered. The two men stood and Simon slung his arm across Max's shoulders and steered him towards the door. 'Put your trust in me, Max. Together we shall sort you out. But first… breakfast. I am starving! Did I tell you about my latest light-o'-love? She is insatiable…'

Max listened with half an ear as Simon sang the praises of his new light-o'-love, Camille, as he wondered with a sense of growing gloom why any woman, let alone an heiress, would choose to wed a debt-ridden earl whose only habitable home was a gatekeeper's lodge.

At Tregowan House, Aurelia reached for a pot of plum preserve to spread on her buttered bread as she reported the bare bones of what had happened at her first meeting with her new half-sisters.

'I can well imagine the surprise when you discovered the truth of your kinship,' Mrs Butterby said. 'I truly hope you will become friends, particularly as we are all to reside together under one roof for the Season.'

'I hope so, too, because I am so happy to find I am not all alone in the world after all. The surprise…oh, I cannot tell you!' Aurelia went on, her joy at meeting her half-sisters overriding her usual caution in talking of her feelings. 'The greatest, most wonderful surprise I could have imagined. Better, even, than the inheritance. Although, of course, *that* news is most welcome, too. Not one of us had any inkling of the others' existence, nor had we any idea of our connection with the Tregowans.

'As to my sisters—I can only speak of my impression of them during that brief meeting. We had little opportunity to speak afterwards, as the post-chaises were waiting to transport the others home. But… Leah Thame struck me as a no-nonsense sort of woman, but in a good way. I liked what I saw. She appears intelligent and is restrained, yet unafraid of speaking her mind when necessary.'

'And her appearance?'

Aurelia conjured up Leah's image. 'She is tall, slender and has beautiful red hair—'

'*Red* hair? How unfortunate. It is not a popular colour with the gentlemen, I fear—'

'*Popular?*' Aurelia bristled on Leah's behalf. 'And what has the opinion of any *gentleman* to do with my sister's merits, pray?'

'Oh! I meant to cast no aspersions, my dear. Only I am conscious you must all find husbands this year and the more gentlemen you attract, the better.' Mrs Buttterby's grey eyes fixed earnestly on Aurelia's face. 'Sarah—the late Lady Tregowan—was my friend as well as my employer and I owe it to her memory to see you all happily married.'

'How long were you her companion?'

'Oh…it must have been twenty-three years, at least. Sarah took me on after Beatrice's mother left due to her condition, although Sarah was unaware of that at the time, of course. Anyway, as I was about to say, I only want the best for all of you and I am determined you shall have ample opportunity to meet well-born and well-connected gentlemen during the forthcoming Season. That is why

Sarah stipulated you must spend the Season in London—to give you the best opportunity of making a good match. You may even attract the attention of a *nobleman*.' Mrs Butterby gave an excited little shrug of her shoulders. 'How perfect *that* would be.'

Aurelia frowned. Augustus had been born into a noble family. She had no intention of putting herself—or her fortune—in the power of such a man. Her preference would be for a self-made man. One who had worked for what he had. A man who could command her respect. A man she could trust.

'Leah is *beautiful*,' she emphasised, keeping her thoughts about prospective husbands to herself. There was no need to antagonise the chaperon just yet, but she was in for a surprise if she imagined Aurelia would meekly fall in with *her* definition of a suitable spouse. 'She will have no trouble attracting male attention if that is your fear. And I liked her.' She had admired the way her half-sister stood up to the solicitor. 'Although I dare say the truth about our paternity will put off some gentlemen when it becomes known, despite our wealth,' she added.

'Oh, I would not advise making that fact public. Better that all three of you retain an air of mystery. It is fortunate that Miss Thame differs from yourself in appearance... people are less likely to guess at the connection.'

Aurelia held her tongue. If the decision were hers alone, she would choose to be honest and open about Lord Tregowan fathering her...tell the truth and to hell with the consequences. But it was not solely her secret and she would wait to see whether Leah and Beatrice would agree with her that they should tell the truth or whether they would prefer to conceal it.

'And Miss Fothergill?' Mrs Butterby asked when Aurelia did not respond to her comment. 'What did you think of her?'

Aurelia thought back to the scene in Henshaw's office where Beatrice almost fainted. Luckily, Leah had the presence of mind to pass her smelling salts to her sister.

'She is a touch timid and reluctant to speak her mind, unlike Leah or I. But she seemed sweet-tempered and I hope we may help her to come out of her shell.' Anticipating a question concerning Beatrice's appearance, Aurelia added, 'She and I do share a familial resemblance, however. Her hair is a darker hue—more of a golden-brown—and her eyes are paler, a misty shade of blue, but they are just like mine otherwise...it was one of the first things I noticed about her. And our faces and features are similar, too, although Beatrice is plumper than me.' She huffed a self-deprecating laugh. 'Well, it would be difficult for anyone *not* to be plumper than me, would it not?' She had finished her bread and reached for another slice. 'Are you not hungry, Mrs Butterby?'

'It is a little early for me yet, my dear. I shall break my fast later.'

'I liked Beatrice,' Aurelia went on, 'although I definitely do *not* like the sound of the brother with whom she lives. She sounded almost frightened of him.'

'Ah.' Mrs Butterby sipped at her tea. 'That is what Sarah discovered, once your circumstances prompted her to send an investigator to find out what had become of the others.'

'*My* circumstances? I never set eyes on Lady Tregowan, although I do know she visited my mother's shop in Bath once.'

'Well, Sarah was well aware of the existence of all three of you. When the late Lord Tregowan—your father—realised he was dying, he confessed his peccadilloes and how he had arranged marriages for each of your mothers. Without the slightest concern about the pain it would cause his wife, I might add. *His* only consideration was to clear his own conscience before meeting his maker! And although he did not say the words, the implication was that his need to stray was Sarah's fault—she, poor woman, was a semi-invalid following an illness soon after their marriage and she was unable to bear children.

'Anyway, she blamed herself for the ruin of your mothers' lives and nothing I said could disavow her of that notion. After he died, Sarah had you all traced and, although neither you nor Beatrice were in ideal circumstances, you were safe enough. Leah was living with the man who'd brought her up as his own—a vicar—and they were very close.'

Her words brought back Leah's distress when she realised the man she had loved as her father had not been her true sire. Aurelia had envied her new half-sister the loving, secure childhood she had never known.

'At that time we still lived at Falconfield Hall,' Mrs Butterby continued. 'Oh, how Sarah adored that place. She brought it to the marriage as part of her dowry, along with this house—which she renamed Tregowan House as a salve to her new husband's pride—and *that* is why they were not part of the entail. His Lordship left them to Sarah in his will and so only the title and Tregowan estate in Cornwall passed to the current Lord Tregowan when the old Earl died.'

'Mr Henshaw told us that the old Earl had fallen out with the current Lord Tregowan's father and refused to leave his heir any more than he was forced to by law.'

'That is true. Max's father—'

'Max?'

'That is the current Lord Tregowan.' Aurelia thrust

aside the handsome face that instantly invaded her thoughts. There was no point in thinking about the man, for there could be nothing between them even if they both wanted it. 'We got to know him quite well. Anyway, Max's father was a gambler. Ran up huge debts, using his position as heir of Tregowan as guarantee. After bailing him out several times, the old Earl put his foot down, which is why he left all his unentailed property to Sarah. Anyway, to continue—last year, Sarah grew weaker and we moved to Bath, where she learned that your mother had passed away and that you were in dire straits.'

Aurelia's throat thickened at the memory of Mama and her final illness.

'Sarah hired an investigator to discover what had become of your half-sisters and she learned that they, too, were in unhappy circumstances although neither as badly off as yourself. She fretted so, worrying that any or all of you might follow in your mothers' footsteps and that more lives would be ruined, so she changed her will and asked me to send it to Mr Henshaw for safekeeping. I did not send it immediately in case she changed her mind again, but she died shortly afterwards.'

'Mr Henshaw admitted the current Lord Tregowan was Sarah's beneficiary before the will was changed, but why did Sarah leave him nothing? She could have helped us without depriving him of everything.'

'As I said, she adored Falconfield Hall, having lived most of her life there, and she loathed Tregowan Place, blaming it for her ill health. In the early days of their marriage it was the only thing that caused arguments between them—*he* wanted to sell Falconfield Hall and invest in Tregowan, but Sarah would not hear of it. The income from Falconfield was used to keep the Cornish estate running at first, but when Max's father revealed his true character—

they were only very distant cousins, you understand—the old Earl stopped all investment in the entailed property.

'Max seemed so different. He visited Sarah often and she believed Falconfield Hall would be safe in his hands. But then, about the same time she learnt of your circumstances, rumours also reached us of Max gambling—a throwaway remark about a gamble he had lost and that debts were accruing. Sarah's sole concern was for the future of Falconfield Hall and she feared Max would sell it to pay off his debts and invest in Tregowan—the very thing she had fought against since her wedding day. That is why there is a condition in the will that, if any one of you—or, to be accurate, your husbands, because the property would be in their names—wishes to sell, the others would get first refusal. She prayed at least one of you would make it your family home.'

Part of Aurelia didn't want to hear Tregowan was a gambler and she silently scolded herself. Her mother had been like that—always making excuses for Augustus as he frittered away what little money they had. Aurelia had sworn never to be so blind to any man's faults, but she sensed herself teetering on the brink of danger by even wanting Mrs Butterby's words to be false. By wanting Max Tregowan to be the decent man she believed him to be.

Not that it matters, for he is off limits.

Aurelia would not risk forfeiting her inheritance. Not for anyone. Her experience of the past months—the poverty and the hunger and the sheer desperation—would haunt her for some time. And she could not wait for the chance to confront that disdain felt by aristocrats such as Augustus for those they deemed beneath them. She would stand tall before them and she needed her inheritance to do it.

'Is that why Lady Tregowan stipulated that if one of us

should marry Lord Tregowan she would forfeit her share of the inheritance?'

'It is.' Mrs Butterby finished her second cup of tea. 'Now. You must be exhausted. Are you ready for your bath and a rest?'

Aurelia cocked her head to one side. She could not wait to begin her new life but, seized by an inexplicable determination to look her best when next she met Lord Tregowan, she had no desire to set foot outside until she was suitably attired.

'Do you know,' she said slowly, 'I feel quite refreshed. I did manage to sleep on the mail coach. I should welcome a bath, but…' she plucked at the bodice of her shabby dove-grey gown 'I only have this to my name and I should like to begin my new life by ordering some new clothing. After all, if I am to attract the attention of the gentlemen of the *ton*, I cannot be seen out in public dressed like a pauper.'

Mrs Butterby beamed. 'Splendid. I shall send a note to Madame Fleury to attend us in one hour. I have already forewarned her that she will have three heiresses to dress for the Season, so I make no doubt she will drop everything to answer my summons.'

Chapter Seven

'**W**ell? What do you think?' Mrs Butterby turned to Aurelia, her brows raised in query, after the final applicant for the role of lady's maid left the drawing room.

It was the day after her arrival and Aurelia braced herself against the weight of Mrs Butterby's expectancy. She had already learned enough about the chaperon to know she would instinctively favour Miss Brace—Aurelia's least preferred of the five applicants. Aurelia had not warmed to Miss Brace in the slightest, but the question was—did she make her choice to keep Mrs Butterby happy, or to please herself?

'I preferred Miss Hopper.' A sweet woman, with a hint of a West Country accent that made Aurelia feel instantly nostalgic. She had taken to Miss Hopper's kind eyes as soon as they met.

'Miss *Hopper*? But...my dear Aurelia...such informality. She even made a *joke*.'

Aurelia rolled her eyes. 'Hardly a joke, ma'am. She merely passed a pleasantry about the weather.' It had been raining hard all day. 'I should vastly prefer a friendly maid to assist me. Miss Brace was too formal.'

'No, no. I cannot agree. Miss Brace knows her place

and will take the appropriate degree of pride in her mistress's appearance. Her age and her wealth of experience will stand her in good stead and benefit you enormously. She will be a far superior lady's maid for an heiress such as yourself. Do not forget all eyes in the *ton* will be upon you once you make your debut. Miss Hopper is *much* too inexperienced.'

'I have little experience either. We shall learn together.'

'But she has only had *one* prior post,' Mrs Butterby almost wailed.

'I am sorry if my choice upsets you but, really, it *is my* choice, is it not?' Aurelia disliked laying down the law, but she could not allow the chaperon to browbeat her over this, or what further decisions about Aurelia's life would she deem it her right to determine? 'And, yes, Miss Hopper might have only held one prior post, but it was with Viscountess Melksham, who is a lovely lady. She was a regular customer at Mama's shop in Bath and if *she* was satisfied with Miss Hopper's skill…' Aurelia did not complete her reproach by saying *who are you to object?*, but the unspoken implication hung in the air between them.

Mrs Butterby's mouth firmed. 'Very well. I can see you are determined to get your own way and ignore my advice—proffered, might I add, with the best of intentions as well as the benefit of my many years of experience. But. There. You know best. On your head be it…but pay heed…do *not* come crying to me when you find yourself an object of ridicule in the *ton*.' Her bosom heaved. 'I pray you will not prove this intransigent when looking for a husband.' She pivoted and stalked to the door, where she paused. '*You* may deliver the verdict to Miss Hopper and the others, Aurelia. *I* am going for a lie down.' She pressed her hand to her forehead. 'I have the headache, so I shall leave instructions I am not to be disturbed.'

Aurelia sighed as the chaperon closed the door behind her. She had not meant to upset her, but she'd had no choice unless she was prepared to allow Mrs Butterby to overrule her every decision. Which she was not. It was surely better to start as she meant to go on than to try and change tack later, but she anticipated a bumpy few weeks ahead until the two of them resolved their differing ideas about Aurelia's new life.

The five women waited downstairs in the entrance hall.

'Thank you all for coming here today and for your patience,' Aurelia said. 'It has been a hard choice but... Miss Hopper, I should like to offer you the position of my lady's maid. I am sorry it is not better news for the rest of you.'

She hardened her heart against the other four women's disappointment as they trooped towards the front door, held open by Vardy in the manner of one seeing undesirables off the premises.

Miss Hopper appeared suitably stunned. 'Me, Miss Croome? Are you...are you *sure*?'

'I am positive, Miss Hopper.'

'Would you call me Bet? If that is allowed,' she added hurriedly. 'Or Hopper.'

'Bet it is,' said Aurelia with a smile. 'Now. How soon are you able to start?'

'Right away, miss. Oh, I am *so* pleased. Thank you.'

'Vardy?'

The butler closed the front door. 'Miss Croome?'

'Please instruct Hall to drive Miss Hopper to collect her belongings and bring her back here.' Hall was the coachman. 'And a room will need to be prepared in the servants' quarters.'

Vardy bowed. 'A room is already prepared, miss, and I shall send a message to the mews at once.'

'Good. Thank you. If you wait here, Bet, the carriage will come round for you.'

Bet curtsied. 'Thank you again, Miss Croome.'

Aurelia smiled at her, then climbed the staircase again to the drawing room. Once inside, with the door closed, her shoulders slumped. Would she ever become accustomed to this? Giving orders to others did not come naturally to her, yet she justified it to herself by recalling her own despair when she sought employment after the Bath landlord had given her that despicable ultimatum. And the strain of having to stand her ground with Mrs Butterby did not help. Aurelia was beginning to understand that her own inclination when anyone gave her an order was to argue, even though she wanted to be accepted and liked. She vowed to be more conciliatory where possible, although it would not be at the expense of her own happiness and peace of mind.

At least she had her own maid now and an acceptable gown and pelisse—thanks to Madame Fleury's girls working long into the night to alter already made garments destined for another customer—as well as a warm cloak and matching bonnet, so she would no longer be confined to the house.

Two days after Max's arrival in London, Simon joined Max at the breakfast table. Max watched his friend pile his plate high with bacon, kidneys, chops and eggs and take his seat at the table. The footman on duty—James—filled his coffee cup.

'Good morning,' he said. 'You actually slept in your own bed last night, did you?'

His friend had been conspicuous by his absence throughout the previous day, after keeping Max company on the day of his arrival.

Simon grinned. 'Indeed. I needed to recoup my strength. What did you get up to yesterday?' He swigged his coffee down in one gulp and James stepped forward to refill it. 'Did you find out anything about those women who ousted you as beneficiary of Lady Tregowan's will?'

'Not yet.'

Simon eyed Max. 'Have you *tried* to find out?'

'Not really.'

If the truth be told, Max had not set foot out of the house, instead spending his time thinking about his situation and trying—without much success—to think of an alternative to marrying for money.

'So you've been brooding? Oh, don't turn that black scowl on me, Tregowan—you forget I know you only too well. You loathe the idea of admitting you cannot remedy your situation through sheer pig-headedness and your own hard work. But some things, my friend, are too important to leave to hope and happenstance. You need to accept the reality that marrying money is the only solution to your woes.' At least Simon's smile this time was sympathetic. 'You're not the first man to be forced to do so and you won't be the last. Accept your fate with good grace, my dear chap.'

Max sighed. 'I know you are right. I was merely catching my breath, that is all. I know I must do something.'

Mama and Letty would be in London next week. He would still have to admit his failure to them both for there was no way he could find a bride before then because hardly any families were in town as yet.

'Well, no matter. Between us, we shall find you a wealthy bride. The first item on our agenda must be to discover the identity of the three Tregowan heiresses.'

Max glared at Simon, signalling with his eyes towards the silent footman.

'Oh...' Simon waved his fork in the air '...don't fret about the servants. I pay them exceedingly well for their discretion. Isn't that right, James?'

'Indeed, sir.'

'But,' Simon continued with a wink, 'their discretion only works in *my* favour, as I am the one who holds the purse strings. Gossip can and does come *into* this house. So, James, tell us. What is the word downstairs about who has inherited Lady Tregowan's fortune?'

James cleared his throat. 'They say there are three young ladies who have each inherited an equal share.'

'There you are, Max. One third each. Better than a kick in the bollocks, is it not? Are the heiresses in residence yet, James?'

'Only one, sir. A Miss Croome. Arrived a couple of days ago.'

Max's breath caught in his lungs and a warm glow flowed through him. So she *was* one of them. Was this a sign? He recalled her bright blue eyes and full pink lips, and the feeling of her body snuggled into him as she slept. But his delight at knowing she might be within his reach was tinged with caution, leaving him feeling torn. Why had she concealed the truth and why had Sarah left her fortune to the daughter of a milliner?

'There,' said Simon with great satisfaction. 'All sorted. Go forth and court Miss Croome.'

Max frowned. 'Have you heard anything downstairs about Miss Croome herself, James? Where she comes from? Who she is?'

That last question was still eating into him because only once he knew who these women were could he begin to understand and, maybe, forgive Sarah's deception in cutting him out of her will entirely. The anger and, yes, bitterness still simmered deep inside even though he had tried

to move on past that initial shock and that was another
reason why he had not ventured out the day before to find
out for himself about Miss Croome, in case he could not
disguise his resentment—hardly the best way to embark
on a courtship of an heiress.

'Nobody knows, milord,' James replied. 'The staff there
are all new and too scared of losing their jobs to say much
as yet. But I do know the staff were hired by a Mrs Butterby.'

'Butterby? She was Lady Tregowan's companion. *She*
must know the truth of why Sarah changed her will.' Still,
it rankled. He had *trusted* Sarah. And now see where that
blind trust had led him. He pushed his chair back and
began to rise to his feet. 'I shall call on her.'

'Whoa!' Simon held up his hand while he hastily swallowed his mouthful of food. 'Not so fast! It is far too early
to call on *anyone*, my dear chap. Finish your breakfast first
and let us ponder our strategy.'

Max looked down at his half-eaten plate of food and,
reluctantly, sat down again, but pushed the plate away, his
appetite gone as his stomach churned again with all that
unspent resentment. 'You are right. But I *shall* call upon
her this afternoon.'

'And I shall accompany you,' said Simon.

'You? There is no need...'

Max eyed his friend—handsome, good company and
wealthy beyond belief. *What woman will look at me with
Simon around*?

'There is *every* need,' declared Simon. 'You need not
worry I shall encourage this Miss Croome, Maximilian.
I am in no hurry to get leg-shackled. But someone has to
be there to rein you in when your anger at Lady T.'s betrayal reveals itself. As it will. You, my friend, are not as
inscrutable as you like to think you are. It's that passion-

ate Italian blood that runs through your veins—no good ever comes of allowing your heart to rule your head, as you have discovered more than once, if memory serves.'

And with that, Simon rose to help himself to a second helping of breakfast while Max forced himself to sit still and drink his coffee, quietly simmering inside even as he acknowledged the truth of his friend's observation.

As it happened, there was no need to call at Tregowan House. Shortly after noon, Simon suggested a ride in Hyde Park and, cheered by the thought of fresh air and exercise after his long overnight journey and his subsequent inactivity, Max agreed. Mounted on one of Simon's impressive horses, a frisky chestnut called Stanley, with Simon on his favourite mount, a black that went by the name of Liverpool—named for the current Prime Minister—they let off steam with a fast canter, only slowing as they approached a sedately driven barouche.

As they neared, Max recognised the heart-shaped face of Miss Croome and identified the lady by her side as Mrs Butterby. There was already a world of difference in her appearance when compared to the impoverished young woman he had met in Bristol. Now, wrapped warmly in a blue velvet fur-lined cloak with a matching bonnet, with her hands tucked inside a fur muff, she looked every inch the wealthy young woman she was.

'That is…er… Mrs Butterby,' he whispered to Simon, remembering just in time that Simon did not know he had met Miss Croome. 'That must be Miss Croome.'

'How fortuitous. She looks a diamond of the first water. She could be your salvation, dear boy, and Stanley here will ensure you don't allow your emotions to get the better of you—he will have you off if you upset him, you know.'

Max didn't dignify that warning with a reply—he was

experienced enough to recognise the horse's skittish nature. He reined Stanley to a halt as the barouche drew alongside, his gaze riveted to Mrs Butterby's face as he raised his hat, giving her no option but to acknowledge him.

'Hall,' she called to the coachman. 'Please stop.'

Max flicked his attention to Miss Croome, whose cheeks were stained pink, but whose nose was definitely elevated in an *I don't care what you think of me* kind of way. He thrust down his already simmering annoyance that she had lied to him. Well…lied by omission.

'Good day, Mrs Butterby. We meet again. I was sorry to learn of Sarah's passing.'

'Good morning, my lord. Yes, it is sad but, as you know, her health had been failing for some time.'

Her gaze moved to Simon, and Max performed the introduction.

'May I introduce Miss Croome, gentlemen? I am standing as her chaperon for the Season.' She touched Miss Croome's gloved hand. 'Aurelia, my dear, *this* is Lord Tregowan.'

'I am delighted to meet you both.' Those brilliant blue eyes met his and clung for a moment—sending the thrill of desire coursing through him—before they moved on to Simon.

Aurelia. Such a lovely name. A lovely name for a lovely woman for—even in the short time since he had last seen her, Miss Croome's complexion had brightened. Max swallowed thickly as he bowed. Her eyes were on him once again when he looked up and he read her clear warning before her gaze flicked sideways to indicate her companion.

So. She hasn't revealed we met on the journey to London. I wonder why?

But that suited Max, as he hadn't told Simon either.

'Might we accompany you for a short distance, Mrs Butterby?'

Max wasn't totally surprised at the indecision that flitted across her face for, after all, she had always been loyal to Sarah and, if Sarah had taken against him sufficiently to change her will, then he could well believe Mrs Butterby had, too.

'Of course, my lord,' she said graciously. 'We shall be honoured by your company.'

Chapter Eight

Upon Mrs Butterby's acceptance, Simon immediately manoeuvred Liverpool around to her side of the carriage, and engaged her in conversation, leaving Max free to ride alongside and talk to Aurelia who sat like a statue, staring straight ahead, a crease between her fair brows.

'Is this your first time in London, Miss Croome?'

'It is.'

Max glanced beyond her to Mrs Butterby who, to give her credit, was clearly trying to resist being drawn into Simon's web of charm in order to watch over her charge. Max waited until the chaperon was further distracted by his friend before speaking again. He kept his voice low.

'Between ourselves, we cannot ignore how and when we met,' he said. 'But why—?'

'I have no intention of ignoring it, Lord Tregowan,' she said. She managed to sound fierce even though her voice was barely more than a whisper and her lips—full and tempting—curved in a serene smile. 'That is not my way.'

'Yet you did not admit your identity on that mail coach.'

'I did not conceal my name.' She elevated her nose. '*If* you care to recall, Mr Austerly introduced us.'

He narrowed his eyes at her. 'You know what I mean.

I was not speaking of your name, but of your circumstances.'

One shoulder hunched. 'My circumstances were… *are*…nobody's business but my own.'

A disbelieving laugh escaped him and Mrs Butterby's head whipped around. He threw her a disarming smile and Simon immediately drew her attention back to him while Max soothed Stanley, who had started to snatch at his bit.

'You are upsetting your horse.' Aurelia's superior tone needled Max even further as he battled to keep his emotions in check and relax his touch on the reins.

'It is unworthy of you to pretend you are unaware of the impact your circumstances have had upon mine,' he said, as soon as Stanley had settled. 'You know full well that your good fortune has resulted in a reduction of *my* prospects. Your situation is therefore very much my business.'

She stared at him then, not flinching away from the scowl that he knew furrowed his brow.

'You are an *earl*.' Her tone was incredulous. 'You have status and property. I had nothing. And I mean *nothing*. And, as a woman, I had few remedies open to me. And yet *you* resent *me* for being the beneficiary of a bequest you somehow believe you were entitled to? Listen to me, Lord Tregowan. *I took nothing from you. It was never yours.*'

And she was right. And yet… 'And, as an earl and a landowner and an employer, I have responsibilities that you cannot even begin to comprehend, Miss Croome. Entire families are dependent upon me.'

'Then you should have thought about that before you gambled away their futures and their well-being, shouldn't you?'

'*Gambled?*'

She folded her arms and stared straight ahead once more as Max seethed at the injustice of her remark.

'Excessive gambling is a curse on all decent people.'

'Miss Croome!' Mrs Butterby looked horrified. 'I must protest! What *will* the gentlemen think?'

'Well, this gentleman is amused by a lady who does not hesitate to speak her mind,' said Simon. 'Max?'

'Oh! Well, yes…but I might be more impressed if the lady in question made certain of her facts before flinging wild accusations around.'

Aurelia glared at him. 'I—'

'Miss Croome… Aurelia…hush, I beg of you, please consider the unseemliness of being seen to argue in public with His Lordship and Mr Effingham.'

'There is no one to see. And Mr Effingham said he found me amusing.'

'*Mr Effingham* is being polite—'

'Or provocative,' muttered Max with a hard stare at his friend, who returned his look with an innocent smile.

'And His Lordship is most definitely *not* amused,' Mrs Butterby continued. 'I beg we *all* leave the subject there. It is not an appropriate discussion.' She indicated the coachman's back.

'For your information, Miss Croome, I do not gamble,' Max bit out between gritted teeth, as Simon rode around the barouche to join him.

He ignored his friend's hissed, 'Max! Steady on!'

'I am *not* my father.'

Aurelia's brows rose, infuriating him further. 'Your father?' She shook Mrs Butterby's restraining hand from her arm. 'I know nothing of your father, sir, other than your predecessor did not trust him.'

'Aurelia…my dear…' Mrs Butterby put her hand to her brow. '*Please…*'

Max stared at Aurelia—her delicately carved cheekbones, flashing eyes, the defiant jut of her chin. Dear God, she was gorgeous.

'Then why do you assume I gamble?' he growled before pinning Mrs Butterby with his gaze. 'What have you told her? And *what* did Sarah believe of me?'

The chaperon's face paled, but her tone was resolute. 'This conversation is over, my lord.' She raised her voice. 'Hall! Home. Now, please.' She bowed her head to Simon and then to Max. 'Good day to you, sirs.'

Aurelia, Max noticed, appeared to feel no inclination to follow normal societal behaviour, for she did no more than send him a fulminating glare as he raised his hat and bid her farewell and completely ignored Simon's mild 'Good day, ladies'.

'Well,' said Simon, as the barouche sped away. 'That seemed to go well.'

'Go well? If I did not know better, I would accuse you of being foxed. It could not have gone *less* well if it tried.'

'Oh, Maximilian, you innocent, you.' Simon grinned at Max as he turned Liverpool's head for home. 'Do you really understand so little of the fairer sex? She's smitten with you. It's written all over her face. And a very beautiful face it is, too, you lucky dog. Why, she barely even glanced at me and, by the end, I swear she had forgotten my very existence. A huge blow to my self-esteem, as I am sure you will realise, but an excellent omen for our plan to find you an heiress to wed, would you not agree? Unless, of course, you decide she is not biddable enough for you to contemplate for your wife?' He sighed, a smile forming on his face. 'Life would never be boring, of that I am sure.'

Deciding Simon's question was rhetorical, Max did not reply and they rode on in silence as he pondered Simon's words. Life certainly wouldn't be boring with a woman like Aurelia Croome, who clearly knew her own mind

and had revealed a refreshing lack of the submission in-
stilled in so many young ladies. He couldn't help but admire the way she had stood up to him, even though her
accusation had stung, being as unjust as it was untrue.
But he still couldn't credit Simon's claim that her nee-
dling him somehow indicated she was interested in him,
although it was true she had seemed genuinely oblivious
to Simon, even with his charm and his good looks. And
his wealth although, of course, she would likely not know
about that. Mrs Butterby would no doubt enlighten her at
the first opportunity.

He tried hard not to foster the hope that marriage to Aurelia Croome might be the answer to his financial woes,
determined to remain practical and not allow himself to
take off in flights of fancy.

'What I cannot quite fathom, though,' said Simon,
thoughtfully, as their horses plodded on towards the gate,
'is why she would hurl such an accusation at a virtual
stranger.' He turned to Max. 'Unless, of course, you have
met the delightful Miss Croome before?'

Max couldn't control the heat that built in his cheeks
and Simon crowed with delight.

'You *have* met her before! I knew it! Tell me all, this
very minute.'

There was no longer any reason to keep up the pretence,
so Max told him about their meeting outside the solicitors
and their overnight journey on the mail coach.

'And you are already halfway in love with her.'

'Don't talk rot, Simon. It is impossible to love someone you barely know.'

'Not for me.' Simon winked. 'I fall in love all the time.
Just one look and I'm lost.'

'That, my friend, is lust.'

'Lust. Love. It's all the same, is it not? After all, you

would not wish to marry a woman you could not lust after. Would you?'

Miss Croome's heart-shaped face and delicate features appeared in his mind's eye and his pulse kicked, speeding the blood through his veins. The lust part was easy. And he liked her, despite her prickliness and her accusation that he was a gambler. *Excessive gambling is a curse on all decent people.* And that, surely, gave them something in common? An abhorrence for gaming and the devastation it could wreak in people's lives.

The difficult part would be to convince her that whatever she had heard about him was untrue. Mrs Butterby would be an obstacle, but now he understood better why Sarah had changed her will if she believed he had fallen into the vice of gambling, as his father had. Somehow, he must find a way to talk to Aurelia in private. And that, he was aware, would prove no mean feat.

'No,' he said to Simon, who was patiently waiting for his response. 'I most definitely would not.'

Two days after their drive in the Park—and her first official meeting with Lord Tregowan—Aurelia was alarmed to be informed by Bet as she broke her fast that Mrs Butterby had taken ill in the night. She hurried upstairs to the chaperon's bedchamber, knocked softly and entered. Mrs Butterby was reclining in bed, propped up by pillows, wearing a pink bedjacket, her lace-edged nightcap tied beneath her chin. She turned puffy, red eyes and an even redder nose towards Aurelia.

'Stop!' She half sat and held up her hand, palm out. 'Do not come closer, I beseech you. *You* must not catch my wretched cold.' As though the effort was too much for her, her eyes closed and she collapsed back against the pillows, groaning.

Aurelia had initially halted by the doorway, but now she moved towards the bed and the invalid. 'Hush. I shall be fine—I have the constitution of an ox, I promise you.'

'Oh!' Mrs Butterby's eyes slitted open. 'I am so sorry, my dear,' she croaked. 'I know you were looking forward to visiting Hookham's—as was I—but we shall have to postpone our outing for another day.'

'Do not fret, ma'am.' Aurelia straightened the coverlet. 'Is there anything I can get you, or do for you?'

'No. I just need to rest. Mrs Burnham has assigned Janet to look after me, so I have all the help I need. I only hope you won't feel too neglected, staying indoors with no company.'

Aurelia fleetingly wondered if Lord Tregowan might call but dismissed the idea immediately. Mrs Butterby had roundly condemned her forwardness during their encounter in the Park and had warned her that no decent gentleman liked a female who was too free in voicing her opinions. Well, and if she had given Max Tregowan a disgust of her, it was for the best. No matter how attractive she found him or how much she—secretly—liked him, there was no point in hankering after the man in the face of that condition in Lady Tregowan's will. Besides, she'd already decided she wanted a man who had worked for his riches, not one born with a silver spoon in his mouth. Although she now realised that meeting such men might prove problematic as it was becoming clear they would not move in the circles deemed suitable for herself and her sisters.

'I am sure I shall survive,' she said. 'But I might not say the same after a few days of my own company, so I suggest you hurry up and get better. Which means sleep! I shall leave you in peace.'

* * *

By the next day Aurelia was already bored with her own company. Mrs Butterby was still confined to her bed and had progressed to sneezing and coughing, according to Janet. There were no books in the house—one of the reasons they had planned to visit Hookham's Circulating Library—and she was thoroughly fed up with embroidery and sewing, both of which reminded her too forcefully of the long hours spent helping her mother make hats and bonnets, turbans and caps.

By late morning, Aurelia had had enough. She knocked on Mrs Butterby's door and entered.

'How are you today, ma'am?'

Mrs Butterby sneezed in reply and shook her head.

'Only… I have come to tell you I plan to visit Hookham's today.'

'What? You *cannot* go out alone, Aurelia.' Mrs Butterby blew her nose vigorously and then groaned, putting her hand to her neck. 'Oh, my poor throat.'

Aurelia handed her the glass of water from her nightstand. The chaperon drank gratefully, her eyes closed, and then she sank back against her pillows, her face flushed.

'Please do not worry,' Aurelia said. 'You forget I was living alone and looking after myself until recently. I am four-and-twenty and I've led a vastly different life to a cossetted miss straight from the schoolroom.'

Mrs Butterby shook her head and opened her mouth. Aurelia took her hand. 'No. Please do not try to speak. You will only make your throat worse. Bet will be with me and Hall will drive us. It will be perfectly respectable.'

Mrs Butterby's eyes screwed tighter as another moan emerged from her lips.

'I shall not stay out for long,' Aurelia went on. 'I cannot wait to read that novel you told me about…the one by the author of *Sense and Sensibility*. I *must* find something other than embroidery to occupy my time, especially while you are confined to bed.'

'*Emma*,' whispered the invalid. 'It is *Emma*.'

Aurelia took that as the chaperon granting her permission. Mrs Butterby's eyes opened a crack.

'Promise me you will go straight there and come straight home, Aurelia. *Please*.'

'I will return as soon as I have the book,' said Aurelia truthfully. 'Go to sleep and please do not worry about me…save your energy for getting better.'

'I knew I should never have agreed to go for a drive in the Park in such damp, cold weather,' Mrs Butterby complained croakily.

Aurelia, though, was pleased they had gone, for at least she had weathered that first meeting with Tregowan and he now knew the truth. And, strangely, she had enjoyed their verbal sparring—his reaction when she accused him of being a reckless gambler had the ring of truth about it, making her wonder if the rumour Lady Tregowan heard had been false.

She tiptoed from Mrs Butterby's room and hurried to her own bedchamber, where Bet awaited her, already clad in her cloak and bonnet. Aurelia hastily pulled on her new deep pink pelisse and matching bonnet and picked up her kid gloves before pausing a moment to admire her reflection in the cheval mirror. She was still coming to terms with this complete reversal in her fortunes. She stroked the soft leather of her gloves. Such luxury. Such indulgence. She need not worry about a thing…and the absence of fear, and of despair, was the greatest bonus of all.

You could still lose it all. If you fail to marry…

But I will not fail!

In the mirror she saw her determination reflected back

at her. She would marry come hell or high water...but it might not be to the sort of man Mrs Butterby deemed suitable.

What do I care what she says? It is I who will have to live with the man.

And, like clockwork, an image of Max Tregowan materialised in her head, as it did without fail every time the conundrum of whom she might wed entered her thoughts.

'Miss?' Bet's voice came from the door. 'The carriage is here.'

Aurelia shook Tregowan's image from her head as she did every time, reminding herself yet again of the futility of yearning for the man who had made such an impression on her when she already knew they could never be, even if he did prove innocent of the charge of being a gambler.

'I am ready.' She pulled on her gloves and picked up her reticule. 'Let us go.'

Before visiting Hookham's Circulating Library, Aurelia instructed Hall to drive them to Harding, Howell & Co., on Pall Mall. When she had first arrived, Mrs Butterby had tempted Aurelia with a promise to visit the store—which she described in glowing colours—but that had also been postponed due to Mrs Butterby's illness. But Aurelia, with spare pin money for the first time in her life, could wait no longer. Besides, she wished to buy Mrs Butterby a gift and where better than a shop described by the chaperon as a cornucopia of treasures?

Aurelia was entranced the minute she and Bet set foot in the store, which stretched a considerable distance back from the entrance and was divided by glazed partitions into four departments. She happily browsed the furs and fans in the first department before heading to the haberdashery in the next section, then venturing further into the third department, stocked with all different kinds of perfumery on one side and jewellery and ornamental items on the other.

She purchased an expensive bar of lightly fragranced soap—very different from the home-made soft soap she had grown up with—plus face and hand lotions for her toilette, and then selected another bar of scented soap and a pretty pair of coral bracelets for Mrs Butterby, partly to cheer her up when she was so poorly, but also to assuage Aurelia's guilt at her determination to make decisions for herself and not to meekly fall in line with whatever the chaperon decreed.

She then—with the assistance of a helpful shop assistant—spent a happy half-hour sniffing the contents of the many flasks of perfumes available. Finally, she found the perfect scent, with a hint of orange blossom, but spicy, warm and sensual, suggestive of exotic, faraway lands. She bought a dainty enamelled bottle of the fragrance with a thrill of excitement. Never before had she used anything more glamorous than a home-made lavender rinse for her hair. The fourth and final department was for millinery and female attire, but she did not linger there because she'd already ordered so many items of clothing from Madame Fleury.

As they headed back through the departments and with the joy of generosity still warming her heart, Aurelia stopped in the haberdashery to buy a pair of fur-lined gloves for Bet who, despite the cold weather, was not wearing any.

'Oh! Miss Croome…you must not…oh, but they are so lovely and warm… I cannot accept—'

'You *can* accept them, Bet, and you shall.' The door-man bowed as they exited the shop. 'I am unable to give you an old pair of mine, for they are full of holes—' Aurelia had made no secret of her circumstances before her good fortune '—and I know only too well the misery of cold, chapped hands.'

'Thank you, miss.' Bet had tears in her eyes.

'Hookham's, please, Hall,' said Aurelia as they climbed into the carriage. 'Mind you—although they are not a bribe, Bet, I shall rely on your discretion and loyalty when it comes to my activities. Mrs Butterby already has enough to worry about. Let us not add to her burdens,' she added with a wink.

'Of course, miss. You can rely on me.'

For the first time since her arrival in London, Aurelia felt in control of her own destiny and her spirits lifted.

Chapter Nine

In Old Bond Street, the carriage stopped right outside Hookham's Circulating Library. Hall opened the door and lowered the step but, as he offered his hand to assist Aurelia down, a tall figure appeared next to the coachman.

'Miss Croome. We meet again.'

Aurelia looked up into Lord Tregowan's dark brown, thickly lashed eyes and her heart leapt. She quashed that frisson of excitement, exasperated by her involuntary reaction to the mere sight of him.

She tilted her chin and managed a cool 'Good afternoon, my lord' in response before putting her hand in his and allowing him to hand her to the pavement.

'What a happy coincidence,' he said. 'That is... I assume this *is* your destination?'

He indicated Hookham's with a flick of his head as one corner of his mouth curled in a half-smile. She eyed him suspiciously, their last meeting in the Park looming large. Where had his anger and resentment gone? How much easier it would be to resist him if he was still annoyed with her.

'You assume correctly, my lord.' She raised her brows. 'And yours, too?'

'Indeed.' His deep voice stirred odd sensations deep inside her, irritating her further. What chance did she have keeping a cool head as she sought a husband if her own body could betray her like this? 'I intend to read the newspapers in the reading room.'

Aurelia puzzled over his friendliness. Was it due to her being one of the Tregowan heiresses and his idea that he could solve his financial problems by marrying one of them? She knew, as he did not, that that plan was doomed and her conscience awoke as she stood irresolute on the pavement. She might despise the aristocracy as a whole, and gamblers even more so, but, somehow, Tregowan did seem different. She recalled his ease chatting to the Austerlys—and to her—on that journey to London. He had not been too high in the instep to ask questions of and learn from a man such as Mr Austerly. Augustus would never have lowered himself in such a way.

She recalled her vow to tell him the truth about that clause in Lady Tregowan's will and realised this might be the perfect—possibly her only—opportunity.

'After you.' Tregowan gestured for Aurelia to precede him into the library, which was also a bookseller. 'Where is your chaperon today?'

'She is unwell, hence my maid accompanying me as I wish to purchase a novel to help pass the time until Mrs Butterby recovers.'

The scent of leather and ink assailed Aurelia as she gazed around the interior of Hookham's at the bookshelves crammed with books, their spines tooled with gold lettering. It looked wonderful—a real treasure trove of stories and adventure and knowledge.

Tregowan remained by her side as an assistant guided her to where she might find a copy of *Emma*. Small touches—a cup of her elbow, a hand at the small of her back—as he guided her through the other customers raised both the tiny hairs on her skin and her awareness of him as a man. She made no doubt he was being the gentleman in escorting her thus, but the effect upon her was unsettling and *that* scared her because, despite her better judgement, she enjoyed his attentions. Too much.

She also became aware of several female customers swiftly appraising Max Tregowan as they passed and the hint of envy in their eyes as they glanced at Aurelia. She was woman enough to enjoy that envy although it made her wonder once again at his motive. Were these attentions genuine, or solely because she was an heiress? The idea his interest might be totally fake disappointed her because she could not deny the visceral tug deep inside her every time their eyes met.

And that was despite still being unsure whether or not to believe his denial of gaming debts. The strength of her desire to believe him troubled her and she again resolved to tell him about that condition in Lady Tregowan's will without delay. Once he knew the facts, he surely would not go out of his way to pay her attention and, although she would be disappointed, at least the truth of his motives would be in the open.

And at least she would no longer be so scandalously tempted to stroke her fingers along that dark-shadowed jaw and explore that fascinating cleft in his chin, or to touch his mouth to discover if his lips were as soft as they looked, or to lay her head on his shoulder and breathe in his musky male scent with its hint of sandalwood.

She thrust such thoughts away, feeling her cheeks heat.

'I have something I must tell you, my lord,' she said, having purchased the book.

They were heading towards the door, Tregowan still

escorting her, having made no move towards the reading room.

He paused and looked at her, his head cocked to one side. 'I am listening, Miss Croome.'

Customers entered and exited the library, moving past them in a never-ending stream, eyeing them curiously.

'Not here. I...' Aurelia bit her lip. 'Would you escort me home? That way we can talk without being overheard.' She gave a little shrug. 'It is a somewhat delicate subject, but I feel it is only fair you are made aware of the truth as soon as possible. I believe it is not far to South Street and my maid will follow behind us. That would be respectable, would it not?'

Tregowan frowned down at her. 'It would. I confess I am intrigued, Miss Croome, although...' and he smiled ruefully '... I suspect what you are about to tell me will not be to my advantage. But...yes, I should be delighted to escort you home.'

Outside, Aurelia handed the book, wrapped in brown paper and tied with string, to Hall and dismissed him, telling him she would walk home. He opened his mouth—she suspected to remonstrate with her—and she shook her head, holding his gaze imperiously until he looked down.

'Very well, Miss Croome.'

'*Thank* you, Hall. And there will be no need to worry Mrs Butterby with this. Do I make myself clear?'

'Indeed, miss.'

Hall bowed. He climbed up on the box of the town coach and drove away. Aurelia was sure she could trust his discretion—she had made a point of subtly impressing the point upon the servants that, ultimately, *she* was their employer. Being under Mrs Butterby's chaperonage did not, in Aurelia's view, mean obeying every single one of her rules. She would also follow her own common sense, as long as she was not stupidly reckless, and how could walking along the street in broad daylight with a gentleman, accompanied by her maid, be deemed reckless?

She placed her hand on Tregowan's proffered arm and they crossed the road before walking along Old Bond Street. His Lordship set a brisk pace, for which she was grateful as, although it was not raining, it was cold. But the speed of their march raised a slight misgiving, even though it seemed overly dramatic to even think it.

'Be warned, sir,' she said, teasingly, although not entirely joking, '*I* might be a stranger to London streets, but I can assure you that my maid is not. I trust you to follow the shortest route to South Street.'

He chuckled. 'You have my word as a gentleman.'

'Then I shall put my trust in you.'

His arm flexed, squeezing her hand briefly into his ribcage, and her stomach fluttered in that way she was getting used to when she was in his company. She cleared her throat.

'Bet, would you please drop back? I wish to talk to His Lordship without being overheard.'

'Yes, miss.'

'Well?' Tregowan's arm flexed again beneath Aurelia's gloved hand. 'What is it you wish to tell me? I am suitably braced.'

She glanced sideways at him to find him gazing down at her with a smile playing around those fascinating lips of his…a smile that provoked another tug of awareness deep inside her. Why did this man, of all men, have to be the one to arouse such feelings in her? Tempted to wallow in a melancholic *It isn't fair* mood, she reminded herself that life itself was rarely fair. Look at what had happened to her.

Had it been fair that Augustus had left Mama and her penniless? No.

Had it been fair that Aurelia had been left destitute? No.

Had it been fair that Aurelia had been plucked from the brink of disaster to be given wealth unimaginable just six days ago? Again, no.

Just as it wasn't fair that the ragged-clothed crossing boy up ahead had to sweep away the dung and detritus of the street to allow fabulously wealthy ladies and gentlemen to cross to the other side without soiling their footwear and hems.

She thrust aside her self-pity, reminding herself she was doing this to expose Tregowan's motives.

'You are aware, of course, that I am one of Lady Tregowan's beneficiaries?'

His expression remained one of polite interest, but Aurelia caught the sudden twitch of the muscle in his jaw and she was aware his forearm was now rock hard beneath her fingers.

'I am.'

'What you are unaware of, though…'

She sucked in a breath, on a sudden swell of apprehension. This man was still a stranger to her. What if he lashed out in anger, as Augustus used to? They had turned into a side street—much quieter than the main thoroughfare—and her nerve faltered. There was no need to tell him now, this minute. She could wait…tell him when there were other people around to call upon for help if needs be. She looked up at him and her breath caught again as their eyes met. *How can I doubt him?* The thought came unbidden, followed by an upwelling of sorrow that she had no wish to examine too closely, already fearful of what it might mean.

He smiled at her, raising his brows. 'Must I beg? You tease me with the lure of revealing a secret and then you leave me waiting…and waiting…and *waiting*…' He put the back of his hand to his brow, in imitation of a swooning maiden. 'You are *too* cruel.'

Aurelia couldn't help but laugh, but sobered all too quickly. There was only one way to tell him and that was to do it. 'I hesitated because it is an uncomfortable topic for me to raise. But you have a right to know. Before... before...'

She shook her head at her uncharacteristic awkwardness. She never usually had difficulty in speaking her mind. In fact, her fault was usually the opposite—a tendency to speak her mind *too* freely. She sucked in a deep breath.

'There are three beneficiaries and there were conditions attached to our inheritance.' She could not reveal the whole 'half-sister' thing. Not yet. Not until she knew if Leah and Beatrice wished to reveal their kinship. But he must understand that the same conditions applied to all three of them. 'We each inherit a one-third share of Lady Tregowan's entire estate on condition that, one: we marry within one year; two: we spend the Season in London under Mrs Butterby's chaperonage and remain under her care until we marry; and three...' she forced herself to meet his gaze '...*three*: that we do not marry the current Lord Tregowan. That is...*you*.'

Max slammed to a halt as Aurelia's blunt words reverberated through him. He stood stock still as he scrambled to make sense of that final condition.

'Good God,' he muttered. 'Sarah must truly have grown to hate me. But...why?'

A carriage turned into the road at that moment, jerking him back to an awareness of his surroundings.

'My apologies, Miss Croome.'

He started to walk again and she remained in step with

him, her right hand still tucked through his arm. His stomach roiled with nervous energy as he slowly came to terms with what that condition meant for him. There would be no courtship of Miss Aurelia Croome. And there was no denying the dismay that spread through him as he accepted that fact.

'That revelation, as you will have realised, has come as something of a shock. But…*why*?'

Aurelia said nothing, but he felt her left hand come across to pat his left arm. She left it there, joined to her right and, briefly, she hugged his arm into her side. Wordless comfort. And it did help, that brief moment of sympathy. But did she realise exactly how huge a blow this was?

'You may not be aware of this, Miss Croome…' She had been honest with him. He would do her the same courtesy. 'But Lady Tregowan took pains to reassure me that she did not share her late husband's prejudice against my branch of the family and would not allow my father's sins to be visited upon me. She said she was happy to entrust her estate to me and I believed her. I have racked my brains, but I do not understand why that changed.'

'I only know what Mrs Butterby has told me.' She hesitated and Max had the sense of her gathering her courage. 'And we return to our exchange of the other day. It seems Lady Tregowan heard of your gambling debts—'

'Gambling debts? That is untrue,' he ground out. 'I do not gamble—well, only friendly games, for pennies. Never for high stakes. You can ask anyone… I saw how an obsession with gambling ruined my father and hurt my mother.'

'But that is the reason she changed her will. And…'

She was chewing at her lower lip, distracting him with a wave of desire that rippled through him despite his dismay. He wrenched his gaze from her.

'And because Lady Tregowan discovered that my

mother had died,' she went on, 'and that I was in…in difficult circumstances.'

He frowned at the sudden hitch in her voice and recalled her appearance when they first met…his assessment that she had not eaten a square meal for some time. Shame curled through him. She, at least, was surely deserving of her good fortune. How could he begrudge her? Yet accepting that did nothing to help his situation. Mama and Letty were due to arrive this week and he still could not decide how best to confess his circumstances without making Letty feel obliged to refuse the Season he desperately wanted her to enjoy. God, what a tangle.

'If you wish to know more,' Aurelia continued, 'you must ask Mrs Butterby. But, even if gambling was not the cause, you have admitted yourself that you are in debt.'

And now he must humble himself before this beautiful woman. His gut tightened, but he would not lie to her or mislead her.

'Yes, I am in debt. The late Earl invested nothing in the Tregowan estate with the result that by the time I inherited the title—my father died the year before the old Earl—the land was in poor condition and the house and buildings… well, rundown is a charitable description. There is a mine there—tin and copper—but that had been closed several years by the time I took over.'

'I did hear some of your conversation with Mr Austerly about your mine.'

Max scrubbed his hand across his jaw as he pondered how much to reveal. There was no need to appeal to her sympathies by speaking of the debts his father left when he died…debts to tradesmen as well as gaming debts. Debts that Max had felt honour bound to clear.

'I raised a loan almost straight away to reopen the mine. It is a lifeline for local people, providing year-round work for them.' No matter what Simon said, Max was pleased he had done so even though it had left him in difficulties from the start. 'But Sarah knew all that. She *knew* I needed money to put the estate right. Maybe, in the end, it was the thought of her fortune being used to refurbish Tregowan that changed her mind…she never did like the place. She blamed it for her continuing ill health.'

'I am sorry.'

Their eyes met and the honest sympathy in those stunning blue orbs thickened his throat.

'It is not your fault. How can I begrudge your good fortune? But…' and he forced a smile '…it seems you and I are in the same boat. We each need to marry. In my case, I need a wealthy wife. In yours…you need a husband so you don't—' He frowned. 'What happens to your inheritance if you do not meet the conditions of the will?'

He despised the sudden hope that had lifted the timbre of his voice. As did she, judging by the darkening of her expression.

'Do not pin your hopes on that happening.' Her voice was frosty. 'But, even if it did, the inheritance still would not be yours. That is all you need to know.'

'My apologies. I did not mean to… I spoke out of turn, maybe, but please believe I would not wish ill upon you or on the other two beneficiaries simply to enrich myself.'

They turned into South Street.

'Apology accepted, my lord.' Her expression was wary now. Could he blame her? 'I am happy I have had this opportunity to advise you of the conditions attached to my inheritance. As you say, we each need to wed—for differing reasons—but at least you now know not to waste your time on me, or on the other beneficiaries when they arrive in town.'

They halted outside Tregowan House. Aurelia's eyes

were guarded as she held out her gloved hand. He clasped it, unable to resist stroking his thumb across her knuckles.

'I appreciate your honesty. Thank you.'

Inadequate words to convey his feelings as shock still churned in his gut, but it proved impossible to conjure up anything more succinct. On an impulse, he raised her hand and pressed his lips to it.

Her intake of breath whispered through him, sending a shiver of desire down his spine.

She snatched her hand away. 'Good day, sir.'

Her movements were as abrupt as her farewell as she pivoted on her heel and disappeared through the now-open front door. As Max strode away, regret erupted at the injustice of meeting a woman who could affect him the way Aurelia had, yet she was the one woman he could never have. She would be hard to get out of his head, but he must try.

Chapter Ten

'Ooh, miss.' Bet eyed Aurelia, worry creasing her brow. 'That Lord Tregowan has upset you, hasn't he? You look as sick as an egg-bound chook.'

Aurelia had hurried straight upstairs and now sat slumped on the side of her bed. She forced a smile as she untied her bonnet strings. 'No. Yes.' She flung the bonnet aside. 'Yes!'

Which was, of course, unfair when it was the circumstances she found herself in that caused her distress.

But he did *sound hopeful when he asked what would happen if I didn't meet the conditions of the will.*

And that rankled, despite his attempt to acquit himself. And it hurt. Even though her main reason for telling him about those blasted conditions had been to expose exactly this. At least she now knew his true motives.

Fool!

She stood up and removed her pelisse, handing it to Bet to put away. The maid picked up the discarded bonnet, then hesitated.

'I know I am only your maid, miss, but if talking about it will help, then I promise I would never betray your confidence.'

She did not wait for Aurelia to reply but headed to the wardrobe to put the clothes away. Loneliness welled up inside Aurelia. She had been alone ever since Mama died and it had been hard to have no one in the world to lean on. No one to confide in. No one to say, *There, there. It will be all right.* Even though, deep down, she knew that was the need of a child, not of a grown woman. She had hoped—*still* hoped—that her half-sisters would fill that gap in her life. Self-pitying tears blurred her vision and she dashed them away, furious at such weakness. What did *she* have to cry about?

'Thank you, Bet,' she said, grateful the maid had her back turned. 'But—'

She paused, considering. It would be a relief to talk to *someone* and she knew she could never bring herself to confide such personal feelings to Mrs Butterby. At least, not until she was absolutely certain the chaperon could be totally trusted. Her mother had been the only person in her life so far who had never betrayed her trust and, although she now understood why Augustus had rejected her— often referring to her, within her hearing, as *that little bas- tard*—she was still reluctant to make herself vulnerable by exposing too much of herself to anyone. Especially to anyone in a position of authority over her.

'It is nothing, really. It is just… I am so lucky, I know. It feels so wrong to be unhappy about anything…and yet…'

She went on to tell Bet about the conditions attached to her inheritance. By the time she finished, Bet was perched on the bed next to her, wide-eyed.

'Ooh, miss! So, you think Lord Tregowan was only nice to you today because of your money?'

'I suspected it, which is why I wanted to tell him about that condition. But…if am honest, I don't want it to be true because I like him. I enjoy his company. And I don't like to think of him as so…so…avaricious.' She shrugged and huffed a mirthless laugh. 'Silly, is it not, when there could never be anything between us no matter how much either of us might wish it?'

'Love is not silly, miss.'

Aurelia took in Bet's shining eyes. 'You are a romantic, then, Bet? You believe in true love, hearts and flowers, and happy-ever-afters, and all of that?'

'Of course, miss. Don't you?'

Max's face materialised in her mind's eye, tempting her to believe the impossible.

'No, of course not,' she said. 'That is not the real world. In the real world we must be practical and make the best of things.'

Head bowed, Aurelia contemplated her hands, entwined in her lap, as a host of unrelated thoughts and feelings flitted through her.

'What would happen to you if you didn't obey those rules in the will, miss?'

Aurelia recalled Mr Henshaw's explanation about the conditions attached to the inheritance.

'If I should fail to abide by them, I will lose most of my share of the inheritance, which would then be divided between Miss Thame and Miss Fothergill. I would have to return any purchases, other than purely personal items such as clothing, and a cottage on the Falconfield estate would be provided for me to live in, together with a yearly allowance of two hundred pounds.'

'*Two hundred pounds?* That is a fortune!'

And, only six days ago, Aurelia would have agreed. Two hundred pounds was paltry, though, compared to the wealth that could be hers if she only stuck to a few rules. Chief of which was to find a husband. And she had established her own criteria for him—steady, kind and, most importantly, solvent—a man who could offer her the safe, secure future she craved. And now there was Leah and Beatrice to consider, too. She had only just found them. The inheritance would make them all equals. She could not bear to think of them drifting apart, which could easily happen if one of them failed to wed and ended up living such a different life to the others.

It took all of his resolve for Max not to call on Aurelia over the next couple of days, but no amount of willpower could keep her from his thoughts. He had told Simon about the condition preventing any of the heiresses from marrying him and Simon—after a suitably expletive-ridden curse aimed at Sarah Tregowan—typically then applied all his energies to nosing out which of the young ladies expected in town for the Season boasted the most generous dowries. Two of them were already in London with their families, so he cajoled and bullied Max into accompanying him to any events they were likely to attend.

By the third evening following his encounter with Aurelia, Max had ceased to care where he was and whose event it was. Those evenings had congealed into a single mass of forgettable conversations and unremarkable faces as he trod up the stairs to yet another salon, guided by the hubbub of conversation that drifted through the open door.

'Miss Harker is over there,' hissed Simon as they paused on the threshold. 'And there is Miss Rowlands. You are in luck! I shall be in the card room if you need me.'

I must try. Surely there will be someone I can face marrying?

Max crossed the room to the Harkers, his heart heavy.

'Lord Tregowan. Such a pleasure to see you again.' Mrs Harker simpered as she dropped a curtsy and her eldest daughter, her cheeks blushing rosily, followed suit.

'Mrs Harker. Miss Harker.' Max bowed. 'The pleasure is all mine.'

He felt dead inside. What was he doing? He had no interest in Miss Harker, despite her ten-thousand-pound dowry. He had nothing against the girl, but she was too young, too biddable, too colourless—all the things Aurelia Croome was not. He cast a surreptitious look around the room even though he already knew Aurelia was unlikely to be present because Mrs Butterby—according to the servants' grapevine—had only risen from her sickbed the day before.

Hopefully they would begin socialising soon and then at least he could look forward to seeing Aurelia, even if they did have no future.

'Would you care to stroll with me, Miss Harker?'

Even as he proffered his arm, Max cautioned himself to pay attention to other unmarried females here tonight, including Miss Rowlands. Societal expectations were unforgiving—if a bachelor paid marked attention to an unmarried lady and then failed to *come up to scratch*, it was not the man who would suffer the consequences, but the girl. People would speculate, often with spiteful glee, as they wondered what was wrong with her that she had failed to elicit a proposal. He had no wish to be responsible for such gossip. His lack of enthusiasm was no fault of these girls.

'It's early days yet, Maximilian,' Simon said later as they arrived home at the end of the evening. They headed for the drawing room where Simon poured them both a brandy. 'Do not despair. By mid-March, the Season will liven up, and the balls will start, giving you more choice. You *will* find somebody.'

Max closed his eyes at that and Aurelia's smiling face

materialised in his mind's eye. So tempting. So painful. So damned impossible. He longed to banish her from his thoughts for good but, instead, he found himself wondering about her...what had happened to her to bring her to those 'difficult circumstances' she had spoken of?

The threadbare clothes and the hunger that had sharpened her cheekbones and given the illusion of eyes too large for her face. Her eyes...those beautiful, bright blue, perceptive eyes—were not too large at all. They were perfect. As was she. He longed to know all about her. He needed to know if his impression of a fiercely guarded vulnerability was correct. He wanted—intensely—to protect her, even though the only practical way of doing so would be to marry her, yet he knew that would be the quickest way to put her once again at risk.

'Max, my dear chap.'

Max opened his eyes at Simon's soft words.

'You are brooding again.'

Max ignored him.

'Is it Miss Croome? Is she the reason for your lack of enthusiasm?'

'I told you I can take no pleasure in searching for a wife using the size of her dowry as the overriding criterion,' Max growled, even as he wondered if Aurelia would be at Lady Pewsey's party the following night. The Austerlys would surely have made sure she had an invitation, just as they'd made sure he was on the guest list. 'Forgive me if I cannot laugh and joke about it as if I did not care.'

Simon sighed. 'What am I to do with you? You do not have the luxury to think with your heart. Or with your cock, for that matter. It is time to accept that Miss Croome is out of the running and to concentrate on the perfectly acceptable girls who will solve your money worries once and for all. Would that not remove a huge weight from your shoulders?'

'Yes, of course,' Max lied.

The following morning a letter addressed to Max was handed to him as he and Simon broke their fast. Max broke the seal and scanned the missive.

Dear Maximilian,
I have news of your mother and your sister. It would seem their arrival is delayed. Please attend me at noon and I shall apprise you of their circumstances. Do not be disturbed, for they are both quite well.
Your affectionate godmother,
Veronica Langbrook

'I am summoned,' he said to Simon. 'Lady Langbrook. Noon today. It seems Mama and Letty have been delayed.'

He knew they had reached France, for Letty had written to him when their ship docked at Marseilles—they had opted to sail the first leg of the journey as crossing the Alps at this time of year was nigh on impossible. Their intention had been to then travel up through France by road before sailing across the Channel. He had no need to wonder why his godmother had not told him the reasons in her letter. This way, he would be forced to visit her and face her inquisition. By now, she would no doubt know all about him being cut out of Sarah's will.

'So the dreaded moment is delayed?' Simon forked eggs into his mouth.

Max sighed. 'I might not look forward to telling them the truth, but that doesn't mean I won't be delighted to see them again.'

'I am sure they will understand.'

'I know they will, but that makes it worse. I've let them down and Mama, unless she has changed, will forgive me instantly.'

'Why should she not forgive you? Your predicament is your father's fault. He is the person who let you all down.'

Max scowled into his coffee. 'In the end, it doesn't matter who bears the blame. Mama can barely walk with her damaged lungs. She needs a safe, warm home. And Letty...' He sighed. 'She has sacrificed so much to care for Mama and I know that as soon as she understands my circumstances she will refuse a Season and claim to be happy to remain as Mama's companion for ever more.'

'That sounds a challenge.' Simon cut into his ham and raised a forkful, but paused as he was about to put it in his mouth. 'At least it'll take your mind off the luscious Miss Croome.'

Max glared at his friend, now chewing contentedly, his eyes wide with innocence. How he regretted telling Simon about his meeting with Aurelia...and about that impossible condition that—amazingly—had no power to completely quash the longing in his heart.

The longcase case in the hall struck noon as Max was shown into Lady Langbrook's drawing room where she sat by the fire.

'Godmama.' He bowed and kissed her scented, wrinkled cheek. 'I trust I find you in good health?'

'Silly question. I am old, Maximilian. Of course I am not in good health.' She gestured at a chair. 'You have only just arrived in town, I collect?'

Max sat down. 'I arrived last week.' There was no point in lying. He knew his godmother well and such a pointed question could only mean she knew very well how long he had been in town without calling on her. He stifled a sigh. 'I have been a little preoccupied and I neglected to call and pay my respects. For which I apologise.'

'Hmph. Now, what is this rumour I hear about Sarah Tregowan? Is it true she has cut you out of her will?'

'It's true. She has left her fortune in equal parts to three young ladies.'

'Who? Why?'

Max shrugged. 'Does it matter? It is a fact and there is nothing I can do to change it. Now, please tell me…what has happened to delay Mama and Letty?'

'Mr Casbourne is indisposed. They have been forced to halt their journey until he is able to travel.'

'Mr Casbourne?' Max racked his brains, but could not recall having heard the name before. 'Who the de—?' His mouth snapped shut at his godmother's raised brow. 'I beg your pardon, but *who* is Mr Casbourne?'

'Did your sister not mention him in her letter?' Her eyes gleamed, relishing the power of knowing something Max did not. 'He was a fellow passenger on the ship they sailed from Naples to Marseilles. He offered to escort them on the journey through France and, as your Mama was uncomfortable with having only servants to accompany them, they accepted. But the foolish man has fractured his leg—so very careless of him—and your Mama and Letty have opted to wait until he recovers before continuing their journey. They still hope to be here by Eastertide, however.'

'I dare say Letty will have written to me at Tregowan,' said Max. 'My housekeeper will no doubt forward her letter on to me.'

'Now then. Back to this inheritance business.' She cocked her head to one side. The sympathy in her eyes scraped at him. 'Have you told your mother or Leticia about the state of Tregowan?'

'Not yet. And I would appreciate it if you do not say anything to them until I get the chance to tell them myself.'

'But—'

'Godmama...' He took her hand. 'Please. I do not want Letty to feel she cannot enjoy her Season because of the expense. You *know* what she is like.'

'I do. Selfless to a fault. And that is why I wish to help. Send her bills to me. I am your godmother. Look upon it as getting part of your inheritance before I die.'

Max shook his head. 'You know I cannot accept, although I am grateful for the offer.'

'Cannot or will not? Max...you are like a son to me. I should like to help.'

'There is no need. I plan to marry.'

She leaned forward. 'Who? One of these Tregowan heiresses?'

'No!' He could not bear to talk about that. He stood up. 'It is all in hand, Godmama, and I promise you will be the first to know as soon as I have any news. Now, it is time I took my leave. And thank you for offering Mama and Letty a place to stay in town.'

'I shall be glad of the company.' She eyed Max. 'I am planning a small, quite select soirée next week. Monday. I shall send you an invitation. And I expect you to attend.'

'I would not dream of missing it, Godmama.' He took her outstretched hand and kissed it, wondering what she was up to, for her face held a familiar smug expression. 'Until then.'

Max was haunted by a mix of guilt and dissatisfaction as he left the house. Now he had told his godmother that his plan to resolve his financial problems revolved around marriage he was committed. It was time to put Aurelia Croome out of his head and direct all his energy towards finding a wealthy bride.

Icy rain mixed with sleet slanted down, blown by a bitterly cold breeze. Max pulled the collar of his greatcoat high and tilted his hat so the brim protected his face as he headed for Portman Square, his spirits plunging deep as he contemplated his loveless future.

Chapter Eleven

'It was most gracious of Lady Pewsey to invite us to her
party tonight, was it not, Aurelia? Especially when your
acquaintance is with her parents rather than with her. Most
gracious indeed. Have you decided which gown you will
wear? Ooh! Who knows *whom* you might meet...? I had
not thought to receive any invitations yet, as it is so early,
and yet here we are, attending a baroness's party.'

Aurelia laughed at Mrs Butterby's barely contained
excitement. They had seen the Austerlys at church last
Sunday morning—the day before Mrs Butterby had been
struck down with her cold—and had been introduced to
their daughter, Emma, Lady Pewsey, and her husband, the
Baron. And then, two days ago, an invitation to an evening party at Lord Pewsey's house had been delivered.
Mrs Butterby had not stopped crowing about it ever since,
viewing it as an early entrée into polite society, and Aurelia was convinced her determination not to miss the event
had hastened the chaperon's recovery.

'I have admitted her graciousness a total of...let me
see...it must be at least a dozen times by now, ma'am,'
Aurelia said.

Mrs Butterby stiffened. 'I am sorry if I am boring you,

but you clearly do not fully understand the importance of such particular attention.'

'It is probably more to do with making up numbers than any great desire to include us,' muttered Aurelia.

'Nor,' said Mrs Butterby repressively, 'do you appreciate how many well-connected people you will meet there. All of which is vital if you are to *get noticed* this coming Season.'

'I thought you were of the opinion an heiress will always attract notice?'

'I am. She will. But…your age will count against you, of course. You will be up against all the young ladies in their first foray into society and, although I concede that your looks are exemplary, your age…' Mrs Butterby allowed her words to drift into silence as she gave a despondent shake of her head.

Aurelia bit back her irritation, knowing it would do no good to voice her thoughts. Mrs Butterby was utterly enchanted by the entire prospect of the Season ahead of them but, the more Aurelia understood about what was to come, the more she viewed the whole thing as a nonsense. A marriage mart? It had more in common with a horse market to her mind—with the young debutantes as the brood mares to be haggled over.

All she wanted and needed was a decent man to marry so she did not lose her inheritance, but she was left cold by Mrs Butterby's hierarchy of desirable characteristics for potential spouses. The chaperon's sight was set on peers for all three of the half-sisters, with nobly born gentlemen lacking a title but still related by blood to an aristocratic family at the bottom of her list of candidates.

'It is far too early to even think about meeting my future husband yet,' she said. 'I should prefer to wait until my sisters join me…it will be more fun.'

'*Fun?* Marriage is a very serious business, my dear. If a lady does not wed, what is she for?'

Aurelia frowned, but held her tongue, aware that she and the chaperon would likely never agree on that subject.

'I know you think I am hopelessly old-fashioned in my views, Aurelia,' Mrs Butterby went on, 'but I promise you I only have your best interests at heart.'

'And that includes marriage to a nobleman regardless of his character?'

'No. Of *course* I should want you all to be happy with whomever you marry.' She tilted her head, her grey eyes brimming with sympathy. 'I do not understand why you have this idea in your head that all aristocrats are un-trustworthy, my dear. They will not *all* be like Augustus Croome.'

Aurelia shot to her feet. 'I believe I shall wear that new ice-blue evening gown tonight.'

'It might help you understand your prejudices better if you talked about him, you know, Aurelia.'

Aurelia ignored the concern in Mrs Butterby's eyes. She could not talk about that man. Not to anyone. All she wanted was to forget him. 'I shall see you at dinner.'

As she climbed the stairs the thought that had been nib-bling away at her ever since that invitation had arrived—the thought that, try as she might, she could not keep at bay—erupted once again.

Would *he* be there?

Every inch of her skin heated at the thought, despite telling herself the fewer times they met the easier it would be.

Later that evening, as she and Mrs Butterby chatted to Mr and Mrs Austerly, Aurelia searched the faces of her fellow guests at Lady Pewsey's party and tamped down her disappointment at Max Tregowan's absence. She had begun to think of him as Max in her head, enjoying the feeling of intimacy it engendered, even though she knew it was a foolish fantasy.

With his wife and Mrs Butterby deep in conversation about the management of servants, Mr Austerly turned his attention to Aurelia, saying, 'Lord Tregowan will be here shortly, Miss Croome. I make no doubt you will be happy to renew your acquaintance with him.'

Her heart gave a funny little flip and it beat just that bit faster. She used her eyes to flick a warning glance towards Mrs Butterby. Mr Austerly nodded and turned away from the others. Aurelia mirrored his movement.

'Indeed I shall,' she said.

Mr Austerly placed his finger alongside his nose. 'Neither Mother nor I have forgotten your request, my dear.'

'Thank you. I am grateful, sir.'

After church on Sunday, Aurelia had managed a quiet word with the Austerlys, and begged them not to reveal to Mrs Butterby that she had met Lord Tregowan on the mail coach.

'Although...' His forehead wrinkled anxiously. 'There is nothing untoward is there, Miss Croome? I mean, we should not like to be a party to...to...' His cheeks turned red. 'After all, Mrs Butterby *is* your chaperon.'

'Rest assured there is nothing improper about my request, sir. You are aware by now of my good fortune?'

'We are. We did wonder why you were so secretive during the journey but, as soon as we heard you had inherited the Tregowan fortune, I said to Mother, "There you are. Depend upon it, *that* is why Miss Croome did not tell us why she was going to London".'

'And you were right, dear sir. I was afraid that revealing the truth could only make our journey uncomfortable.'

'And your thoughtfulness does you credit, my dear,' he said, patting Aurelia's arm.

'But...when I arrived, I failed to tell Mrs Butterby I had met Lord Tregowan and then we met him in the Park. She introduced us, and neither of us revealed we had met before, and...' She gave a helpless shrug. 'There was no real reason for secrecy, but if she finds out now it would be sure to raise awkward questions.'

'I understand.' Mr Austerly winked. 'You may rely upon us. Oh, look, here he is now.'

Aurelia glanced over to the door where Max now stood, scanning the room, a deep crease carved between his dark brows. His gaze collided with Aurelia's and she felt the physical jolt deep inside her as his expression softened and his lips curved in a smile.

'Well, he looks delighted to see you, my dear. Oh! Does he now know the truth about your inheritance? Will it be awkward for you two to meet?'

She tore her gaze from Max.

'He knows the truth, sir.'

Mr Austerly beamed. 'Jolly good. And it appears he bears you no grudge, so that is splendid.' He raised his arm and waved at Tregowan. 'Now.' He rubbed his hands together briskly. 'Please forgive me, Miss Croome, but you will have to wait before renewing your acquaintance with His Lordship, I'm afraid. I have come up with a splendid notion concerning his mine and I simply cannot wait to tell him. It'll be deadly dull talk for a female, so I shall leave you with the other ladies for now, but I promise I shan't detain him for long.'

He trundled across the room and Aurelia turned back to Mrs Butterby and Mrs Austerly, her emotions a tangle of contradictions. Happiness at seeing Max battled with the annoyance and hurt that still lingered after their last conversation, and also with the awkwardness of what she would say and how she should behave when—as they inevitably would—they spoke. And, deep inside, there was that heavy weight of knowledge that, whatever she said, whatever she might feel for him, they could never belong together. Ever.

It's a silly schoolgirl crush. That is all.

But the memory of the comfort he had offered during that long, cold, jarring journey was not easily dismissed. She had felt safe and protected, and he had been the perfect gentleman. She cast a surreptitious glance to where Mr Austerly and Max were talking and felt her cheeks heat when, again, her eyes met Max's dark gaze. She became aware of Mrs Butterby's scrutiny and speedily schooled her expression into one of interest as she joined in her conversation with Mrs Austerly, which had moved on to fashions and shopping. Before long, however, they were joined by Mrs Austerly's daughter Emma, Lady Pewsey.

'Please excuse the interruption, ladies, but I thought Miss Croome might like to meet some of the other young people here tonight.'

'Thank you,' Aurelia said as she walked with Lady Pewsey towards a group of three girls. 'I appreciate the chance to meet some people nearer my own age.'

Although, to be fair, Lady Pewsey was closer to her age than the girls in the group, who looked young enough to only recently have left the schoolroom. Barely had Aurelia been introduced to Miss Glaston, Miss Deborah Glaston and Lady Portia Paxford when two gentlemen joined them. Aurelia was conscious of their assessment of her and she stretched her lips in a smile, understanding that introductions to such men, who would then feel entitled to openly appraise her, were to be her fate until she wed.

'Lord Sampford, Lord Ibstock, this is Miss Croome.

It is her first time in London. Lord Ibstock is the Miss Glastons' brother, Miss Croome.'

Aurelia curtsied, aware of Mrs Butterby watching from across the room with an approving smile. After a few minutes of small talk, Lady Pewsey excused herself to go and greet more arrivals, leaving Aurelia with these strangers. The presence of the two gentlemen, she soon realised, had the effect of silencing the three young ladies, who simply stood there with demure smiles on their faces.

'Always a pleasure to meet a new face, especially one as pretty as yours,' said Sampford, a slightly built man of around thirty, of medium height, with a pleasant countenance, fair hair and huge ears. 'Where have you been hiding yourself until now, Miss Croome?'

Aurelia kept her smile pinned to her face, conscious in the periphery of her vision of Mrs Butterby keeping her eye on her. 'In Bath, my lord.'

'Bath?' Ibstock tittered, setting Aurelia's back up. 'Is that not full of dowagers and invalids these days?'

Aurelia elevated her nose at His Lordship, who was stouter than his friend, with close-set eyes she immediately distrusted. 'Not entirely, my lord,' she said sweetly. 'After all, *I* lived there and I am neither a dowager nor an invalid. As you may see.'

She was aware of a whispered gasp of horror from the three girls. She did not care.

Ibstock scowled disapprovingly down his nose. 'Croome? Are you one of the Wiltshire Croomes?'

She raised her brows. 'I have absolutely no idea and, may I say, I could not care less.' She had already decided not to even try to conceal where she had come from, because someone was sure to find out and reveal the truth. 'My mother was a milliner and I was too busy helping her in her shop to concern myself with distant relations.'

Ibstock's nostrils flared. 'A *shop* girl?'

Aurelia bridled at his tone and at the way he moved to place himself between her and his sisters. Sampford stepped forward as she opened her mouth to retort, deftly cutting between her and Ibstock.

'I apologise on behalf of my friend, Miss Croome. Rest assured that not *every* gentleman will hold your past against you.' He crooked his arm. 'Would you care for a turn around the room?'

She wouldn't, not really. But neither did she wish to stay near Ibstock, especially now she seemed to have given him a disgust of her within such a short time of their first meeting. So she nodded, placing her hand on Sampford's arm, and they walked away, leaving Ibstock behind.

'We heard your father was Augustus Croome,' Sampford said.

'That is correct, but I should prefer not to discuss him.'

She might as well not have spoken, for all the notice he took.

'I did not know him,' he said, 'but I do know his nephew. The family do not speak of him. He was—'

'He was the black sheep of the family,' Aurelia interrupted. 'Disowned by them. Which is why I know nothing about them. Pray tell me, Lord Sampford—if you were both already aware of my father's identity, why did Lord Ibstock ask if I was one of the Wiltshire Croomes?'

Sampford halted and stared down at her. 'My, you are forthright, are you not? But you must know there are rumours flying around about the young lady who has taken up residence at Tregowan House. Is it true you have inherited the Tregowan fortune?' He chuckled. 'Poor Tregowan.' There was no sympathy in his voice. Rather, there was something akin to glee, as though he relished others' misfortunes. 'He has been anticipating that inheritance for the past eight years. Such a blow—it has put him in an unholy tangle, especially now his mother and sister are returning from Italy.'

'His mother and sister?'

'Oh, yes. Any day now. They are due to stay with Lady Langbrook for the Season. Did you not know…it is the very latest on dit—together with *your* inheritance, of course. His mother is an invalid, you know. In a wheelchair. And the sister gave up any chance of marriage to care for her. *Poor* Tregowan…that really is piling on the pressure, don't you agree? The word is that Tregowan Place is a very ruin…uninhabitable, even…so quite where he plans to house his womenfolk is a mystery now he has no hope of the Tregowan properties, or income from the investments.' He cast Aurelia a sly grin. 'It must be a considerable sum?'

Aurelia set her jaw. Damned cheek of the man. 'I am not the sole beneficiary, Lord Sampford. There are three of us.'

'Ooh! Three of you? Who? Do tell…any confidences will go no further…'

Aurelia silently berated herself for giving even that much away, although it would be common knowledge once Leah and Beatrice joined her.

'You will find out soon enough, my lord.' She elevated her nose. 'I do not approve of gossip.'

'Oh, neither do I, dear lady. Neither do I,' he said, comfortably, as he secured her hand on his arm once again and continued their stroll, out of the drawing room and on to the spacious landing. 'But…did you hear…'

Aurelia blocked his voice out as they walked up and down and he droned on, telling her titbits of news about people she had never heard of before. His monologue appeared to require no response from her, so she pondered what he had said about Max. Was it true? Would he soon have his mother and sister to provide for? And his mother…an invalid… Sympathy for him gathered in her breast as she recalled his vehement denial that he had accrued gambling debts. But *something* had caused Lady Tregowan to take against him—there was no smoke without fire, as Mama used to say.

A different voice—a deeper voice that spoke her name with some urgency—penetrated her musings and she came back to her surroundings with a start to find herself already halfway down the stairs with Lord Sampford.

Chapter Twelve

'**M**iss Croome!' Max Tregowan was striding along the
landing above them. 'Your chaperon is asking for you.'
He ran down the stairs, halting on the step below the one
on which she and Sampford had halted, blocking their
progress. 'Sampford.' He inclined his head, but a hard
glint in his dark eyes suggested he held little regard for
the other man.

'I was taking Miss Croome to view the library.' Sampford glowered at Max. 'She told me she enjoys reading.'

Did I?

Aurelia had no recollection of saying anything much
at all to His Lordship after he launched into that ocean of
gossip. The humiliation of almost allowing herself to be
walked into disaster while daydreaming made her sharp.
'That is correct, Lord Tregowan. I adore books and librar-
ies are such fascinating places.'

'Nevertheless, Mrs Butterby is anxious that you do not
stray out of her sight. *Thank* you, Sampford.' Max thrust
his hand out, clearly expecting Aurelia to take it. 'I shall
escort Miss Croome back to her chaperon.'

Aurelia ignored his outstretched hand and stuck her

nose in the air. He needn't think she had forgotten their last meeting so readily.

Sampford's lips compressed. 'No need for you to trouble yourself, Tregowan. I shall return her myself. Right away.'

Despite her irritation at Max, Aurelia found herself hoping he would insist. She would far rather be escorted by him than by Sampford, but stubbornness stopped her from accepting his hand. Instead, she turned on the stair, saying, 'Thank you, Lord Sampford. I am obliged to you.'

She felt the burn of Max's gaze between her shoulder blades as she walked back up the stairs on Sampford's arm. He delivered her back to Mrs Butterby who was not, as Aurelia expected, watching out anxiously for her charge's return, but was deep in conversation with a Mrs Barrington, telling her all about Lady Tregowan's final illness.

As Sampford strolled away, Mrs Butterby broke off her conversation to say, 'Lord Sampford! An *earl*, my dear. I just knew you would take. Rumour has it he is hanging out for a wife this Season. How exciting if he chooses *you*.'

'If he does, I shall refuse him,' muttered Aurelia, earning herself a sharp reprimand from her chaperon and a severe look from Mrs Barrington who, although not titled, was evidently *well connected*—that phrase Aurelia was beginning to dread.

As the two ladies resumed their conversation, Aurelia found herself questioning whether the chaperon had, in fact, asked Max to find her at all. She soon decided she had not, a conclusion that thrilled her for it could only mean that he had been watching over her. Protecting her.

Some time later, bored out of her wits as Mrs Butterby and Mrs Barrington discussed yet more people Aurelia had never heard of, she swept her gaze around the room for the umpteenth time and there he was. Max. Standing alone on the edge of a group of people, sipping a glass of champagne. Aurelia murmured to Mrs Butterby that she was going to find the Misses Glaston and Lady Portia and the chaperon broke off her conversation to pat her hand.

'I am delighted you are making friends, Aurelia,' she said—somewhat patronisingly, in Aurelia's opinion— before resuming her conversation.

Aurelia weaved her way around the room until she was close to Max. The leap of joy in his expression as he noticed her sent shivers of delight chasing over her skin.

'Mrs Butterby did not send you to find me. Did she?'

Max's jaw set. 'What makes you think that?'

'I can easily ask her.' Aurelia made to walk away.

'Wait!' He sighed. 'No. You are right. But I saw you leave the room with Sampford, and I was…do you not know better than to wander off with random strangers?'

'Yes. Of course I do. I… I wasn't paying attention. He was droning on so, about people I do not know and do not care to know, and I didn't notice where we were going.'

'Sampford,' he growled, 'is the very worst of all tittle-tattles and he has a spiteful streak. You should not believe all he says and you ought to watch what you say to him. He will twist your words to enhance the stories he likes to spread, simply to elicit a sharper intake of breath from his audience.'

'He told me your mother and sister are soon expected to return from Italy. Is that true?'

His eyes glinted. 'So you did pay attention to some things he said?'

Aurelia shrugged carelessly, determined not to give him reason to suspect how happy she was simply to talk to him. 'Yours was one of the few names I recognised. Do not read anything more into it.'

He laughed. 'That has put me in my place, has it not?

Well, yes. That is correct. As they have lived in Italy for the past decade, Letty never had a Season.' His head dipped, as did his voice, giving the impression he had almost forgotten Aurelia was there. 'She deserves the chance to enjoy herself. And maybe even meet someone who will make her happy.'

'And will they return to Italy after the Season?'

'No.' Max drained his glass and beckoned a footman who was circulating among the guests with a tray of drinks.

'A glass of champagne?' he asked Aurelia as he set his empty glass on the tray and selected another.

She nodded and took the glass he offered her, sipping as she wondered at his brusque reply to her question.

'You do realise that if Sampford had taken you to the library and you had been seen, that you would be hopelessly compromised and bound to marry him?' Max speared her with a disapproving look. 'Is that how you wish to gain a husband, or do you wish to have some say in the matter?'

She frowned up at him. 'Of course I wish some say in the matter. What a ridiculous thing to say.'

'Then you need to exercise more caution.'

She was angry because he was right. 'There is no need to be so smug about it. I admit I made a mistake. I shall take more care in future. Satisfied?'

'Satisfied?' His lips—those fascinating lips—pressed together firmly and he sighed. 'It is not my place to be either satisfied or dissatisfied about any aspect of your life, is it? But having said that, I should hate to see you suffer through an unwitting transgression of the rules that bind society.'

'Then do not watch,' she teased.

He held her gaze for several seconds over the rim of his glass as he drank. His look reached deep down inside her, gathering her insides into a ball of anticipation that set her pulse racing and dried her mouth. She sipped her drink, searching for something…anything…to break the tension that stretched between them, yet the simplest solution of tearing her gaze from his did not seem to be an option.

'I cannot *not* watch.' He looked down at his glass, then, and she could breathe again. He took her glass from suddenly nerveless fingers and placed both glasses on a side table. 'Come. Let us walk.'

He did not offer his arm as Sampford had done, but they strolled around the perimeter of the room, side by side, not speaking. Her head was full of past meetings. What had been said. The glances. What they meant. What she felt. And curiosity as to what he was thinking. What he felt… and why they were both playing with fire when the only outcome was that they would both be burned.

'We have not spoken since the day we met at Hookham's,' he said. 'I regret my clumsiness. I upset you unintentionally.'

He walked through the open door on to the spacious landing and she followed. There were few people out there, but servants were coming and going constantly and she felt safe enough. She bit back the denial that he had upset her. It would be a pointless lie, its only purpose to soothe her silly pride. Somehow, she yearned to be honest with him. Always.

'Do not fear I shall try to entice you to the library.' His voice held the hint of a laugh, but it then turned sorrowful. 'We both know that would spell disaster for us both.'

She could not answer, afraid emotion would choke her words and reveal too much of herself and her inner feelings, even to him. Especially to him, for she suspected he had the power to hurt her. Unbearably.

'I want to thank you again for your frankness that day,'

he went on when she offered no reply. 'I did appreciate it. It took courage.' He halted by a window set back in an alcove and faced her. 'Are you still cross with me?'

'Cross? Why should I be cross?' she asked, even though she knew what he meant and she relived that sinking sensation in her stomach at the sudden hope that had lifted his voice as he asked about those conditions.

He held her gaze for several long, fraught moments. 'You know why,' he said eventually and the warmth and intimacy in his deep voice kindled a flicker of awareness deep in her belly that in turn lit a spark that darted through her, causing her breath to catch in her lungs. She bit her lip, desperate to hide her reaction to him, and tore her eyes from his.

'I was not angry that day. I was merely taken aback at your blatant hope that if I fail to meet the conditions attached to my inheritance, you might then benefit.' She elevated her nose, striving for the ladylike conduct deemed essential by Mrs Butterby. 'I did not anticipate such ungentlemanly behaviour.'

A strangled noise, stemming from his throat, reached her ears and she snapped her gaze back to him. The wretch was clearly trying not to laugh. At her!

'Well? Can you deny it?'

'No. I shall not insult you with a denial but, in my own defence, any hope was heavily weighted towards the benefit for me. The minute I realised that my good fortune would be your *mis*fortune, that hope evaporated like mist in the wind.' A slight frown creased his forehead as his eyes searched hers. His voice lowered to a whisper. 'It is important you believe me. Please.'

It was her turn to frown and her stomach clenched uneasily. This was too intimate. Too risky. She ought to run.

Get back to safety and to Mrs Butterby. But she could not tear herself away. Not yet. 'Why?'

He moved closer and she stepped backed into the alcove. He propped one hand against the window frame behind her.

'I do not want you to think badly of me.'

'Then why, pray, were you desperately trying not to laugh just now?'

His smile turned crooked. His eyes though…they shone with the genuine light of admiration and a warning whispered through her. This was unwise. So very unwise. But it was…addictive.

'It was the way you said, "I did not anticipate such ungentlemanly behaviour".' His brown eyes twinkled. She had to look up to meet them. He was close. So very close. His scent—all male, with a hint of sandalwood—invaded her and set her nerve-endings tingling. 'You sounded as though you had swallowed a dictionary.' His voice deepened still further, stirring yet more unfathomable feelings deep inside her. 'Not at all like the young woman I met in Bristol ten days ago.'

Aurelia swallowed. She should step away now. Move past him out on to the landing. Find her way back to the other guests. But she did not move. 'You think me pompous, Lord Tregowan?'

He might be right. In her eagerness to conceal her attraction to him, she had assumed the mantle of a highborn lady. Which she was not and he knew it. Heat washed across her chest and up her neck, and she watched his eyes follow the progress of that blush. His absolute focus did nothing to cool her down. And then he licked his lips, provoking a tightness in her belly and a swift tug in that intimate flesh between her thighs.

'Max,' he murmured. 'call me Max. And I would not

be so *ungentlemanly* as to describe you as pompous, Aurelia.' A smile curled the corners of his mouth. 'It was an attempt to put me in my place for which I cannot blame you.' He leaned towards her, his lips close to her ear, and her heart hammered against her ribcage even as her breath caught, yet again, in her lungs. 'Hoity-toity, maybe. Spirited, definitely. Pompous? Never.'

His hot breath whispered across the bare skin of her neck and upper chest, raising goose pimples in its wake. She could not deny he was flirting with her, although to what purpose she could not begin to guess. And neither could she deny she was enjoying his attention, or that she wanted to continue and longed to see where these thrilling feelings might lead. But self-preservation was ingrained in her and she feared losing everything she had gained if she failed to meet those conditions set in Lady Tregowan's will. If they were seen…

'This…' The words stuck in her throat, and she cleared it. 'I must go. I must find Mrs Butterby.'

'Why?'

'You need to ask why? This… Oh! I cannot say it. You know very well what I mean.'

She placed both hands on his chest and pushed him back. To his credit, he did not resist. She slipped past him and hurried towards the salon, beckoned towards safety by the hubbub of voices sounding through the open door.

Chapter Thirteen

*W*hat the—?

Max shoved his fingers through his hair and paced along the landing, away from the salon. What in God's name had he been thinking?

You weren't thinking. At least, not with your brain. You mindless idiot.

He halted, staring blindly, his chest heaving as self-recrimination engulfed him.

Supposing someone had seen us? What then?

He shuddered. Thank goodness she'd had the good sense to stop before they had gone any further. He...*he* had forgotten everything other than the bewitching woman he was with. Every. Single. Other. Thing.

I should apologise.

But how? What words? She had been right. Again. It was impossible to put into words. And, once they had vocalised it, and admitted to that invisible thread that seemed to link them—a link she surely felt as vividly as him— how then could they go back?

I need to avoid her. That is the only solution. Now Mama and Letty are delayed, I should go back to Cornwall and only return to London at Easter so I can escort

Letty to balls and so forth. And, by then, maybe Aurelia will have met a man whose attentions will not result in the loss of her inheritance.

Sampford's smirking face materialised in his mind's eye and the urge to obliterate that stupid grin had him curling his hand into a fist. Well, he'd warned her about the man and she did not seem enamoured of him, so hopefully she would look elsewhere for a spouse. Find a decent man who would treat her well and with respect.

Respect? Like you did not five minutes ago? *That* sort of respect?

He swallowed his growl of frustration as he pivoted on his heel and stalked back to the salon to seek out his host and hostess in order to take his leave.

'Tregowan!'

Max swallowed his groan as Mr Austerly hailed him.

'Have you had time to think about my offer?'

Austerly had told Max earlier that he was interested in investing in Max's mine. In fairness, there was little for Max to think about as he had scant choice if the mine was to remain open, let alone thrive. It needed an injection of capital from somewhere and he did not have the where-withal. And an external investment would help ease his own money troubles.

'I have. And, yes, I am interested,' he said.

'Jolly good!' Austerly rubbed his hands together. 'I shall write to Keast and instruct him to be prepared to travel to Tregowan directly to inspect the mine. Keast is a wizard at developing any mine's potential.' He grinned happily. 'Let us hope this will be a lucrative collaboration for us both, my lord.'

'I am still surprised you wish to concern yourself with another mine, sir. I should have thought your existing mines were more than enough to keep you occupied.'

'They would be if I was a man for resting on my laurels. But I miss the thrill of new discoveries and new opportunities. And I *like* you, Tregowan. You're a good man and will make a fine business partner, I have no doubt. Now, do you wish to be present when Keast inspects the mine?'

'Yes, I would like to be. I am sure I will learn a great deal.'

'When do you intend to return to Cornwall?'

Despite his earlier thought that he ought to put distance between himself and Aurelia, he couldn't bring himself to leave. Not just yet.

'I will let you know,' he said.

'I'll tell Keast to stand by.' He nudged Max with his elbow and lowered one eyelid in a wink. 'Neither would I be in a hurry to leave with a lovely young maiden like Miss Croome around.'

Max prayed Austerly was just ribbing him in his bluff way and that his interest in Aurelia wasn't that obvious.

'What is wrong with you, Max? You've been like a bear with a sore head all morning,' Simon said as he and Max climbed into his carriage after a few rounds at Jackson's Saloon on Monday morning. 'I thought our sessions were meant to be friendly bouts. It was all I could do to hold you at bay.'

Max sighed. 'Sorry. I've decided to go back to Cornwall.' He'd wrestled with his conscience ever since the Pewseys' party and it had to be the most sensible suggestion. 'I need to check on the renovations and it makes sense for Austerly's man to inspect Wheal Rowenna as soon as possible.'

'When?'

'Oh...well, I must attend my godmother's soiree this

evening…' *I ought to leave tomorrow.* 'And…well… I thought the end of the week.'

Just a few more days. That cannot hurt. Can it?

'So why is the prospect of leaving London making you grumpy enough to take out your frustrations on me? Could it be anything to do with the glorious Miss Croome?'

'I've *told* you,' growled Max. 'If she marries me, she loses her inheritance. And I need a wealthy wife.'

He had made the fateful error of confiding in Simon when he arrived home from Lady Pewsey's party two nights ago. Plied with Simon's excellent quality brandy, it had not taken long before he had admitted his growing feelings for Aurelia and his despair at the trap in which they found themselves.

'Who said anything about marriage?' Simon waggled his eyebrows and Max reined in the urge to land him a facer. 'The heart, my dear chap, takes no notice of practical considerations such as money. And nor does the libido. Tell me…' he leaned forward, his elbows propped on his knees '…is she as obsessed with you as you are with her?'

'What does it matter?'

Max stared gloomily out of the carriage window. His longing for Aurelia had intensified tenfold since that evening. How had he fallen for her so hard? So fast? Simon was spot on. His heart was deaf to any number of good, solid reasons why he should forget her. Common sense and practicality weren't enough to control his desire and his need for her. He wanted her. As simple as that. And when he wasn't with her, he couldn't stop thinking about her.

'There is nothing either of us can do about it. There is no way out of it. I would have to go to Cornwall soon, in any case, to meet with this Keast fellow. It'll be for the best.' If only he could persuade himself that was true. 'I'll return to London before Mama and Letty arrive.' He eyed Simon and raised his brows. 'May I stay at your house again? I could not countenance living with Lady Langbrook.'

'Of course.' Simon relaxed back against the squabs. 'You know you don't need to ask.' He glanced out of the carriage window. 'The weather seems to be worsening. If you are determined to go to Tregowan, you'd better not leave it too long.'

Max followed his gaze. It had grown colder in the past few days, made worse by the bitterly cold wind. There had even been one or two flurries of snow, but not enough to settle, thank goodness.

'I'll keep an eye on it,' he promised.

'If I happen to be away when you return you must treat my place as your own and, if you will take my advice, you should take the opportunity to use it for discreet meetings with your Miss Croome.'

'That I will not do. She would face ruin!'

Simon shrugged. 'Only if you are caught. If she feels for you as you do for her, why not if you're careful? You have no choice but to look elsewhere for marital partners, so why deny yourselves a little pleasure first?'

Max caught the mischievous glint in his friend's eye in the nick of time to stop himself from launching that punch at him.

'When will I learn?' He sighed.

'Never, I shouldn't think, if you still struggle to recognise a little friendly mockery when it is offered.'

That evening, Max and Simon—who had been included in the invitation—presented themselves at Lady Langbrook's house for her soirée. His godmother—dressed in rich ruby red, which set off her grey hair to perfection—was at the top of the stairs, greeting her guests.

'Maximilian! And Mr Effingham. I am so pleased you both found time to attend my little soirée.'

Max took hold of his godmother's outstretched hands and kissed her cheek. 'Godmama. We would not miss it for the world.'

She laughed up at him. 'But of course.' She turned to Simon. 'I hope you are well, sir?'

'All the better for seeing you, ma'am.' He looked her up and down and blew her a kiss. 'You look charming, as usual.'

She beamed. 'You always were a wicked flirt. Now, off you go, for I have something I wish to say to Maximilian.' She gestured towards the drawing room from where the sound of voices and laughter could be heard.

'I thought this was to be a small, select soirée?' Max said as Simon walked away.

'And so it is! When one has lived as long as I have, one must be judicious in the selection of one's guests. There are many, many names excluded from tonight's guest list.'

Max laughed, shaking his head. She was incorrigible. And up to something. He could feel it in his bones.

'I have decided you need my help, Max,' she went on and apprehension pooled in his gut. 'So, I have invited a few of the young ladies with the most generous dowries out of those who are already in town. It is time we began to whittle your list down so you can make your choice.'

Max scowled. She was interfering. Of course she was. 'Firstly, I need no help. Secondly, what makes you imagine any of those girls, or their parents, would accept an offer from me? I have nothing to offer.'

'Maximilian!' She slapped his arm. 'You are an earl. A peer of the realm!' She leaned closer. 'None of these gels are from titled families. They would kill one another for a chance to be a countess.'

Max gritted his teeth against an unwise retort.

'I have also compromised my own high standards by inviting Miss Croome, the only one of the three Tregowan heiresses who is yet in town. After all, the Tregowan fortune should be yours by rights and, with five thousand pounds a year, I did not think we could ignore her as a possibility.'

Joy leapt through him at the news Aurelia would be here, but he was careful to hide his reaction.

'I have already met Miss Croome, but there is no possibility that she and I might make a match.'

'Oh? You do surprise me. She has yet to arrive, but I shall look forward to meeting her and seeing for myself what has set you against her, for I hear she is quite pretty.'

Max sighed. She really left him with no choice.

'If you think marriage to Miss Croome will rectify matters, you are mistaken.' He took a deep breath. 'The conditions of the inheritance are that if any of the three beneficiaries was stupid enough to want to marry me, she would lose everything.'

The shock on his godmother's face did nothing to soothe the raw betrayal he still felt. 'That is...*oh!* Just utterly vindictive. I wish I could give Sarah Tregowan a piece of my mind.'

Max smiled ruefully. 'As do I. I wish even more that I understood it. But... Godmama...whatever Sarah did, please remember it is not Aurelia's fault. I know how brutal one of your put downs can be.'

Her head tilted. 'Aurelia?'

Max gritted his teeth again as he suffered his godmother's scrutiny.

Her lips quirked in a half-smile. 'Very well. I can see you are determined to enlighten me no further, but I confess I am more intrigued than ever to meet Miss Aurelia Croome.'

Max bit back his retort. It would achieve nothing other than to further pique her curiosity. 'You have more guests arriving,' he said lightly. 'I shall leave you to greet them.'

He headed for the drawing room and then prowled from room to room, unable to settle for any length of time at any of the activities available for the guests. As well as the main room, there was a card room plus another room set aside to listen to various talents such as singing or readings of—to his ears—hopelessly mediocre poetry. There was also the opportunity to dance in the dining room, the centre of which had been cleared of furniture for the purpose. Aurelia had arrived, with Mrs Butterby, and Max had thus far managed to avoid being in the same room as her and his godmother at the same time.

'Lord Tregowan?'

He came to with a start and with the realisation he had been standing to one side of the dining room, staring blindly at the handful of couples on the floor. He looked down into Aurelia's lovely face, gulping in her sweetly curving pink lips and her stunning blue eyes like a man dying of thirst in a desert. Her gown of gauze over golden-yellow shimmering satin clung to a figure that made his mouth water.

'You are putting off the dancers, glaring at them in such a ferocious manner.' She searched his expression. 'Has one of them upset you?'

'You are speaking to me then, after the last time we met?'

He was in no mood for banter, or for keeping up the pretence—with her—that nothing was happening between them. That they did not share some undeniable connection that, in his case, only grew stronger despite all the excellent reasons he should resist it with every fibre of his being.

Her smile was crooked, but the lift of one brow still managed to give her an air of ladylike control. 'Clearly I am speaking to you, for here we both are. Will you dance with me?'

Powerless to refuse, he extended his hand and led her into the line of dancers. There was little time to do more than snatch a few whispered words while they danced and, at first, neither of them even made the attempt. From Max's point of view, a few whispered words were not nearly enough to say what he longed to say...what was in his heart. But he knew those words ought never to be said. It would be unfair on them both. So, instead, he watched her in silence, telling himself this must be the limit of finding his contentment.

He studied her every movement—the graceful arc of her arm; the smooth spin on her heel, her hem flaring slightly to reveal a glimpse of slender ankles; the tilt of her head; the curve of her lips; the sparkle in those mesmerising blue eyes. He drank it all in, tucking them into his memory together with her scent—an exciting, evocative, spicy perfume that stirred his senses and his body and made him yearn to wrap her in his embrace and explore every inch of her with his hands, his lips, his tongue.

The patches of colour on her cheeks deepened as the dance progressed.

'Do not stare at me so...so...intently,' she whispered at one point when they circled one another—their hands touching—in the centre of the two ranks of dancers. 'It makes me feel—'

She broke off as they moved apart, but her cheeks were an even hotter pink when their hands met at the next move-

ment of the dance. 'You look as though you want to de-
vour me.'

Her words…the image they conjured in his mind…
jolted through him like a bolt of lightning, firing and thickening his blood.

'You do look good enough to eat,' he murmured in her
ear after the music ended as he escorted her from the room.
'And you are tempting my appetite in so many ways…'

What am I doing? Am I mad, to make this harder?

He reined in his passion. Such talk would help neither
of them.

'My apologies,' he said. 'That was inappropriate.' But
her hand on his arm felt so right, even though her touch
was featherlight. He could not bear to deliver her back to
her chaperon so soon. 'Shall we walk a while? I need to
warn you about Lady Langbrook. She is my godmother
and is taking an altogether unwelcome interest in my need
for a wealthy wife.'

The pressure of her fingers on his arm increased. 'Ah.
So that explains the invitation that seemed to come from
nowhere. I met her briefly on our arrival, but she seemed
more interested in the people who arrived after us. A Miss
Rowland, I think it was. But why do you believe there is
a need to warn me about her?'

'She invited you because she had the idea that the
Tregowan inheritance is rightfully mine and that justice
would be served if I wed one of the heiresses. I told her
we had already met and that there was no likelihood whatsoever of a match between us. And the reason why. She
was…' he gave her a rueful look '…unhappy. And I cannot promise that she will not make her displeasure known
to you, even though I reminded her it was not your fault.'

Aurelia shrugged, giving a light laugh. 'Oh, do not

worry about me—I shall not wither if she gives me a set-down.'

Max frowned, her carefree response giving him pause. His feelings for her, and the regret there could be no future for them, grew stronger every day, but *her* feelings were still something of a mystery to him, keeping him off-kilter. He racked his brains, reliving all their encounters. She had always been friendly, but did she really feel anything stronger or was that merely wishful thinking on his part? He did not doubt that beneath the nonchalance with which she faced the world there beat the heart of a passionate woman and that her cool outer shell was just that. A shell. But that did not mean those powerful emotions swirling beneath her surface involved him.

'Another staircase.'

Aurelia had halted and Max saw that they were, indeed, at the head of the staircase. He stared down into the hall below. All the guests had arrived and the servants were busy elsewhere, other than a solitary footman seated just inside the front door. His arms were folded and his chin rested on his chest.

'The question is,' Aurelia murmured, 'did you lead me here, or did I lead you?' Heat flashed in her blue eyes as they searched his and his pulse leapt in response. 'You see how easy it is to lose oneself in one's thoughts and be taken unawares?'

'As Sampford did to you the other night?'

'As Sampford did to me the other night,' she agreed. 'And now...' She caught her bottom lip between her teeth, sending another jolt through him. 'The question is...do we go forward, or do we go back?'

'Literally? Or metaphorically?'

'Both?'

The clamour in his head to play safe and to retreat

never really stood a chance. Maybe he was fooling himself. Maybe she was simply toying with him, recognising that she held him in thrall and enjoying her position of power. Maybe he was heading for heartache, but he thrust aside his misgivings, driven by the stronger urge to learn as much as he could about her. To pierce her guard and discover the true woman beneath.

'Would you care to see the library, Miss Croome?'

'I do so love a library, Lord Tregowan,' she said, with warm laughter in her voice.

Max stepped down the top stair and then raised his brows as he held out his hand for hers. Joy flooded him when she placed her hand in his and descended the stairs by his side. He collected an already lit candle from a table by the library door and led her inside.

'Why?' He moved away from her before facing her, still unsettled by that need to understand. 'Why risk your reputation when you know if you were seen in here with me it could ruin your chance of marrying well? You could lose your inheritance.'

Her head tipped to one side as she contemplated him, her hands loosely linked in front of her. 'My concept of marrying well does not necessarily concur with that of most people in society. Including you, I suspect.' She tucked her lips between her teeth, looking thoughtful. 'Do not misunderstand me, Max—' his heart twitched with pleasure at hearing his name on her lips '—there is no doubt in my mind that I *shall* meet the conditions of the will. I must. And that means I will marry. But there is no condition that my husband must be of a certain class. I would be perfectly happy to marry a businessman of some sort, so the danger of being seen is not as acute as you may believe. After all, no one has the power to force a marriage between us when we are both aware of the disaster that would be. But I have come here with you—risked my reputation, if you care to think of it like that—because I have a proposition for you.'

Chapter Fourteen

M̲ax's stunned expression prompted Aurelia to add, 'Proposition is a poor choice of word. A suggestion might be better.' The idea had come to her as she'd cast around for an answer to his question as to why she would risk her reputation when the truth was she had just wanted to talk to him—to be with him—where there were no eyes to see and no ears to overhear.

He rubbed his hand across his jaw. How stark and handsome and...*passionate*...he looked, standing there in his immaculate evening clothes with those intense dark eyes of his burning into her. He was all male and the urge to touch him and to be touched sent waves of longing through her. She might still be innocent—more or less, barring a few kisses—but she knew enough about men to recognise when one found her attractive and she did not even try to deny his interest was reciprocated. She wished she were bold enough to actually proposition him—to go further than a tête-à-tête in his godmother's library—but she was not.

'I need a husband,' she said instead. 'A decent, prudent man who will not fritter my inheritance away once he has control of it. A man I can like and respect. I ask for no more than that.'

'And is Lord Sampford a suitable prospect?'

'Do not be—' Her jaw shut with a snap when she saw the playful glint in his dark eyes. She laughed. 'I must learn not to take everything you say on face value, mustn't I?'

He shrugged, a teasing smile curling his lips.

'And you,' Aurelia continued, determinedly ignoring the feeling that her heart was being clawed to shreds, 'need a wife with a large dowry. No. Do not poker up as though I have landed a terrible blow to your manhood. Facts are facts and we must both face them.'

A crease knitted the skin between his brows. 'Go on.'

'My suggestion is we help one another. You will know the true character of many of the gentlemen who will pay court to me. And I will have the opportunity to learn more of the true character of the young ladies I meet—which of them are hopelessly dull and which hide a nasty streak behind smiles and sweet words.'

He moved nearer. 'That sounds an excellent idea.'

His deep voice vibrated through her and she fought the urge to step back. Out of danger. Where his scent could not reach her and muddle her thinking and weaken her resolve. To step back so he was out of reach. So that her hand could not simply rise and place itself against his chest. His heart.

She raised her eyes to his and tumbled into those smouldering depths. Dimly, she felt him take one hand and, one by one, loosen the fingers of her evening glove. Slowly, he slid it from her hand before raising her palm. He bent his head, pressing warm lips to her skin, and her heart turned a somersault. Without volition, her other hand rose to comb her fingers through his thick, soft, dark locks.

She barely noticed the transition, but of a sudden she was in his arms, his mouth seeking hers. She tilted her head up and met him willingly, delighting in the glide of his lips over hers and the hint of controlled power she sensed as he gently kissed her. She moaned in her throat, pressing closer, her legs turning to jelly as she thrust her fingers through his hair and clamped his head still in case he had any thought of stopping.

His arm around her waist tightened, lifting her, pulling her into his hard, muscular body, and she felt the proof of his desire moulded against her belly. His tongue nudged at the seam of her lips and she opened to him, pure excitement racing through her as she lost herself in the best kiss she had ever experienced.

She lost all sense of time as his mouth dragged across her jaw and neck, kissing and licking, but with the odd gentle nip followed by a low growl of frustration. Her breasts were full and heavy, her nipples hard and aching. A feeling of pure anticipation built deep in her belly, a need that spurred her on, urging her to follow wherever this glorious craving might lead. She clung closer as he caressed every inch of the naked skin of her shoulders and smoothed a gently circling hand down her spine to her bottom, where he squeezed, sending a spear of hopeless longing through her.

When he finally released her from his embrace, she shivered as the cool air replaced the heat of his body. Her lips throbbed and tingled and she touched them, wondering if they looked as swollen as they felt. Her breasts heaved as she fought to steady her breathing.

'I...' Max cocked his jaw to one side, frowning. 'We had better get back, before people notice our absence.'

She frowned back at him. 'Is that all you have to say?'

He thrust his hand through his hair and took a couple

of paces towards the door before facing her again. 'What do you want me to say? That was a pleasant kiss? Well, yes, it was very nice. Or do you want an apology from me for kissing you? You did not raise any objections at the time...or did I miss them?'

Pleasant? Nice?

Anger stirred, deep in her belly, smothering any lingering desire. She would not allow herself to be dismissed so carelessly.

'A simple acknowledgement that we had shared a kiss might have been nice. Possibly a few words about how our friendship might change as a result of it?'

'To what purpose? We both know a kiss cannot lead anywhere. We know the truth. This changes nothing.'

The starkness of his words punched the air from her lungs. She dragged in a breath. She felt stupid. Humiliated. Deflated. A foolish, emotional woman. What had she expected? A miracle to happen? A heaviness settled in her chest. She sighed.

'I am sorry. You are right.'

She just wished he did not suddenly seem so distant... standing there, stern and tall and unemotional—no sign of the passion that so often signalled his inner feelings. Doubts assailed her where before she'd had none. Had she been so wrong about his feelings for her? 'I do not need an apology and, yes, you are right—' and how she hated the fact that they must be driven by the expectations of others '—we ought to return. Immediately.'

The harsh lines etched into his face softened. 'It is the only way, Aurelia.'

How she loved to hear her name on his tongue. She raised her hands to check her hair, although she was sure he had not touched it while kissing her.

'Your hair looks perfect.'

She drew in a long breath, wishing he would say some-thing, *anything*, to indicate the kiss had meant something to him, too, even as she knew he would not because there was no point. She pushed down her hurt and stalked past him to the door.

'You had better wait down here a while,' she said. 'We ought not to return together.'

She opened the door a crack and peeked out. The foot-man was still dozing on his chair. She glanced back at Max.

'Are we still to help one another to find suitable spouses?' It would still give them an excuse…a reason…to talk.

'Yes, of course.'

Aurelia climbed the staircase, pain squeezing her heart. How she wanted to be angry with him. Enraged. But all she felt was cold and empty and numb. Alone. And lonely.

She swallowed past the thick lump in her throat and painted a smile on her face before seeking out Mrs But-terby.

'Where have you been? Lady Langbrook wishes to meet you properly.' The chaperon gripped Aurelia's arm as she joined her, moving them both out of earshot of any other guests.

That is all I need—Her Ladyship blaming me for steal-ing Max's inheritance.

'Nowhere. The ladies' retiring room. I had a slight headache.'

'Oh. I… Do you wish to go home? I am sure Lady Lang-brook will understand.'

But Aurelia refused to slink away like a dog in the night. That had never been her way. She still had her pride and she had always stood up for herself. 'No. It is gone now. I am fine.'

* * *

Within five minutes, Lady Langbrook joined them.

'Prudence! You have found her.' Their hostess examined Aurelia from head to toe. 'And Miss Croome—finally we get the opportunity to have a chat.'

Aurelia curtsied, smiling warily at Her Ladyship as she straightened. And then her smile broadened as her brain caught up with what she had heard.

Prudence! Mrs Butterby's name was Prudence. It suited her, for prudent she most definitely was.

'Thank you for your invitation this evening, Lady Langbrook.'

Max's godmother inclined her head. 'I am...*interested*...to meet you properly, Miss Croome. I understand you are a considerable heiress, courtesy of the late Lady Tregowan.'

Aurelia only hesitated a couple of beats. 'And I understand that you are Lord Tregowan's godmother, my lady.' She ignored Mrs Butterby's hand of warning on her arm. 'But if you expect me to cower in the face of your...um... *interest*...you will be disappointed. I did not steal that inheritance from your godson. I had never even met Lady Tregowan.'

Mrs Butterby's grip turned into a clutch. 'Miss Croome! No. Please...'

But Lady Langbrook waved her hand imperiously, a gleam of amusement lighting her eyes. 'Do not fret, Prudence. I have no objection to a woman who is unafraid to speak her mind.'

Despite her irritation, Aurelia felt one corner of her mouth quirk up.

'Is what he tells me true? That there is a condition in the will preventing any of the three heiresses from marrying him, on pain of losing her inheritance?'

'It is true.'

Her Ladyship rounded on Mrs Butterby. 'Do you care to explain, Prudence? What in God's name was Sarah thinking? Why did she turn against Maximilian?'

'I... I... We heard he had been gambling and that he was in debt.' Mrs Butterby had paled, but she did not cower in the face of Her Ladyship's wrath either and Aurelia's opinion of her increased a notch. 'She was ill...fretting about Falconfield and its future...she couldn't bear for it to be sold to support the Tregowan estate after all her years of fighting against it. And so she made a new will. Just before she died.'

'And who told you he had been gambling?'

'I do not recall. It was a rumour we heard. A gamble that had been lost and a loan that could not be repaid.'

'A rumour? My godson was cut from her will for a *rumour*?' Her Ladyship's voice shook with anger. 'The *gamble* was that he raised a loan to expand that wretched mine of his—he was *trying* to do the right thing by providing jobs for the local people. That gamble failed—the loan was not enough and he had to abandon the search for more tin. Or was it copper? I forget. That mine has never made him a profit,' she muttered, shaking her head. 'It's been nothing but a burden on him ever since he opened it. But—' and her voice rose again '—that is by the by! He may have allowed his heart to overrule cold, hard business sense on that occasion, but he is no gambler in the sense *you* mean it. He abhors gambling, after his father—'

She fell silent, then drew in a trembling breath. 'My apologies, ladies,' she said stiffly. 'You are guests in my house and I have allowed my emotions to run away with me.' She squared her shoulders. 'I shall not allow it to happen again.'

Her diatribe had had the ring of truth about it and gave

Aurelia much to mull over. She now felt even more guilty about that inheritance. Even though it was legally hers, she could not help but think that, morally, it should belong to Max. Might he also believe that? Could his actions—leading her on and kissing her like that before turning cold—be meant as some sort of punishment? She did not think he would be so petty. But how well did she really know him?

'Now, Miss Croome,' Lady Langbrook said, 'is there anyone here you have yet to meet? Lord Runcorn, perhaps?'

She indicated a dark-haired gentleman at the far side of the room, standing on the edge of a group of people that included Lord Sampford, Mr Effingham and the elder Miss Glaston.

'We have not yet been introduced, my lady.'

Anything that took her mind off Max would be welcome.

'Then, come and I shall make the introduction.'

'Miss Croome!' Runcorn scanned Aurelia from head to toe and back again. 'I am honoured to meet you. The tales I have heard of your beauty, in truth, barely do you justice.'

He bowed over her hand and it was all Aurelia could do not to roll her eyes. As she joined in the general conversation, she noticed Max come into the room and she acted her heart out, flirting with both Runcorn and Sampford, keeping all her emotions battened down, determined to show nothing of her hurt to anyone. Especially not to Max.

Let him wonder what that kiss had really meant to her.

Let him think of it as an aberration on her part.

Let them both concentrate on finding suitable marriage partners and forget that kiss had ever happened.

It was a relief when Mrs Butterby came to tell her it was time to go home.

Chapter Fifteen

The weather turned noticeably colder the next day, and Mrs Butterby proved reluctant to drive in the Park with Aurelia, who was bored of being cooped up in the house. How she wished her sisters would come, then she wouldn't have only Prudence to rely on for company. Not that she disliked the chaperon, but she couldn't help but chafe at being under her strictures. She could be such a fusspot.

'But you know I ended up with that horrid head cold the last time we went for a drive,' Mrs Butterby said, peering at her embroidery and tutting before reaching for her scissors. 'Do you want to see me take to my bed again?'

'Of course I do not.'

Aurelia took a turn around the room. Really, this was like being in a cage. Besides, there was no chance of seeing Max if they stayed indoors all day and, despite what happened between them the night before, she still yearned to see him. She returned to Mrs Butterby and knelt down before her. The chaperon laid her embroidery down, giving Aurelia her full attention.

'I am not unsympathetic, my dear. Look…if you *promise* not to leave the carriage, why not take Bet with you? I am sure that will be better than nothing.'

Aurelia took Mrs Butterby's hands and looked pleadingly into her eyes. 'Just a *very short* walk? Please? I promise faithfully to remain in sight of the carriage. What on earth could happen to me in broad daylight?'

Mrs Butterby sighed, her smile resigned. 'Very well, then. But please have a care for your reputation, Aurelia. I shall send Hall and one of the footmen and he, as well as Bet, will accompany you on any walk. Is that agreed?'

Aurelia grinned and leaned in to kiss Mrs Butterby's cheek.

The Park proved thin of company when the carriage turned in through the gates and Aurelia tried hard to quell her disappointment there was no sign of Max. After one circuit, she decided to take a stroll anyway, even if she had no one to walk with or to talk to. Bet knocked on the carriage roof to signal to Hall to stop the carriage and Gareth—one of the two footmen at Tregowan House—opened the door to hand down both Aurelia and Bet.

'Keep the horses moving, Hall. We shall let you know when we have had our fill of fresh air,' Aurelia said to the coachman. 'Bet and I will be perfectly safe with Gareth here.'

She set a brisk pace along the edge of the carriageway and only slowed when she was hailed by name. She turned, her heart soaring, only for it to plummet as she identified Mr Effingham astride his huge black steed. There was no sign of Max on his chestnut.

Her smile, however, did not falter. 'Good day, Mr Effingham.' She bobbed a curtsy.

Mr Effingham leapt down from his horse, looping the reins over its head to lead it. 'Good day,' he said. 'I trust you will not object to my walking with you for a while?

I am pleased to see you, for you have saved me calling upon you.'

'You intended to call upon *me*?'

'Indeed.' He glanced back at Bet, who had dropped back to walk beside Gareth, and he lowered his voice. 'I wasn't certain if you knew…'

He paused and Aurelia's pulse picked up a beat. Instinct warned her this would not be good news. She swallowed. 'Pray continue.'

'Are you aware Lord Tregowan has returned to Cornwall?'

Aurelia felt as though her world had crashed down around her ears. 'Cornwall?'

'Yes. He left early this morning. I did not know if he told you of his plans last night?'

'No. Why would he?' Amazing that her voice sounded quite normal even while her insides were in such turmoil. 'We barely know one another.'

'Ah. Of course not. Silly me.' The sympathy in his glance scraped at Aurelia's already raw nerve-endings.

'I am sure he will come back shortly,' she said, 'for I understand his mother and sister are due to arrive in London any day. He will wish to be here to greet them, I assume.'

'Ah.' Mr Effingham sounded uncomfortable. 'He might not have mentioned…there has been a delay. They are unlikely to arrive much before Eastertide now.'

Eastertide? That was Leah and Beatrice's deadline to come to London and, as she had been counting the days and weeks, Aurelia knew that was precisely eight weeks and five days from today.

He's gone.

Why had he not told her he was leaving? Or had he not known? But he must have known…must have made plans…and yet he had not breathed a word of it to her. He had kissed her, but he had not told her he was going.

I thought we were friends.

Admit it…you thought you were *more* than friends! Or why were you foolish enough to allow him to kiss you? In fact, why were you *scandalous* enough to *encourage* him to kiss you?

She closed her ears to that taunting inner voice as an aching lump took up residence in her throat.

I must not allow Mr Effingham to see I am upset. I will not allow anyone to guess how much this hurts.

For hurt it did. More than she would ever have guessed. But she pinned an expression of polite interest to her face as she talked a little longer with Mr Effingham, who then mounted his horse and cantered away. Aurelia carried on walking, putting one foot in front of the other by rote, until large snowflakes began to fall, swirling in the brisk breeze. The change in the weather reminded her about Hall and the carriage, which was by now following behind them.

She stared blindly out of the carriage window during the short drive home and, once they arrived, she hurried through the front door with her head high and straight up the stairs, calling over her shoulder to Bet that she would manage without any help and that if Mrs Butterby were to ask, she was having a rest until dinner and would prefer not to be disturbed.

As they sat in the drawing room awaiting dinner that evening, Mrs Butterby said, 'What do you wish to do later, as we are spending a quiet night at home?'

And thank goodness for that…

Aurelia could think of nothing worse than attending yet another *quiet pre-Season event* as the hostesses insisted on labelling their soirées, routs and so forth, always eager to excuse the fact there weren't enough people yet in town to make every event a *veritable crush*—an accolade that was the pinnacle of every hostess's ambition, according to Mrs Butterby.

'I shall write to Leah,' she said, on impulse. 'She gave me her address when we met. I long to know when my half-sisters will join me.'

And I pray it will be soon, for I don't know how I shall bear it if they do not arrive until Eastertide.

She missed them, she realised. How peculiar, when they had only met the once but, somehow, knowing they shared the same blood had forged an unbreakable bond between them already. At least…and she bit her lip…it had as far as she was concerned. What if they did not feel the same? All her newfound confidence wavered. What if they did not like her? What if they rejected her? As Augustus had done. As *Max* had done.

I must do all I possibly can to prove I am worthy and their equal. I cannot risk losing them as well as Max.

'Is there something wrong, Aurelia?' Mrs Butterby's eyed her anxiously and Aurelia stiffened.

'Of course not. What could be wrong?'

She instantly regretted her snapped response. She knew the chaperon was only being friendly but that, to Mrs Butterby, meant sharing feelings…talking about the past, and Aurelia's childhood…speculating about who Aurelia might marry. All things Aurelia simply could not bring herself to discuss. A wave of panic swept through her at the very idea of laying bare the reality of her childhood and admitting to the anguish of a child at the incomprehensible rejection by her father. Anguish she had, in time, learned to hide behind a wall of defiance.

She could not make herself vulnerable by exposing any of her inner feelings, especially now with this different pain so close to the surface. *Oh, Max. Why did you go?* Grief ripped at her heart but, even through her torment, a small part of her realised that none of this was Mrs Butterby's fault and she softened her tone.

'There is nothing wrong, Mrs Butterby, I promise.'

The chaperon smiled, but Aurelia could see she had not fully set her mind at rest. If only Leah or Beatrice were here, maybe she could confide in them? But the instant that thought arose, she dismissed it—how could she tell *anyone* about her feelings for Max? It was all so hopelessly complicated. There could never be a future for them. Not when she was terrified of losing everything she had so recently gained and being catapulted back into poverty. And not when Max needed a wealthy wife to rebuild his estate, to provide for his invalid mother and unmarried sister and to secure those miners' jobs.

Besides, he clearly did not care about her feelings or he would not have left London without a word. The very next morning after kissing her, too. And what about their agreement that they would help one another find suitable spouses? Well, that would not happen now. Even when he returned, her pride would not allow her to broach the subject again.

She swallowed her sigh…everything was *so* complicated. A labyrinth with no way out.

'Well, if you are sure, my dear,' Mrs Butterby said. 'Although I hope you know you can trust me if there is anything worrying you? I only wish to help.'

Aurelia smiled. 'I know that. Thank you.'

'Well, anyway, I think it a splendid idea to write to Leah. I do hope the three of you will be friends. Shall you write to Beatrice as well?'

'No. She did not tell us where she lives.'

'Oh!' Mrs Butterby leapt to her feet. 'I can help with that. I have her brother's address here somewhere.'

'No! Thank you, but it would not be wise. Beatrice was adamant neither of us should contact her and I shall respect her wishes. She seemed afraid of her brother finding out about her inheritance. He sounded quite horrid.'

'I believe he is something of a despot, from what Sarah was told by the investigator. Hopefully her inheritance will give Beatrice her chance to break free of him. Ah, Vardy—' as the butler entered '—is dinner served?'

'It is, ma'am.'

After they ate, Mrs Butterby read while Aurelia sat at the mahogany secretary in the drawing room and tussled over the wording of her letter to Leah. Although she began it innocuously enough, she soon found herself pouring her heart out to the half-sister she had only met once. Once she began, the words flowed and, by the time she reached the bottom of the sheet and had then continued by crossing her lines, she felt considerably calmer. There was no power on earth that could persuade her to actually send the letter but, not wishing to arouse Mrs Butterby's suspicions, she folded the sheet and sealed it anyway.

'I think I shall retire now,' she said.

'Goodnight, my dear. Sleep well. If you leave your letter in the hall, Vardy will ensure it is taken to the post office for you.'

'Thank you.' Aurelia picked up the sealed letter. 'Goodnight.'

In her bedchamber, she knelt by the fire and pushed it into the flames with the poker.

'Miss Croome?'

She started at Bet's voice. She hadn't heard her come into the room.

'Let me see to the fire. You shouldn't be doing that. I... Oh.'

Bet paused by Aurelia's side and stared at the folded, sealed paper slowly curling at the edges from the heat of the flames. She moved away and began fussing around the bed, turning down the covers. 'Are you going to bed now, miss?'

Tears prickled Aurelia's eyes. She blinked them away, telling herself the brightness of the flame caused them, but she knew that was a lie. She gulped. 'Yes. I am.' Her voice sounded strained, but Bet, mercifully, said nothing, simply supporting Aurelia to her feet and helping her to undress and sitting her down to brush her hair with long steady strokes.

It was comforting. If she closed her eyes, it was almost as though Mama... Mama... The tears could no longer be blocked and they spilled quietly, wetting her cheeks, dripping from her chin.

'There now.' Bet stood her up, with an arm around her, and guided her to the bed. 'I shall go and ask Cook to make a hot posset for you. That's what my ma always gave us when we were children', and she bustled out of the room, giving Aurelia precious time to regain control of herself.

Later, as she sipped the comforting drink, Aurelia said, 'Thank you, Bet.'

The maid smiled. 'It's my job to look after you, miss. I only fetched you a warm drink.'

'The thanks were for not asking questions, Bet.' She rubbed her forehead. 'It is not like me to cry so easily. I am sorry if I embarrassed you.'

'Bless you, miss. I'm not that easy to embarrass. And you have good reason to feel wibbly-wobbly at times.'

'Wibbly-wobbly?' Aurelia laughed.

'It's what my pa says, miss, if Ma gets teary-eyed. It's been a big change for you, coming to London. Learning to lead a new life. No one could blame you if it all seems a bit too much at times.'

'It's not that,' Aurelia said before she could stop herself.

'Ah.' Bet began to tidy away Aurelia's clothes, and straighten the dressing table. 'Then it is a man? I heard what that gentleman told you about Lord Tregowan.' She didn't pause for a reply, but went on, 'I often wonder if they're worth the trouble they cause us females, miss.'

Aurelia sipped her drink, then wriggled slightly to move herself further down into the warmth of the bed, taking care not to spill her drink. It was soothing to listen to Bet without needing to reply. Her eyes half closed, her mind draining of all thought.

'Now, don't get me wrong, miss. My pa is a good man. Lots of them are. But the ones that aren't…well, the heartache they can cause to us women is never worth it, to my mind.'

'But I must trust one man, Bet.' She lifted heavy lids to eye the maid over the rim of her cup as she drained the last of the milk. 'I have to marry, or I lose all this.'

Bet paused in her tidying and came to stand by the bed. 'And if it doesn't make you happy, miss? You told me what would happen if you don't marry. You won't go back to starving, or to the fear of not having a roof over your head.' She took the empty cup from Aurelia. 'Maybe you should compare the life you would have then with your life of a few weeks ago, rather than with this life of luxury. Then, you would feel yourself rich indeed.'

Will I ever feel rich without Max? Although, even if he wanted me, two hundred pounds is not enough to solve his problems.

There would be no easy answer to her dilemma. Utterly exhausted, Aurelia did not reply as her eyes drifted shut. She felt Bet tuck the bedclothes around her, but she did not even hear her maid leave the room.

Chapter Sixteen

The long journey back to Cornwall gave Max far too much time to ponder his hasty decision to leave London and to regret not heeding Simon's warning about the weather. It worsened considerably during the journey, making it even slower and more hazardous than usual. Max was grateful he had secured an inside seat as the poor souls riding on the roof had to be helped down at each stop, they were so stiff with the cold.

The decision was so sudden, and he left at such an early hour, that Simon was the only person he had told and *he* had still been half-asleep, so Max hadn't even had to fabricate an excuse for going. He had written to his godmother, out of courtesy, promising to return to London in time to greet Mama and Letty when they arrived.

He spent most of the journey with his hat tilted down over his eyes and his arms folded across his chest, feigning sleep, not caring that his fellow passengers would think him rude. He had no wish to discuss the snow, or speculate as to the chances of the coach foundering in a snowdrift, or wonder if their journey might be delayed. But the drawback of his failure to join in with the small talk meant he had too much time to brood about his lack of finances and his need for a wealthy wife. And *far* too much time to think about Aurelia and about that kiss and about how he was a scoundrel of the lowest order.

No good castigating himself now for his lack of control, however. He had kissed her because he couldn't *not* kiss her. Not when she stood so close…so temptingly close… her face tilted up to his and her evocative scent wreathing through his senses. He had been lost from the moment she spoke of a proposition. His mind had leapt unerringly to Simon's suggestion of liaisons in his house—spoken half in jest, but so tempting none the less—before she had corrected herself to make it clear she meant they might help one another find suitable spouses. Every fibre of his being had rebelled at the thought of her in the arms of another man, and had clamoured to make her his, to possess her.

His fingertips still tingled at the memory of her silken skin as he'd caressed every exposed inch of her shoulders and upper back. His hands cupped involuntarily as he remembered the soft, round globes of her bottom as he squeezed them and he could still taste her lips, and still hear her quietly whispering his name as he kissed and nibbled her neck. It had taken all of his resolve to release her and not to swing her into his arms and carry her to the rug before the fire that still smouldered in the hearth to finish what they had started.

'Are you quite well, sir?'

The voice jerked him from his memories and he raised the brim of his hat to meet the worried look of his neighbour. Max realised he had groaned out loud.

'I am fine. I apologise if I disturbed you,' and he tipped his hat back over his eyes before the man attempted to draw him into the general conversation.

After the soirée, he had lain awake half the night, utterly shaken by that kiss. No good telling himself to put it from his mind…to forget it…to forget *her*. No good whatsoever, because he *wanted* her, now more than ever, and because Simon's words still echoed through his head, enticing him, and because that kiss had removed any lingering doubt about Aurelia's feelings for him. She wanted him, too. There was danger there for them both, but, in particular, for her and he must protect her.

His only solution had been to put distance between them by returning to Cornwall. Immediately. And so he had woken Simon. Written to his godmother and also written to Mr Austerly to advise him that Keast might visit him whenever proved convenient.

And to leave without saying goodbye to Aurelia? *That* had been deliberate. An act of selflessness. She had already been hurt by his reaction after their kiss and he had built on that, relying on her to be hurt and even infuriated that he had gone without even a goodbye. That could only help her anger, helping her to banish him from her thoughts.

By the time the short stagecoach from Launceston to Liskeard dropped Max at the road junction nearest to Tregowan Place, he was utterly exhausted and more despondent than he had ever been in his life.

After Aurelia had learned that Max had left London, she spent the first few days hoping Mr Effingham had been mistaken. Foolishly, she clung to the expectation he would suddenly appear and it would all prove to be a mistake. But that miracle did not happen and she sank into a low mood, exacerbated by the snowy weather that severely curtailed their activities by confining them indoors. More than once she caught Mrs Butterby eyeing her anxiously, but she ignored all of the chaperon's efforts to persuade Aurelia to confide in her.

She told herself she hated him for kissing her when it meant nothing to him and when he knew it could lead nowhere, and for then leaving London without even saying goodbye. That hurt more than anything. They had agreed they would help one another find a spouse and yet, the very next morning, he had gone without a word.

Aristocrats. They are not to be trusted. I was right all along.

She dug deep to rouse her anger at his shabby treatment and yet, although anger came when she concentrated hard on finding it, mostly she just felt numb inside.

By the end of that week, however, Aurelia finally released her forlorn hope and accepted that Max had gone and that the feelings he had aroused in her were not reciprocated. Henceforth, she vowed, she would present a bright and carefree image to the world, allowing no one to suspect the true depths of her pain and despair.

'I rather thought Miss Thame might have written back to you by now, my dear,' said Mrs Butterby one afternoon, a week after Max's departure. 'I wonder if your letter was delayed by the weather?'

Aurelia started guiltily for, after burning that letter in which she had poured out her heart, she had not even thought about writing another.

'I shall write again in case the first one went astray,' she said and went straight to the secretary.

This time, she wrote only of the people she had met and the places she had been and avoided anything of a personal nature, like feelings. It was only after she signed the letter *your affectionate sister, Aurelia*, that she realised that not only had she not mentioned meeting Max, but she had also omitted any mention of Mr Effingham or of Lady Langbrook. Leah would, of course, be interested that Au-

relia had met Lord Tregowan—and she had every right
to know about him—but Aurelia simply could not bring
herself to even write his name. What would Leah think
when she arrived in London and learned Aurelia had already met Max and not told her? She loathed the idea her
sisters might guess she had fallen for the one man she was
expressly forbidden to marry, but she could think of no
reason to suggest to Mrs Butterby they should keep her
introduction to Max a secret. Any such request would be
bound to prompt questions as to why.

She pushed aside that problem for now, trusting she
would think of something eventually.

She sealed the letter and wrote Leah's direction on the
outside and put it in the hall for a footman to take to the
post office, before heading to her bedchamber to choose
a suitably stunning gown for her first evening out since
Lady Langbrook's soirée. It was time to dazzle the *ton*.

She threw herself into every evening party they attended, exhausting herself so that, when she went to bed,
she was asleep the minute her head hit the pillow. She
danced every dance possible at every event and, in between, she drove herself to entertain with conversation
that sparkled and with flirtatious and enticing glances,
using her fan to great effect. The cluster of admirers sur-
rounding her every evening increased, Lords Sampford
and Runcorn prominent among them, but the more those
gentlemen rose to her bait, showering her with increasingly extravagant compliments, the more Aurelia secretly
despised the lot of them.

Prudence, though, seemed delighted to witness her pop-
ularity and Aurelia hoped her performance was convinc-
ing the chaperon there was nothing amiss after all and

that her recent low mood was simply the absence of social events to attend.

When they arrived home one night, Mrs Butterby asked Aurelia to join her in the drawing room for a cup of tea before they retired. Curious—for the chaperon's normal practice was to head straight to bed after an evening out—Aurelia agreed.

Janet had brought in the tea tray and Mrs Butterby poured their tea before speaking.

'I cannot help but notice the change in you, my dear. I have puzzled over possible reasons for it, but I cannot reach a conclusion.'

'What manner of change?' Aurelia sipped her tea, her mind working furiously. Had Prudence guessed her high spirits were all an act?

'I was so worried about you after Lady Langbrook's soirée. You seemed to sink ever deeper into the doldrums and I wondered if maybe you were fretting about what Her Ladyship said about your inheritance. But now… I do not believe I have ever seen you in such high spirits. You had half of those young men hanging off your every word. Yet I cannot rid myself of the suspicion that you are not serious about a single one of them.'

Aurelia bit her lip. Could this be her chance?

'You are right about some of it, ma'am. I did fret about what Lady Langford said, especially when I remembered something you said when I first arrived.'

'I?'

'It was about Sarah and when she changed her will. You said you did not send it immediately to Mr Henshaw after she signed it in case she changed her mind again.'

'Oh!' Mrs Butterby placed her cup in its saucer and placed them back on the tray. 'Yes, I did wonder if she might have second thoughts, but then she passed away and so I sent it immediately. And is that what was bothering you? You silly goose. It is all legal and correct. Lord Tregowan has no grounds to contest the will. Mr Henshaw was confident of that.'

'I hadn't thought of it in terms of him contesting the will. But I cannot help feeling guilty because Lady Langbrook sounded so sincere and so it seems to me that Lady Tregowan cut His Lordship from her will over a misunderstanding. He had not been gambling, but investing in his mine for the benefit of his workers.'

'But there is nothing to gain from fretting about it, Aurelia. It is out of your control. Under the law, the inheritance belongs to you and your sisters.

'I know, but that does not stop me feeling guilty and I could not but dread the thought of facing Lord Tregowan again.'

'Is that why you were so quiet? You were worrying about meeting him again? Oh, my dear.' Mrs Butterby moved to sit next to Aurelia and put her arm around her. 'He is a gentleman. He will not knowingly upset you.'

Aurelia tamped down her guilt at misleading Mrs Butterby when she was being so kind. But…needs must… 'You asked why I have changed, though, ma'am, and it is because Lord Tregowan has returned to Cornwall. It is the relief that I do not need to dread meeting him wherever I go.'

'Oh, good heavens! I had no idea…well, thank goodness he *has* gone if he had that effect on you, my dear.'

'But now… I cannot help but worry that if *I* feel this guilty, how will Leah and Beatrice react when they find out? I should not like my sisters to suffer.'

'Then we shall not mention him again. As far as we are concerned, he is just a name…some gentleman you have never met.' She released Aurelia and smiled. 'There! Is that better?'

Aurelia smiled, guilt tangling with the sense of relief in her belly. '*Much* better. Thank you, Mrs Butterby.'

It didn't take Max long to settle back into the normal routine of his life and he was grateful the severe winter weather that had near-paralysed the rest of southern England had not ventured beyond the River Tamar, as that meant the building work could continue on the Place. Max couldn't have returned to London if he wanted to—tales of roads blocked by snowdrifts abounded, removing any temptation to go back, but also delaying Mr Keast's visit just in case the snow and ice should move further west.

Mr and Mrs Carey still looked after the gatekeeper's lodge for him, meaning he had home-cooked meals every evening when he came home from a day overseeing the building work—where the new roof was slowly taking shape, slate by slate—or dealing with the numerous day-to-day problems that arose at Wheal Rowenna together with Pengelly, his foreman. Hard work meant less time to think, and for that he was grateful, but he was still unable to entirely banish Aurelia from his thoughts and, from time to time, he caught himself wishing he might share something with her—a joke; a thought; a drift of snow-drops on the edge of a spinney; a pair of buzzards soaring majestically overhead; the joy when the final slate was nailed to the roof.

Letters from Simon and from his godmother kept him abreast of matters in London and, in the case of Simon's missive, Max wished he had not bothered, for he wrote at some length about how Aurelia Croome was taking the *ton* by storm. Upon reading those words, Max cursed and hurled the letter into the fire, but it was too late. Her image, once again, haunted him—this time, the spectre of her in another man's arms, laughing and flirting—and no matter how hard he worked to forget her, as she had clearly forgotten him, he could never quite succeed.

Chapter Seventeen

'Aurelia, my dear, do please stop pacing. It will not bring your sister here any sooner.' Aurelia flung herself down on the drawing room sofa at Mrs Butterby's reprimand. 'And do take care. Your gown…it will be hopelessly creased. Do you wish Miss Thame to think you a scarecrow?'

Aurelia stood and smoothed the blue-and-white-striped skirt of her morning gown before sitting again, this time with ladylike poise. No, she did not want Leah to look down upon her. She wanted her to view Aurelia as her equal, and to like her. Be proud of her, even. She sat still for all of two minutes before rising to her feet again, her stomach a tangle of excitement and apprehension. Leah's reply to her letter, received last week, had revealed little of her half-sister's character or inner thoughts. In fact, it had been as carefully worded as Aurelia's own letter to Leah and Aurelia had gleaned nothing of any importance from it, including no definite date for her arrival in London. Then yesterday a second letter, very brief, had arrived, announcing Leah had left Dolphinstone Court and expected to arrive this morning.

'I cannot help but be restless, for I cannot wait for her to get here. I pray she has not been delayed on the road.'

'I am sure she will soon be—oh! That sounds like an arrival. No!' Aurelia halted at Mrs Butterby's command. 'Come and sit down. Do not overwhelm the poor girl by pouncing on her the minute she arrives.'

Aurelia returned to the sofa but could not bring herself to sit. She watched the door expectantly. The handle turned and Vardy entered.

'Miss Thame has arrived, ma'am.'

He stood aside and Leah entered the room, looking apprehensive. Aurelia immediately went to her, her hands outstretched.

'Leah! I am so pleased you are come at last.' Her sister looked tired, her beautiful blue-green eyes haunted even though she was smiling. 'Come and meet Mrs Butterby, our chaperon. I warn you, she takes her role *very* seriously,' she added in a whisper.

'I am happy to meet you again, Aurelia. Thank you for the welcome.' Leah kissed Aurelia's cheek and, in that moment, Aurelia felt sure all would be right and they would be friends.

'And Mrs Butterby.' Leah crossed the room to the chaperon. 'Thank you for taking on the role of our chaperon.'

'I am happy to meet you, Miss Thame. And Aurelia is correct—' Mrs Butterby levelled a stern look at Aurelia '—I do take my role seriously. It is my ambition to see you all successfully wed by the end of the Season and, to that end, you will both do well to remember I have cultivated the hearing of a bat, the eyes of a hawk and a nose for trouble—essential attributes for a chaperon with three wealthy young ladies' reputations to protect.'

Aurelia rolled her eyes, but then frowned, only half listening to the others' conversation as she pondered the shadows darkening Leah's eyes. There was unhappiness there, if she was not mistaken. Well, she knew all about unhappiness and, if she could persuade Leah to confide in her, she would help her sister banish whatever ghost was haunting her. Mrs Butterby was advising Leah that the three half-sisters should keep their relationship and their paternity a secret and, sensing Leah was about to argue, Aurelia gave a quick shake of her head. That was a discussion to have between the three half-sisters, when Beatrice arrived.

Mrs Butterby continued to rattle on about how much remained to be done before Easter and how she hoped Beatrice would not delay much longer, ending with, 'Shall I ring for refreshments? I dare say you are fatigued after your long journey, Miss Thame.'

'Oh, please. Call me Leah. Every time I hear Miss Thame I am transported straight back to the schoolroom and I intend to leave all memory of my time as a governess in the past.'

Aurelia noticed Leah cross her fingers as she said that last, again making her wonder what—or who—she was trying to forget.

'Leah. Thank you. Although I shall stick to the formalities in public.'

'Of course. Might I freshen up first? I feel decidedly grubby.'

'I asked the kitchen to heat water ready for you,' Aurelia said. 'Come. I shall show you up to your bedchamber. Your maid will have unpacked your trunk by now, I dare say.'

'My *maid*?'

Aurelia and Mrs Butterby had hired two lady's maids—Faith and Maria—a fortnight before, ready for when Leah and Beatrice arrived.

'Yes, indeed.' Mrs Butterby's eyes twinkled. 'If you are to take the *ton* by storm you will, first and foremost, need to look the part. Unless you wish to spend hours coaxing your own hair into the latest fashionable style?'

'Of course.'

Aurelia showed Leah upstairs to the second floor. 'My bedchamber and one other overlook the street, so we put you in that one. Beatrice's room, and Prudence's, are at the back.'

Leah's laugh sounded forced. 'Prudence?'

'What's wrong?'

'Nothing. I—I used to know someone called Prudence, that's all.'

'And is *Prudence* the reason you crossed your fingers when you claimed you wished to leave all memories of your time as a governess in the past?'

Leah narrowed her eyes at Aurelia. 'I don't know what you mean. Is Prudence Mrs Butterby's name?'

'Clever diversionary tactic there, Leah. And, yes, although she has not suggested I use it, so I don't call her that to her face.' Aurelia grinned. 'One has to take one's pleasure where one may. Here we are.' She opened Leah's door. 'My bedchamber is next to yours.'

Faith was already inside, unpacking. She turned and curtsied.

'Good afternoon, miss. I am Faith, your lady's maid.'

'I am pleased to meet you, Faith.' Leah turned to Aurelia. 'Thank you. If you will excuse me, I should like to wash and to change my gown. I'll join you in the drawing room shortly.'

Aurelia smiled, feeling content for the first time since Max left London. 'I am glad you've arrived, Leah. I'm looking forward to getting to know you.'

As time went on, Leah's arrival helped ease some of the pain and sense of betrayal Aurelia felt. She would show

Max Tregowan she didn't need him, or his help to find a suitable husband, not when she had her new sister by her side. They spent their time in a whirlwind of shopping, dressmakers, dancing lessons and promenading or driving in Hyde Park in the late afternoon—more of a pleasure than an ordeal as March progressed, although the sky remained grey, and glimpses of the sun were fleeting.

More and more members of polite society arrived in town, bringing with them increasing numbers of invitations to suppers, card parties and soirées. The two Tregowan heiresses were popular with certain gentlemen and Mrs Butterby proved her worth in weeding out the seasoned fortune hunters from the more genuine suitors who needed to marry money, like Sampford and Runcorn, and a Lord Veryan, who had taken a shine to Leah. But Aurelia still chafed at the lack of opportunity to meet any men other than over-privileged aristocrats, who she feared would squander her fortune without a qualm. Even a visit to the theatre, for which she'd had high hopes of meeting people from different walks of life, came to nothing.

'Here we go again,' muttered Aurelia to Leah as they made their way up yet another the staircase to yet another rout, this one hosted by Mr and Mrs Barrington. Mrs Butterby had already spied an old acquaintance and, after cautioning the sisters to stay together, had stopped to chat.

The heat hit Aurelia's face as they entered the salon and she flicked her fan open. Leah, she noticed in consternation, looked wan, her freckles standing out even more than usual. The skin around her eyes was bruised with fatigue and shame curled within Aurelia that she had been so busy trying not to think about Max she had not done more to support Leah.

'Shall we try to find somewhere a little quieter?'

Leah shook her head. 'I am all right. A little tired. It is such a change of pace from Dolphin Court.'

Aurelia threaded her arm through Leah's and, making slow progress, they moved between the press of bodies towards the opposite wall where the tall windows stood open.

'I shall be glad when the balls begin,' Aurelia said. 'At least they will be fun, unlike these events where gossip is the main entertainment, it seems.' There was often informal dancing at the parties they attended, but they were both keen to experience their very first ball. 'Oh, how I wish Beatrice would come and fill that gap in our lives.'

'I know what you mean,' said Leah. 'There are meant to be three of us and until we are all here it will always feel as though something is missing.'

Her eyes momentarily sheened over with tears and Aurelia sensed she was thinking about more than Beatrice, but she curbed the urge to pry. Her attempts to discover what was haunting her sister had been gently rebuffed and, conscious of her own reluctance to talk about her past, or even mention Max's name, Aurelia had to respect Leah's wish for privacy.

But if I ever meet that Lord Dolphinstone, he had better look out!

Lord Dolphinstone was Leah's former employer and, from the number of times his name was casually dropped into the conversation, Aurelia had guessed quite early on that he was the source of Leah's unhappiness.

Aurelia must be a better actress than she realised because she was certain neither Leah nor Mrs Butterby suspected *her* heart was breaking and that was how it must stay, for she could not bear their pity should they guess the truth.

'Miss Croome! Miss Thame! What a beautiful sight to meet our eyes.'

Lord Sampford bowed. As he straightened, Aurelia caught a glimpse of calculation in his eyes before he masked it with a wide smile that looked utterly insincere.

His companion, Lord Veryan—as vain a peacock as Sampford—also bowed. 'Indeed. You brighten up any event with your presence.'

His gaze, which managed to be both lascivious and avaricious at the same time, was on Leah. Aurelia sensed her sister shrink into herself a little and she squeezed her arm. Yes, both men were awful—patronising, entitled and utter bores—but even Aurelia, with her rebellious streak, accepted they could not afford to offend two such prominent noblemen.

'Good evening, my lords,' she said, steeling herself for another bout of condescending conversation. From the resigned look in Leah's eyes, her expectations were no higher than Aurelia's.

'I know I have said this before, Leah,' Aurelia said as they sat in the drawing room after arriving home, Mrs Butterby having retired to bed, 'but can you truthfully stomach the idea of tying yourself to one of those pompous nincompoops for life? You would spend all your time suppressing your own opinions and your true character because, mark my words, men like Sampford and Veryan already look down on us for our pasts—you a governess, me a shop girl.' They reminded her all too painfully of Augustus and his sneering contempt. 'How do you imagine they will react when they discover we are the by-blows of some dissolute earl?'

Both she and Leah had already agreed they would admit

to both their paternity and to their sisterhood, as long as Beatrice was also happy to do so.

Leah huffed a laugh. 'I dare say that will entirely depend on how desperate they are for our fortunes!'

'Indeed. Oh, thank you, Janet.' Aurelia smiled at the maid who carried in the tea tray.

She had come to value these cosy, late-night chats with Leah after Mrs Butterby retired. She poured a cup of tea and handed it to Leah, then poured one for herself.

'That is it exactly,' Aurelia continued. 'Would you not prefer a man who has *earned* his position and wealth rather than one who was merely born to the right parents? Those men are so utterly convinced of their own superiority and will doubtless secretly despise us for the circumstances of our birth, yet Prudence is still adamant we should seek spouses from within their ranks, in the belief good breeding is the only essential characteristic for a successful match.'

Leah sipped her tea, her brow wrinkled thoughtfully. 'Not all aristocrats are like those fortune hunters, Aurelia.'

'I have yet to meet any who are not.' Aurelia batted away the mental image of Max that appeared from nowhere and clawed at her heart. He'd proved as bad as the rest of them, stealing a kiss and abandoning her. He could stay in Cornwall, for all she cared. 'Well, speaking for myself, I can do without a husband who will look down upon me throughout our marriage because of my birth.'

'As your father did your mother? And you?'

Aurelia narrowed her eyes at Leah, who shrugged and held up her hands in a gesture of surrender.

'I withdraw the question, but you cannot blame me for trying.' Her sea-green eyes twinkled. 'Now...' she stroked her chin in an exaggerated manner '...what shall we change the subject to this time?'

Aurelia's smile felt crooked, but at least she'd once again deflected her sister's attention on to her father and her up-bringing for any distress she'd inadvertently revealed. Far better that than for Leah to realise Aurelia's heart was breaking. Still. More than a month after Max left.

'We could speculate about when Beatrice will arrive,' she said.

'Again? Mrs Butterby doesn't seem too worried as yet. But it is still hard for us to settle when our lives feel so incomplete.'

'At least Prudence has eased her stranglehold on me now that you are here. I am sure she views you as a ci-vilising influence on me.'

'She wants to do her best for us, Aurelia. She feels the burden of the responsibility Sarah laid upon her, but she is trying to be less strict since I pointed out you have been looking after yourself for so long.'

'Thank you. I hope we won't clash as often now she is more relaxed over her duties as chaperon. I admit I find it hard not to fight against too tight a rein.'

'And one day you *will* tell me about Augustus Croome,' said Leah, lying one cool hand against Aurelia's cheek, 'for it seems to me he is at the root of your distrust of aristo-cratic men. I can tell your childhood was unhappy—unlike mine—but I pray one day you will find a man who will love you for the person you are and who will not give a fig for your past.'

Aurelia hugged Leah. 'I pray we both will', and her heart ached at the sorrow in her sister's beautiful eyes and the sad smile on her lips.

She vowed to redouble her efforts to look after her sis-ter and to try to make her happy. And woe betide the man who had broken her gorgeous sister's heart.

Chapter Eighteen

Max pointed Caesar's head for home and gave him his head. The great grey stallion's long legs made quick work of the two miles between Wheal Rowenna and Tregowan Place and they arrived at the stables a mere three minutes before the rainclouds streaming in from the west made good their threat of a downpour. The rain drummed on the barn roof as Max leapt from Caesar's back and Jem, his groom-cum-farmhand, ran forward to take charge of the horse.

'Has the gig returned yet?'

'Nay, milord. I dare say they'll get wet.'

Max peered through the open barn door at the lashing rain while Jem unsaddled Caesar and rubbed him down with a handful of straw. 'As will I,' he commented.

One of the many drawbacks of living at the lodge was the half-mile distance from the stables. The estate wasn't sufficiently well manned to spare someone to bring Max a horse every time he needed to go to the mine, so he had long ago opted to walk between the two, comforting himself that it wouldn't be for ever and that one day he would take up residence in the Place itself and could send word to the stables whenever he required transport.

That promise had been eight years ago. Failure once again pressed its weight on him even though, at long last, there appeared a glimmer of hope on the horizon.

'At least Old Tom will drop Mr Keast off at the lodge,' he said now. 'And he took an umbrella with him, so that should give our visitor some protection.'

Mr Austerly had made good on his promise and his mine engineer, Mr Keast, was due to arrive today. He would inspect Wheal Rowenna tomorrow. Max couldn't help but fear it would come to nothing even as he prayed Keast would see some potential in the mine. At least then he would have Austerly's promised investment to help develop Rowenna. He dared not think what would happen if Keast advised Mr Austerly against investing in the mine— it would mean halting any further work on the Place until Max could find himself a wealthy wife.

And, as it always did, without exception, every time any thought of his marriage entered his head, Aurelia's beautiful, heart-shaped face would arise in his mind's eye.

'If you want, take Bess, milord.' Jem's words tugged him back to reality. 'She'll get you there quicker and Old Tom'll hitch her to the back of the gig to bring her back.'

Max eyed the aged bay mare, contentedly munching hay in her stall. 'No,' he said. 'Don't disturb her. Look. It's easing a bit. I'll make a dash for it. We'll see you tomorrow and, don't forget, we'll need the gig at ten.'

He might be happy to walk between the lodge and the stables himself, but he was not about to inflict that on Mr Keast when he was eager to impress the man. He pulled his greatcoat collar up around his ears and settled his hat more securely on his head before striding out of the door. He broke into a jog, the wind at his back giving impetus to his speed and shielding his face from the rain. He was panting by the time he reached the lodge and dashed in through the back door, where he stopped to pull off his boots and hang his coat to drip.

'Here you be, milord.' Mrs Carey handed him a towel. 'There's a fire in your bedchamber if you want to change your clothes.'

'Thank you, Mrs C.'

By the time Max was pulling on a dry pair of breeches, he heard the sounds of arrival. He hastily tied his neck-cloth and buttoned up his waistcoat before hurrying down the steep, narrow stairs. In the hallway a man was divesting himself of his coat, hat and boots. He looked up at the sound of Max's footsteps, revealing a far younger countenance than Max had expected.

'Mr Keast, I presume?' Max thrust out his hand. 'I'm Tregowan.'

'Indeed.' Keast shook Max's hand, then released it, flushing, to step back and bow. 'My lord.'

Max laughed. 'No need for that. Tregowan is fine. You are younger than I expected. From the way Mr Austerly sang your praises I assumed you'd had decades of experience in the mines.'

'I'm five-and-twenty, but I went underground at twelve, so I've had plenty enough experience. Mr Austerly recognised a fellow enthusiast for new ideas and techniques and he made it possible for me to get an education and better myself. I owe him a lot.'

From what Max knew of Austerly, that did not surprise him in the least—his enthusiasm for progress and innovation had been clear in their talks. He'd spoken of Keast as the son he'd never had and it was admirable he'd helped the boy to grow beyond his bleak start in life. From his own mine, Max had seen how miners' younger children worked alongside the women—the bal maidens—above ground, dressing the ore after it was brought to the surface. After the age of twelve, boys joined their fathers underground. Poor families had little choice but to put their children to work early in life.

By the time they had finished eating their dinner, Keast's enthusiasm for his subject had injected Max with the confidence that if anyone could transform the fortunes of his mine, this man could. If his verdict was unfavourable, Max really would have no alternative but to close Wheal Rowenna for good.

The following day they spent the morning down in the stifling underground heat of the mine. Max showed Keast both the main deposit of tin ore and the copper seam they had found last year, a discovery that had generated much excitement, for copper was five times the value of tin. It had been then that Max had taken that fateful gamble and borrowed money to invest in a modern beam engine to drive the wheel that hauled the rocks they blasted out to the surface, but the amount of copper in those rocks had never lived up to its early promise.

Max prayed that Keast would find something...*any-thing*...in Rowenna that would justify Mr Austerly investing money in the venture.

'Well,' said Keast, after they climbed the ladder back to the surface and slaked their thirst before washing their hands and faces at the water pump. 'I will not keep you in suspense. Do you have maps of the tunnels here? I want to show you something.'

'Yes. They're in the office, over there.'

Max caught the eye of his foreman, Pengelly, and saw

his own hope mirrored there. Pengelly knew as well as he did the repercussions for the local men, women and children who worked at Rowenna if the mine could not be made viable.

Half an hour later, Max was driving Keast back to the lodge for something to eat before Old Tom drove him up to the road to catch the short stage back to Launceston. His spirits were lighter than they had been for some time, all due to Keast's belief there was indeed a richer seam of copper just waiting to be found. He had shown Pengelly where to begin cutting a new, exploratory tunnel—not at the face of the secondary excavation, where they had been digging, but about halfway along the access tunnel.

'I cannot thank you enough,' Max said.

'It was my pleasure. And there is, of course, no guarantee I'm right about that seam of copper you've been following not being the main deposit. Only time will tell—but I have enough confidence to recommend Wheal Rowenna as a good investment for Mr Austerly and I shall write to him as soon as I arrive home.'

The agreement was for William Austerly to purchase a one-third share of the mine, which would give Max a sum sufficient to pay off that loan for the beam engine as well as leave a small amount to contribute towards Letty's Season, and to continue with the refurbishment of the Place. It would not solve all his money worries, but it went a long way to alleviate the pressure he was under. He would still need to find a bride with a generous dowry, however, in order to secure the future of the estate. And, with unerring timing, as soon as the thought of a marriage came into his head, so, too, did the memory of Aurelia Croome in his godmother's library, her blue eyes full of promise, darkening as her pupils widened, her lush lips parting in anticipation.

Max forced his attention back to Keast. 'Thank you. I shall be sure to speak to him upon my return to London next week. But are you not worried it is too much of a risk for him to invest until we know for sure there is a richer deposit of copper?'

Keast laughed. 'If we wait until then, why would you need a partner? You would continue as sole owner and reap all the profits. Business decisions like this…there has to be an element of risk for both parties. To be honest, it is that risk Mr Austerly most enjoys. If he did not relish it, he would not be where he is today. He would be content to live on his farm and run his original mine and live a comfortable life.'

His words summed up the man Max knew and his enthusiasm for life. He'd experienced some of that same enthusiasm when the copper had first been discovered and he'd taken out that loan, but harsh reality had quickly obliterated it in his case. He hoped to rediscover it soon. It would not bring him all his heart's desires, but he looked forward to rediscovering some of that earlier *joie de vivre* he had felt during the first few years of his life as a peer of the realm.

Chapter Nineteen

The twentieth day of March, which was a Wednesday, was memorable for a number of different reasons, but it left Aurelia feeling like a mere bystander in her own life.

The previous day had been momentous in itself, when Lord Dolphinstone, Leah's erstwhile employer, had unexpectedly appeared in Hyde Park while the two half-sisters were walking with Sampford and Veryan. Seeing the shocked reaction of both Leah and Dolphinstone confirmed to Aurelia that he was indeed the cause of Leah's unhappiness and, when he then turned up at the Todmordens' rout that same evening, and she saw them together at close quarters, she went to bed that night convinced that the Earl was as smitten as his former governess. He had arranged to call upon Leah the next day, raising the hope he intended to propose. Aurelia was thrilled for Leah even though her sister's joy only highlighted her own emptiness.

On the Wednesday morning itself, Bet woke Aurelia with the announcement that Beatrice had arrived and was taking a bath, and that she had brought a monstrous black cat called Spartacus with her. The relief that flooded her as she washed and dressed told Aurelia just how worried she had been about their youngest sister's failure to appear in London until now. She hurried downstairs to the morning room to find Beatrice—wrapped in Leah's blue and gold paisley shawl, her golden-brown hair damp and curling from her bath—already there and she rushed forward to envelop her sister in a hug.

'I am so happy to see you. We were worried about you.' Aurelia released Beatrice and stood back, clasping Beatrice's shoulders, as she studied her. 'I have gained weight since we met and you have lost it. Now we are more alike than ever.'

In truth, her pretty, plump little sister looked drawn and unhappy and Aurelia hated to see the strain in her eyes. As the four ladies of the household ate breakfast together, Mrs Butterby dominated the conversation with advice to prepare Beatrice for her new life while Aurelia managed to inject a few of her own questions about Beatrice's scoundrel of a brother, Sir Percy Fothergill, who sounded even more despicable than she and Leah had imagined. Leah ate quietly, clearly listening, but taking little part.

After breakfast Mrs Butterby, still talking non-stop, led Beatrice to the drawing room while Leah and Aurelia followed behind, discussing Beatrice and what they had learned of her life at the hands of her brother and his wife.

'At least now Beatrice is here we can finally discuss whether or not we publicly admit to our relationship,' said Leah as they entered the room.

'You know my opinion on that,' said Aurelia. 'I think we should announce it and be damned.'

'As do I, but I can also understand why Mrs Butterby advises caution.'

'Caution?' Mrs Butterby queried from where she and Beatrice sat on the sofa. 'About what did I advise caution?'

'Whether or not to openly acknowledge the three of us are half-sisters.' Leah smiled at Beatrice as she sat down. 'We agreed to wait until your arrival, as the decision will affect you, too.'

The biggest cat Aurelia had ever seen—presumably Spartacus—was grooming himself on the seat closest to the fire, seemingly quite at home. Aurelia elected to remain standing rather than evict him.

'Why should we not admit to our relationship?' Beatrice's gaze darted between the other three women. 'I am *proud* to have you as sisters and I care not who knows it.'

'There.' Aurelia smiled warmly at her. 'Beatrice agrees with me.'

'But…you do not understand, Beatrice,' said Mrs Butterby. 'By openly admitting you are the offspring of the late Lord Tregowan, you are exposing your mothers' morals to the censure of society.'

'Speculation is already rife,' said Leah.

'Ah, but speculation is merely that. Once you acknowledge the truth there will be no going back. And there will be suitors, and families, who will not even consider an alliance if there is a hint of a taint in your bloodlines.'

'If I am not good enough for a man to marry based upon my own merit,' said Aurelia, 'then *he* is not good enough for me to consider.'

'And I, too, am proud to call you both my sisters,' said Leah. 'So I agree we should acknowledge our relationship for, as Aurelia pointed out, to keep it secret would mean a lifetime of lies and surely there can be nothing worse than starting out married life upon a lie.'

Aurelia was pleased Leah agreed with the views she had espoused during their previous discussion of the matter.

'Well. If you are all determined…' Mrs Butterby heaved a sigh, shook her head and then, unexpectedly, she smiled. 'May I say... I applaud your courage and your integrity. And I am also slightly envious you have one another. I hope you continue to support each other and that you become lifelong friends as well as sisters.'

Her voice quivered and she dabbed at her eyes with her handkerchief. Aurelia, who still at times clashed with Prudence over her strictures, realised again how much she had mellowed since Leah had arrived and vowed to treat her with more patience in future, for her admission to a touch of envy of their sisterhood touched a chord. The Tregowan inheritance was one thing, but it paled into insignificance beside meeting Leah and Beatrice. Having them as her family gave her riches money simply could not buy.

'There! I have turned all maudlin!' Mrs Butterby continued. 'Beatrice, my dear, you must be exhausted...why do you not go upstairs to rest now? And—' She shot to her feet. 'Leah! In all the furore of Beatrice's arrival, I quite forgot! Lord Dolphinstone arrives shortly. Oh, my goodness.'

'Lord Dolphinstone?' Beatrice asked.

Leah blushed. 'I will tell you all about it later. Mrs Butterby is right...you do look exhausted. Go and get some rest.'

Beatrice looked scared. 'Oh, no. I couldn't possibly... what if Percy comes here?'

'What if he does?' Aurelia went to Beatrice and hauled her to her feet. 'We are here to support you and he no longer has any authority over you.' She hugged her, hard. 'You are safe, Beatrice. Come along, up the stairs with you. And perhaps you'd better take that monster with you.'

She indicated the cat and Beatrice, blushing, scooped him into her arms, saying, 'Oh. Of course. I'm sorry.'

Spartacus put his ears back and grumbled, but he made no attempt to escape as they went upstairs to Beatrice's bedchamber where Aurelia helped her half-sister out of her gown. Beatrice climbed into the warmed bed.

'Oh, this is blissful.' She snuggled down.

Spartacus immediately moved on to her stomach and began to knead the eiderdown. Beatrice reached to stroke him. Aurelia watched, feeling the love for this new sister of hers already warming her heart and helping to fill the void left by Max.

'Is he not heavy?' she said.

'Yes, but he will not stay there long. It is his way of showing his love.'

'Ah. Then he is worth his weight in gold, is he not?'

'He is.' Beatrice's eyelids drooped. 'Aurelia, who is Lord Dolphinstone?'

'Leah was working for him as governess before she came to London and, unless I am very much mistaken, he will soon be her husband and, hence, our brother-in-law.' She bent and kissed Beatrice's forehead, smoothing her hair back gently. 'Sleep tight, my dear.'

Aurelia soon learned she was not mistaken when a radiantly smiling Leah and Dolph—as Lord Dolphinstone was called by family and friends—came to the drawing room to announce their betrothal. They intended to marry without delay and planned to remain in London, with Dolph's three young children, for the remainder of the Season.

'I want to be here to support you and Beatrice,' said Leah, her blue-green eyes sparkling with happiness. 'I pray you both will find the love and joy I have found... and I am determined to help you achieve it.' She leaned closer and whispered, 'And you will have my full support when you reject both Sampford and Runcorn! Together, we must persuade Mrs Butterby that a match with either man would be a disaster.'

Aurelia hugged her tight. 'Thank you,' she whispered, although her heart was hollow, for she knew she could not have the one man who haunted her dreams.

Aurelia then smiled up at Dolph and held out her hands. 'I hope you will forgive me for my suspicions of you?'

Last night, at the Todmordens' rout, she had confronted him about his behaviour towards Leah.

His sombre countenance broke into a smile. 'But of course.' He bent and kissed her cheek. 'I am grateful you were so ready to defend Leah. Now, please forgive us, but we are eager to go and tell the children our good news.'

'When will we meet them?'

'We shall bring them over later today,' Dolph promised. 'I need to arrange the marriage licence first...we hope to wed the day after tomorrow.'

And the day had not finished with its surprises.

Aurelia and Mrs Butterby—leaving Beatrice to sleep—went out shopping and arrived home to find the front door wide open and Vardy standing at the bottom of the staircase blocking the way of an irate, portly gentleman, standing wide-legged with his hands on his hips while another man—taller, slimmer and dandyish—stood to one side, looking on with a supercilious sneer.

'She is my *sister*!' the stout man bellowed.

Aurelia flicked a look up the staircase, but there was no sign of Beatrice. Hopefully she was still asleep, poor thing, for she had been exhausted, but Aurelia relished this chance to confront the man who had turned her sister into a nervous wreck. She hurried past him and spun to face him, shoulder to shoulder with Vardy. Mrs Butterby, she was pleased to see, followed suit. There was no way this monster was getting access to Beatrice.

'Leave this house, sir,' she said, summoning as much

hauteur as she possibly could. 'You are not welcome here. Ever.'

'And who the devil are you to tell me what to do? I am Sir Percy Fothergill and I demand to see my sister, Beatrice. I know she is here, so there is no use denying it!'

'I do not deny it, but you are still not welcome. I—'

'Percy!'

Aurelia glanced back, and up the stairs, to where Beatrice was descending, with Maria by her side. The determination on her sister's pale face allayed Aurelia's fears. This man might have controlled and bullied Beatrice, but he had not broken her spirit.

'Have you told him yet, Aurelia?'

Aurelia shook her head, and stood aside, watching with huge delight as Beatrice told her despicable brother that he was not her brother, and had never been her brother, and that she owed him nothing. When the other man entered the fray, claiming a betrothal to Beatrice, she roundly dismissed him with the words, 'There is no betrothal, Sir Walter, as well you know.'

As the two men left, Sir Percy still blustering, Aurelia whispered, 'Bravo, Sister. I am proud of you.'

'Well! This *has* been an eventful day,' said Mrs Butterby as the three women climbed the stairs together. 'I trust not every day with you will quite so exciting, Beatrice, for I am quite exhaust—Oh!'

Aurelia followed her gaze to the landing above them, to the tall stranger standing there.

'Ah,' said Beatrice and Aurelia relaxed at her sister's lack of surprise or of fear.

As they reached the head of the stairs, her gaze was first drawn to the sleeve that was pinned up, halfway between the gentleman's wrist and elbow. Then that was forgotten as she took in the shock of dark blond hair above a handsome face with bright blue eyes and a mouth that looked to be on the verge of a smile.

'Lord Jack Kingswood, this is Mrs Butterby, my chaperon, and Miss Aurelia Croome, one of my half-sisters.'

He bowed. 'Delighted to meet you both.' Aurelia watched with interest as he and Beatrice's eyes met. 'I enjoyed watching you rout those pompous asses, Bea.'

By the time Lord Jack—the twin brother of the Marquess of Quantock, no less, and who had escorted Beatrice on her journey to London—left them, Aurelia was convinced he and Beatrice had feelings for one another. Mrs Butterby took herself off for a rest, leaving Aurelia and Beatrice in the drawing room together with Spartacus, who was gently snoring on the sofa. Aurelia teased Beatrice with questions about Jack, but Beatrice demonstrated a surprisingly stubborn streak—which Aurelia had to admire, given all her sister had gone through—and vehemently denied Jack was anything more than a friend before pointedly changing the subject.

'Do you know why Lady Tregowan stipulated we must spend the Season in London? And the reason for the other conditions?'

Aurelia told Beatrice everything she had learned about the conditions attached to their inheritance, including the one forbidding their marriage to Max Tregowan.

'I see,' said Beatrice, as Aurelia swallowed down her pain and battled to keep an expression of scorn on her face. 'He must be very bitter about that if she left everything to him in the first place. That is what Mr Henshaw said, isn't it?'

'It is.' Aurelia shrugged to demonstrate her indifference. 'But what should he expect if he's run up so much debt? I have no sympathy for the man.'

But I do! Oh, I do. And I know Sarah was wrong about his gambling debts. But it makes no difference. It can never make a difference.

She had tried everything to banish him from her heart. And her thoughts. But still he haunted her, despite her acceptance that their situation would be hopeless even if Max did feel the same about her. He must wed a rich wife—no amount of wishful thinking could change that fact and so that wife could never be her even if she *were* prepared to forfeit her inheritance and the thought of that…the possibility of somehow losing everything and sliding back into poverty…still had the power to bring her out in a cold sweat.

She welcomed the sound of an arrival that filtered up the stairs from the hall.

'That sounds like Leah has returned,' she said, with some relief. 'She went to Lord Dolphinstone's house to visit the children as she hadn't seen them since she came to London. *She* was in denial about her feelings, just like you, until Dolph turned up this morning and proposed.'

They talked about the wedding, and the gowns Beatrice would need, until Leah came in, hand in hand with Dolph, who was carrying a little girl. Two young boys and a massive dog with a thick, black-tipped tawny coat followed them. Leah introduced Beatrice to Dolph, who then introduced his children.

'This is my daughter, Tilly…' he indicated the child in his arms '…and these scamps are Stevie and Nicky.'

'This is Wolf,' announced the smaller of the two lads—Nicky—as he pulled the huge animal over to Beatrice and Aurelia.

'Wolf?' Beatrice stroked the dog's tawny head. 'That is a good name for him, as he does look rather like a shaggy wolf.'

'These ladies are to be your aunts, boys,' Leah said, as the dog set off to explore the room. 'Aunt Beatrice you have met. And this is Aunt Aurelia.'

'Well, how lovely to have two nephews and a niece.' Aurelia blinked to disperse the tears that prickled her eyes. How lucky Leah was. How happy she was for her. 'Such a difference to all our lives in so few months. From being alone to having a ready-made family.'

Hiss...

'Oh, dear,' said Beatrice.

Spartacus stood, back arched, on the sofa, his back arched, green eyes almost starting from his head and his fur standing on end, while Wolf, with a small yelp, leapt back, a trickle of blood on his black nose.

'I am so sorry. I forgot Spartacus was even there.'

Wolf licked the blood from his nose and stood, his head cocked to one side, tail slowly wagging, as he and Spartacus locked eyes. Slowly, the cat relaxed his posture until, with a final disdainful look at the dog, he circled and settled back down on the sofa.

Aurelia glanced apprehensively at Dolph, wondering if he might reveal his true colours. She could only imagine Augustus's reaction in similar circumstances. But her future brother-in-law gave her no cause to worry for Leah as a smile tugged at his mouth.

'That,' he said, 'could have been a disaster. However, it seems the victor was agreed with very little bloodshed and peace will now reign. But I am rather relieved the two of them won't be sharing their home in the future.'

Once again, delight for her sister flooded Aurelia even as despair for herself formed a leaden weight in her stomach. How could she ever dream of such a happy ending?

Chapter Twenty

'Welcome back, Lord Tregowan.' Parkinson bowed and stood aside for Max to enter Simon's Portman Square residence. 'I trust your journey was uneventful?'

'It was indeed, Parkinson. Thank you. Is Mr Effingham at home?'

'He is in the salon, my lord.' Parkinson held out his hand for Max's portmanteau. 'If you will follow me, I shall announce your arrival. Oh, and there is a letter for you. I shall put in your bedchamber. Dinner will be served in half an hour and I will ensure another place is set for you.'

Max followed the butler up the stairs, quashing his impatience at Parkinson's stately pace—impatience which was entirely due to the fact he was here, in London, and Aurelia Croome was once again within his reach. It seemed his sojourn in Cornwall had done little to put her out of his mind, for her lure shone even brighter than before.

'Max! My dear fellow. It is good to see you back.'

'Thank you. I'm surprised to find you home. Not dining with the lovely Camille tonight?'

'No. That is over. She was becoming overly possessive, so you are stuck with me this evening.' He grinned. 'We could go to m'club later?'

Max welcomed the distraction. 'Yes, I will enjoy that. I'll go and freshen up for dinner.'

His letter was from Letty. He skimmed it, taking in the news that they had not yet resumed their journey but still hoped to be in London by Easter. Max frowned over her words, noting her frequent mentions of Mr Casbourne, the man who was escorting them through France and whose injury had caused the delay. Something in the way she wrote about him made him wonder if his sister was enamoured of the man. If she was, he hoped for her sake that her feelings were reciprocated.

In the dining room, the table was set with several courses—fish, soup, roast meats and pies, and vegetables in a variety of sauces—and the tantalising smells reminded Max he had not eaten since he broke his fast on the journey, early that morning.

'Well?' said Simon, as he drank his vermicelli soup. 'Was your trip to Cornwall a success?'

'It was, yes.' Max told Simon about Keast's visit and the likelihood of William Austerly investing in Wheal Rowenna.

'Good news!' Simon raised his glass in a toast. 'However, what I really wish to know is if your trip away has helped put a certain heiress out of your mind.'

'Yes,' Max lied.

Simon narrowed his eyes at Max. 'Well, that is also good news because I have found you the perfect girl to marry. Miss Newton. Do you know her?'

Max shook his head.

'From the north. Somewhere.' Simon waved his hand vaguely. 'Father is wealthy as Croesus—mining again, but coal in his case—and he's determined she'll marry a title. She's pretty. Seems well brought up. Perfect for you. I'll introduce you.'

Max's heart sank. 'Thank you.'

He concentrated on his food. He ought to make conversation, but all he wanted to talk about was Aurelia. And he could not. *Should* not.

'I had a letter from Letty. They still hope to arrive by Eastertide.'

'Then there is no time to lose in your campaign to win the hand of Miss Newton. I wonder if her family will be invited to the Smethwicks' ball tomorrow night? Hmmm. Possibly not, given they're *nouveau riche*.'

James and Bell, the footmen on duty, cleared their dishes and then served them with red mullet with capers and scalloped oysters. Parkinson refilled their glasses. Max battled the cloud of dread that fogged his head. The sound of the door closing caught his attention and he looked up from his plate to see that the servants had left the room. Simon was watching him, a frown stitched between his brows.

'I have never known a man like you for wearing his heart on his sleeve, Maximilian,' he said. 'Come on, then. You need to get this out of your head if you are going to win Miss Newton. You are dying to know all about Miss Croome and that thought is getting in the way of all others. And...' he sighed '...there is much to tell. So, I shall apprise you of the latest news and then you, my friend, must accept your responsibilities as the Earl of Tregowan and marry for the sake of the estate and your family.'

'What news is there?'

His stomach roiled with something akin to fear as he wondered if she'd already found a husband, but Simon told him all about the arrival of the other two beneficiaries— Miss Thame and Miss Fothergill—and the news that they and Aurelia were half-sisters.

'That last titbit has only come out since Miss Fothergill's arrival last week. It's said Sarah Tregowan left them her fortune because all three were in precarious positions and to salve her own guilt about never giving her husband an heir. It was old Tregowan who arranged marriages for their three mothers. He couldn't have picked a worse husband than Augustus Croome, could he? Well...' Simon grinned '...other than old Fothergill, I suppose. Don't know much about the Reverend Thame. I dare say old Tregowan didn't much care who wed them, as long as it got them off his hands. And his conscience.'

Max forked some fish into his mouth and chewed without tasting it. He swallowed.

'And...have you seen her? Is she well?'

'Oh, on top form, my dear fellow. Top form. Cutting a dash through society. Got all the chancers eating out of her hand, panting after that inheritance.'

'I am glad to hear she is enjoying her Season. Is she...?' He jibbed at having to ask, but he must know the worst. 'Is she betrothed yet?'

'Not yet, but I doubt it'll be long. The betting book has Sampford as the front runner, with Runcorn a close second. Her sister, Miss Thame, has already been snapped up.'

'Has she? Good God...that was quick. By whom?'

'Dolphinstone. Her old employer. She was his governess. So it wasn't as quick as you might imagine. Love match by all accounts.'

They both continued to eat in silence while Max pondered this news.

'She's still on your mind then, old chap?'

Simon's sympathy cut through Max's reflections. Going to Cornwall had solved nothing, it seemed, as far as Aurelia Croome was concerned. He had only to hear her name...to imagine her with all those fortune hunters hanging on her sleeve...and he was right back where he started.

She was on his mind the whole time. He still wanted her. He loved her, but he could not have her.

'Not at all. Merely thinking over all that's happened since I've been away. I'm pleased for her she has a family and I'm sure she will find a husband worthy of her.' The words grated his throat. 'As I will find a wife to suit my needs.'

'Indeed,' said Simon and helped himself to a large helping of raised venison pie.

'You will enjoy it, miss.'

Aurelia smiled at Bet's reflection in the mirror as the maid dressed her hair in preparation for Lady Smethwick's ball, which she threw every year to celebrate her husband's birthday. It was always one of the first balls of the Season and the first ball that all three sisters would attend together.

'Is that an order, Bet?'

'Have you not sworn for weeks now that you will not mope after His Lordship? All I am doing is reminding you of that vow.'

'You are right, of course. I bless the day I appointed you, Bet, for I could not burden either of my sisters with this—not when I know how much they would long to help and I know there is no solution.' She sighed. 'Besides, why should I mope after him when he has clearly put me right out of his mind? You are right to scold me and I promise you I shall sparkle and dazzle at the ball tonight. Not one soul will suspect that—'

Aurelia's jaw snapped shut. She had nearly said it. Those words that came to her sometimes in the dead of night, when no one was around to witness her misery. The admission that her heart was breaking.

'*No* one will suspect my true opinion of these cossetted lords and gentlemen while I search for a decent man to marry in order that I do not find myself living in an isolated cottage in Somerset for the rest of my days while my sisters live their gloriously contented happy-ever-afters.'

'Miss Fothergill might find herself in the same predicament as you, miss. She is a lovely lady, but she doesn't show to advantage next to you or Lady Dolphinstone.'

Bet pinned a circlet of sapphires and diamonds in Aurelia's hair and tilted her head as she studied Aurelia in the mirror. 'There. A perfect match with your gown. You will outshine them all, miss.'

'Our Beatrice may be shy and less flamboyant than Leah or me, but I suspect she might surprise us all yet, although maybe not tonight. She is petrified of dancing in public, poor thing, despite our lessons.'

Not only had they hired a dance master to teach them the dances, but Aurelia had also been practising with Beatrice. Her sister, though, remained convinced she would make a fool of herself.

A knock sounded at the door and Mrs Butterby, clad in a gown the shade of lilac blossom, entered. Aurelia stretched her lips in a wide smile as she met Mrs Butterby's eyes in the mirror. She was getting better at faking happiness, she mused. She could almost fool herself, were it not for that hard knot of misery in her chest that no number of fake smiles and false laughs could banish.

'You are ready, Aurelia. Good, for Dolphinstone's carriage is outside and he won't want to keep his horses standing.'

Aurelia stood and turned, and Mrs Butterby's eyes misted over. 'Oh, you look exquisite, my dear. Sampford *must* declare himself soon…he has been most particular in his attentions… I can't understand why he is so reluctant to commit.'

Aurelia exchanged an amused glance with Bet, who knew all about Aurelia's efforts to discourage Sampford from such a declaration. She prayed he would not find his courage tonight, for she knew without doubt—and Sampford clearly half suspected—that she would refuse him.

Bet helped Aurelia on with her midnight-blue satin mantle and her evening gloves, then handed her a fan and her reticule.

'There, miss. All done.'

'And well done, Bet,' said Mrs Butterby. 'I don't deny I had doubts about your experience when Miss Croome chose you as her lady's maid, but I see now that her decision was the right one.' Her brow darkened. 'I wish I could say the same for that Maria. She has not the warmth of character a timid girl like Beatrice needs.'

'I agree.' Aurelia passed Mrs Butterby, heading for the door. 'And Bet tells me she is unpopular below stairs, too.'

'Good heavens. No one told me that. I shall speak to Mrs Burnham about it. I cannot have discord among the staff. Perhaps you, my dear, will speak to Beatrice and ask whether we should hire another maid for her?'

'I will,' Aurelia promised. 'But not tonight.'

She joined Beatrice in the hall. She took in her younger sister's huge eyes and the way she worried at her lower lip and her heart went out to her.

'You look beautiful, Bea, and that gown is stunning on you.' It was true…she was a gorgeous woman. She just didn't believe it yet. Aurelia prayed Lord Jack Kingswood would come to see what a treasure was sitting right under his nose. 'Come along.' She slipped her arm around Beatrice's waist. 'Let us go and set that ballroom alight!'

The night after Max's return to London, he and Simon set off from Simon's house to walk to that of his Portman

Square neighbours, Lord and Lady Smethwick. Other than paying a courtesy visit to Mr Austerly—who had happily confirmed his investment in Wheal Rowenna—Max had remained indoors all day, mentally preparing himself for seeing Aurelia again. His spirits had been in a state of flux the entire time—one moment full of eager anticipation and praying she would be there tonight, the next, filled with dread and hoping for her absence.

After exchanging greetings with their host and hostess, the two men followed the sound of the music to the back of the house where His Lordship's annual birthday ball had already begun.

A footman stood at the door of the ballroom with a tray of glasses and they each selected a glass of champagne. Max took one step into the room and froze, his attention drawn inexorably to the only person in the room who mattered. He stood to rigid attention in an effort to disguise—and deny—the utter turmoil in his gut, his veins and his thoughts. Only his eyes moved as they clung to Aurelia Croome—the woman he had tried so hard to convince himself he had no feelings for whatsoever—as she partnered that dog, Sampford, in a cotillion.

The man is a simpering idiot! What is she thinking? What the hell *does she see in him?*

And she…*she* was in sparkling form, clearly having the time of her life and relishing being the centre of attention as she moved with grace and confidence, her smile brilliant and her blue eyes as dazzling as the diamonds at her throat, her golden hair fashioned into dancing ringlets.

Watching her, it felt as though something reached deep inside Max and grabbed a handful of vital organs and squeezed and twisted until he could barely catch his breath. But that feeling broke her spell and, realising he had halted in the centre of the doorway, Max moved aside.

Not to stand inconspicuously against the wall as he had intended, but to stand right on the edge of the dancing area, waiting for the dance to end.

'Maximilian.' Simon was there, at his shoulder, his voice low and urgent. 'Take care. Do *not* allow her—*anyone*—to see what you feel.'

'I don't know what you mean.'

He had to force the words through clenched teeth. He could not tear his eyes from her charade—it had to be a charade. He could not bear it to be anything other than a charade. Jealousy swelled inexorably inside him, spurred on by fury at himself for his weakness in being dragged straight back to the very feelings he had gone to Cornwall to escape.

Simon, by his side, clasped his arm by his elbow. 'Don't do anything stupid, I beg you.'

'I am merely watching the dancers. Have some faith in my good sense, Simon.'

'Ah, but I know you. You might have good sense, but you are also too romantic and too impulsive for your own good, Maximilian. Please. Stay here with me and do not do anything you regret.'

There was no one else in that ballroom but her, as far as he was concerned, and his gaze clung to her as she danced. Anger, and the urge to punish her, joined that heady mix of emotions churning up his insides. It might be unfair to aim that fury at her but she, and only she, was the cause of this feeling of utter, helpless desolation. Desolation because there was still no way out of their predicament. And all the while, there she was, without a care in the world, dancing, flirting, searching for the husband she needed to secure her inheritance.

Any husband as long as it wasn't him.

Chapter Twenty-One

As Aurelia danced with Lord Sampford at Lord Smethwick's birthday ball—her third dance of the evening—
she congratulated herself on her ability to disguise her
true opinion of His Lordship and his ilk. Her smile felt
so forced, yet Sampford seemed taken in—encouraged,
even—by her seemingly rapt attention. As if she would
ever contemplate marrying a man like him...so like Augustus in his entitlement and his condescension and his
waspish manner that she could never put herself in his
power. But she must continue with this farce in order to
keep Mrs Butterby happy until she worked out a way to
meet a self-made man instead of one of these preening
popinjays.

Thank goodness the dance was ending.

Sampford bowed. 'Now, Miss Croome. Might I claim
my second dance?' He reached out and captured her hand.
'It is the supper dance next.'

His smile radiated smug confidence.

'Oh, dear.' *Now I sound like Beatrice. She is always
saying that.* But there were worse people to model modest behaviour on than her beloved sister. 'I am sorry, my
lord, but I am already promised for this dance.' She made

a show of looking around the ballroom. 'I must wait for my partner, it seems.

She had no partner for the next dance, but she fibbed without a qualm because she wanted to join her family for supper and to talk with them about everything and nothing, not make polite conversation with some overattentive and self-satisfied lord.

'I am cut to the quick,' cried Sampford, placing his hand on his heart in a dramatic gesture that made Aurelia cringe. 'You are too cruel. Tell me you have a dance free later.' He waggled his brows suggestively. 'We could take a little air outside. Get away from this stifling heat.'

'I think not, sir.' Aurelia's chin lifted of its own accord, her teeth gritted behind her tight-lipped smile. 'Thank you for the suggestion, but I have my reputation to consider.' She scanned the room now as she spoke, wondering if Dolph might be free to partner her for the next dance and keep the rest of her entourage at bay. But, no, for there he was, just leaving the ballroom. 'Now, please—'

Her breath caught in her lungs at the tall, dark figure standing near the door and her heart soared before she registered he was glowering. At her. How *dare* he?

'Excuse me!'

She did not wait for Sampford's reply. She marched straight across the floor, making straight for Max.

'You are back.'

'As you see.'

'You just disappeared. You did not even say you were going.'

She became aware her hands had clenched into fists as she confronted him, but she was beyond caring what other people thought. The rage…the *hurt* rage…barrelled through her, flattening every silently whispered caution and every instinct for self-protection in its path.

Max raised a haughty brow. 'I was unaware I owed you any explanation, Miss Croome.'

Miss Croome? Oh! 'What happened to Aurelia?' she hissed. 'You called me Aurelia when you wanted to kiss me.'

He shrugged, his face all hard, angular planes, his dark eyes—usually so lively and passionate—opaque. Dismissive. 'Men often say things to achieve their aims.'

Her jaw ached, it was clenched so tight. Her chest heaved. He was so utterly indifferent, just as he had been after their kiss. *Was* this the true Max Tregowan? Just another spoilt aristocrat, cutting a swathe through other people's lives, taking what he wanted without a care for the hurt he caused? Bet was right to reproach her for moping after him.

'You are no gentleman, sir. I thought…' The words caught in her throat, and she had to choke out the rest of her sentence. 'I thought you were different. Better than them.'

She waved a wild arm, indicating their fellow guests, catching a passing gentleman in the chest.

'Take care, Miss Croome. You are allowing your emotions to take control. People are beginning to notice.'

'Better by far to have genuine emotions than to be a cold, dead *fish*. You care for nothing but your own selfish gratification.'

'You are mistaken.'

Still, not a hint of passion or emotion in his expression, but—looking more closely—she could see turbulence in the depths of his dark brown eyes. For the first time she noticed Mr Effingham hovering behind him. She was so furious she could not even respond to his tentative smile.

'And what is it you care about, other than your own pleasure?'

'I care about Tregowan.' He raised a haughty brow. 'As you know, my need for funds dictates that I must marry a rich wife, and I shall do my duty, for the sake of the earldom and for the sake of the people who work for me. That clause in Lady Tregowan's will is unfortunate in that it precludes me taking either you or your sister, Miss Fothergill, as my wife. That, without doubt, would have been the easiest solution for us all.'

Aurelia gasped out loud. 'Easiest? Why, you…you *arrogant* swine! For your information, neither I nor my sister would stoop to consider you as an acceptable match, even if that condition did not exist.'

She managed to stamp her foot and swivel away from him at the same time—how she didn't trip over her own feet she didn't know—and she marched back across the ballroom to her sisters, straight through the couples forming for the supper dance.

'Oh! Insufferable, rude man!' Aurelia flung herself down on to a vacant chair, snatched her fan from the table and plied it vigorously, conscious of a swell of relief that only Leah and Beatrice had witnessed her outburst. Mrs Butterby would have been horrified had she been present.

'Who is he, Aurelia?' Leah's sea-green eyes were troubled. 'What did he say to upset you?'

'Tregowan,' Aurelia bit out through gritted teeth, glaring across the room at him. He, however, was not looking in her direction. He was merely standing where she had left him, glowering into space as Effingham talked rapidly in his ear.

'Oh, heavens. How he must resent us.' Beatrice looked and sounded worried.

'What did he say?' Leah laid her hand over Aurelia's, stilling her drumming fingers.

Aurelia sucked in a deep breath. 'He had the nerve to

imply that, had that clause forbidding marriage to him not existed, he would have taken...*taken*, if you please...either me or Beatrice as it would have been the easiest solution for all. *Easiest!* Arrogant, puffed-up swine! As if all he has to do is click his fingers!'

'I am sure he did not mean it in *quite* that way, Aurelia.'

'Oh, he did. He is selfish and arrogant and—'

'And a swine. Yes, you have already told us. But...how do you know him? I was unaware you had even met Lord Tregowan. You have never mentioned him.'

'No.' She eyed Leah. Beatrice appeared to have disappeared into a world of her own and was clearly not listening. 'And if I claim that was our first meeting...?'

Leah arched one brow. 'Would you really expect me to believe that, Sister dear?'

Aurelia huffed a laugh. 'No. I suppose I would not.'

'Does Mrs Butterby know?'

Aurelia sighed. 'She introduced us, but we... I...' She snapped her fan shut and fidgeted with it, then opened it again to cool her heated cheeks. 'Our paths crossed once or twice afterwards, but Prudence was not always present.' Heat flared across her chest and swept up her neck. 'Anyway...he is infuriating. He returned to Cornwall before you arrived in London and I did not expect to see him back here. Not yet, anyway.'

She felt her cheeks burn hotter. Why did she feel the need to hide their meeting outside Henshaw and Dent and their shared journey on the mail coach? But she knew why. Talking about that would mean delving even deeper into her feelings about him. And there was no point. None at all. Especially now when it was clear he had fooled her into believing he had feelings for her. Well! She supposed he did have feelings for her—feelings of lust. She snorted, and clapped her hand over her mouth. She then caught Leah's eye and they both giggled.

'But… Look, we cannot talk freely here, but may we talk about this again?'

'If we must.'

Leah smiled at her. 'I am on your side.' Her head tilted and her eyebrows rose teasingly. 'I understand you hate him, but with such intensity and passion…'

Aurelia hunched her shoulder and turned away. Leah touched her arm.

'It will help if you talk about it, I promise.'

'As you did, about Dolph?'And the minute those words left Aurelia's lips she regretted them, for were they not tantamount to a confession that she had feelings for the blasted man?

Touché,' Leah said, lightly. 'We will talk soon—oh, hush! Here is Mrs Butterby returning. Beatrice said she met an acquaintance upstairs and stayed to chat…and here is Dolph, too, with our drinks.'

After supper, Beatrice claimed a headache and the newly-weds—who had always intended to leave the ball early—offered to drive her home in their carriage, leaving Aurelia and Mrs Butterby at the ball. As the two of them returned to the ballroom, Lord Runcorn waylaid them. She had promised him the first dance after supper.

'Well met, Miss Croome. Would you care for a breath of fresh air before the dancing resumes? There are several others outside on the terrace taking the air, so you need not fear any impropriety.'

Mrs Butterby egged her on with her eyes and Aurelia quashed the niggle of guilt that told her she was being unfair. She ought to be clear…*clearer*…with both him and

Sampford that they would never stand any chance with her but, even for a woman as forthright as her, it was an impossible subject to broach until one of them plucked up courage to declare himself. Until then, she must play one off against the other. And this was the perfect opportunity to knock Sampford off his stride once again.

Besides, Max might be watching and it would prove to him that she could not care less about him.

'Indeed, my lord.'

Runcorn waited until they were outside. 'I could not help but notice your encounter with Tregowan.' He squeezed her hand against his ribcage. 'The scoundrel upset you, it was clear. I hope you know I am here to help if you need protection.' He lowered his voice. 'No doubt he is still enraged over that business with the will?'

Aurelia swallowed the urge to ask why he hadn't come to her defence at the time.

'I was not upset and I have no need of protection, sir. But thank you, anyway. Lord Tregowan and I were simply indulging in a frank exchange of views.'

They paused by a balustrade, beyond which Aurelia assumed there was a garden, but the combination of a moonless night and a cloudy sky meant nothing was visible. She turned her back on the void, facing back towards the ballroom. At the far end of the terrace, a conservatory jutted out at right angles to the house and, although it was unlit, the light from the ballroom windows illuminated a tall male figure standing inside, watching. Something about his stance told her it was Max and she shivered involuntarily under the weight of his attention even as the hurt anger of before bubbled up again. He'd made no apology. He'd insulted her. He'd ripped her heart apart, yet again. She shivered again and Runcorn closed the gap between them.

'You are chilled, my dear.'

He slid his arm around the back her waist, out of sight of others on the terrace. For one brief moment Aurelia thought of allowing him the liberty…anything to prove to that rogue Tregowan that he meant nothing to her, but her earlier wariness about leading these lords on too blatantly came back strongly, urging caution. She arched her upper body away from him and brought her hands up between them.

'Lord Runcorn! I thought better of you than to try to take advantage in such a way. Do you wish to ruin my reputation?'

'But… Miss Croome…' He moved back a little, removing his arm.

That anger at Max had settled into a cold fury.

Is this what he has brought me to? Allowing a flirtation with a man I care nothing for, just to prove how little he bothers me?

She cast a swift glance at the conservatory. He was still there, watching, his face a pale featureless shape at this distance. 'Thank you, sir. It is time I returned to my chaperon.'

He raised an arrogant brow. 'We are engaged for the next dance, Miss Croome.'

'I have quite lost my appetite for dancing, my lord. If you will excuse me?'

She stalked away, leaving him on the terrace. When she entered the ballroom, however, her steps did not take her to where Mrs Butterby sat with the other chaperons, but in the opposite direction. She strolled around the perimeter of the room, using the dancing couples and the onlookers to shield her from both her chaperon and from Lord Runcorn, if he had presumed to follow her. She did not look back to find out. She slipped out of the ballroom the first chance she got and she looked around, getting her bearings. An unlit passageway at one end of the hall showed promise and, as she entered it, she saw the glazed door of the conservatory before her.

Chapter Twenty-Two

Max stood still, looking out over the terrace, even after Aurelia had gone inside, leaving that cod's head, Runcorn, standing alone. He had managed to escape Simon's vigilance by the simple expedient of giving his word as a gentleman that he would not approach Aurelia for the remainder of the evening. He did not doubt she would avoid him after he had so thoroughly insulted her. Maybe driving yet another wedge between them had been the right thing to do—it would be easier, surely, for them both if this attraction between them were broken irrevocably— and yet he couldn't deny his own wretchedness.

He had hurt her. Again.

At supper, he'd decided to leave the ball immediately afterwards, knowing it was the wisest course of action. Yet the instant he had spotted Aurelia heading out on to the terrace with Runcorn he had made his way to the conservatory to watch her from afar, even though seeing her with other men was like pouring salt into an open wound.

He must accept she would marry—she must, or she would lose her inheritance—and he really did understand her fear of returning to a life of poverty. And he had no choice but to marry money if he wanted to provide a home suitable for Mama and Letty, let alone leave his heir with an unencumbered estate.

But, dear God, this is hard...

He swept his fingers through his hair, turned away from the window and froze.

His heart thundered in his ears, all but drowning out the music from the ballroom. His mouth felt as though it had been sucked dry even as sweat dampened his palms. So much for her avoiding him.

'What are you doing here?'

His voice rasped and he cleared his throat. He breathed in, trying to calm himself, catching a hint of her fragrance as it mingled with the scent of the flowers. Every muscle in his body stiffened and his throat ached with all the feelings he must suppress.

'I came for an answer. You *do* owe me an explanation. You know you do.'

She stood a good ten feet away, her small hands clenched into fists, her chin tilted defiantly as her blue eyes brimmed with unshed tears. His heart cracked at the sight, but what good could come of telling her the truth? The lies, though...the excuses...the harsh words to send her from him hating him even more than she did now... they would not come. Instead, his pulse raced as he battled in silence to hold back the flood of emotions that threatened to burst free.

She moved towards him. One step. Two. Her bosom heaved with emotion, the creamy upper swells of her breast bringing the saliva flooding back into his mouth.

'Why did you not tell me you were leaving?' Her voice quivered and he saw her gulp as though swallowing a cry. But when she spoke again, anger was the only visible emotion. 'You used me! You pretended we could be friends!'

Pure emotion roiled and bubbled inside him. The frustration…the injustice…the sheer impossibility of standing here before the woman he loved, pretending indifference… His blood fired hot…yet still he fought the craving to take her in his arms. To soothe her.

'You said we would help each other…'

It was the sorrow in those last quiet words that proved too much. Two strides and he swept her into his arms, taking her lips in a crushing kiss, deaf to the warnings that shrieked inside his head. But she struggled against him and, as those struggles penetrated his passion, he forced his arms to release her and stepped back, holding his hands up in apology.

'I am sorry… I should not—'

He got no further.

'Shush. You were holding me too tight. Crushing me.'

And then his arms were full again as her fingers speared through his hair and her mouth sought his.

Some time later, and he was unsure precisely how long had passed, he was sitting on a bench with Aurelia on his knee, his arms around her waist and her head on his shoulder.

'Why didn't you tell me you were leaving?' Her voice was small, unsure.

He could no longer lie to her. He could no longer pretend. 'I was rattled after that kiss. I left on impulse. I realised there was…something…between us and I knew there could be no happy ending, so I thought that by making you angry, you would hate me and you would soon forget about me.'

And that had not worked because he hadn't the strength of character to follow it through.

Too romantic and too impulsive for your own good, Maximilian.

Simon's words echoed through his head. He was right... but Max *wanted* to follow his heart. His passionate nature was an intrinsic part of him, but now he must rein it in, for Aurelia's sake. He could not be the cause of ruining her future.

'I do not want to forget about you.'

'But you know you must...*we* must. We cannot change that condition in Sarah's will and although my circumstances have improved a little—' He told her about Mr Austerly's investment in Wheal Rowenna, 'I am still in debt and likely to be for some time if I am to make Tregowan Place a fit home for my mother and my sister. They arrive shortly, so I have no time to delay. I still need to marry money.' A chill went through him. How he hated that fact.

'It is so unfair,' she whispered, pressing warm lips to the corner of his mouth. 'I cannot bear the thought of marrying any of the men I have met. And although I am overjoyed for them, every time I see Leah and Dolph together or I watch Beatrice and Jack tiptoeing around one another—for I am convinced they are both in denial of their feelings—the simple fact of knowing there is nothing other than Jack's stubborn pride standing in the way of their union makes it so much worse that I...*we*...should be denied such happiness.'

'Leah and Beatrice are your sisters? Miss Thame and Miss Fothergill? Is that correct?'

'Yes. Well, half-sisters. You have heard that the former Lord Tregowan fathered us all?'

Max nodded. 'And I was told about one of your sisters marrying Dolphinstone. That would be Leah?'

'Yes. He employed her as his governess before she came to London.'

'And Jack?'

'Lord Jack Kingswood.'

'Quantock's brother?'

'Twin brother, yes. He was gravely injured at Waterloo, but he and Beatrice…' Her voice faltered. 'Well, they look entirely smitten to me, but he is being a typically stubborn, proud man, and she is too unsure of herself to believe he could ever want her.' She sighed, tightening her arms around his neck. 'They are the only two aristocrats I have met who give me faith there are decent gentlemen out there. Somewhere. Oh! Apart from you, of course.'

'You did not think that earlier—about me being a decent gentleman, I mean.'

'I always thought it…*knew* it… I merely kept my true opinion to myself.' She kissed his cheek and then inhaled. 'You smell…delicious.'

His breath caught in his throat at her words. She shifted on his lap to stare into his eyes, her expression serious.

'That argument we had earlier…we could use it to our advantage, Max.'

'How so?'

'Everyone will think we cannot stand the sight of one another, so no one will suspect if we…if we…' Her cheeks bloomed pink and her lids lowered to mask her eyes.

'If we what?' But a sinking sensation in his stomach told him he suspected he knew. How the devil was he meant to keep their friendship within the bounds of respectability? He already craved more of her…more of her company, more of her body. He had relied upon *her* hands on the ribbons to stop them galloping headlong into disaster.

'Well…if we meet…like this…from time to time.' She bit into her full lower lip and his pulse rocketed again. 'You think me scandalous, don't you?'

He rubbed his nose against her cheek. 'Only in a good

way,' he assured her. 'But, just so I understand—are you suggesting we meet, clandestinely? How do you imagine we can do that without being seen?'

'We can be careful. Bet, my maid, is very discreet. We walked home from Hookham's that time…it did not create any gossip.'

'But as soon as one person notices us talking amicably, it will be all over the *ton*. No one will believe we are enemies, and they will be watching us like hawks. Especially when that clause in the will becomes public knowledge. Simon tells me you and your sisters are already the main topic of the gossipmongers.'

'There must be some way.'

She nuzzled his ear, nibbling gently. The blood surged to his groin and he was hard in an instant.

'I will think about it.' He must stick to his guns. Remain resolute. Even though his inner demons were clamouring to take advantage, telling him he deserved a glimpse of happiness before tying himself to some female for her money. 'But I can't risk embroiling you in scandal, sweetheart.'

He stood, lifting her from his lap and setting her on the flagstones before dropping a tender kiss on her forehead. *If only*…but there was no use repining. His finances were better, but he could never provide her with the life she deserved. Or get even close to meeting her need to be protected from worry over debt and poverty.

'We ought to leave. Someone might come in.'

She cradled his face, gazing with tenderness into his eyes. 'Yes. We must take care…but is it so very wrong to snatch some happiness for ourselves?'

She pressed her soft mouth to his. It took all his strength not to sweep her once again into his arms. Instead, he cupped her chin and deepened the kiss briefly, before tearing his lips from hers.

'How can that be wrong?' He drank in her lovely face. 'Promise me one thing, Aurelia. Promise me, from now on, there will always be total honesty between us.'

'I promise.'

'Go,' he said in a tortured whisper. 'Go now, and…will you be at Lady Poole's soirée tomorrow night?'

'Yes.'

'Good. I shall see you there, my darling. My love.'

Her huge blue eyes sheened with tears.

'Whatever you see…if I flirt with other men…know that I wish it were you. Only you.' She tore off her glove, put her fingertip to her lips and then pressed it to his. 'Always remember it is false and I am merely playing a part. Until tomorrow,' she whispered, before hurrying from the conservatory.

Drained of energy, Max slumped on to the bench and waited. When enough time had passed, he left the conservatory and the cloying scent of the flowers that was making his head ache. He soon found Simon and told him he was leaving.

'It is a disappointment you did not get to meet Miss Newton, but there will be other times,' said Simon. 'I shall see you tomorrow. Probably. There is a lady here tonight…'

He waggled his eyebrows suggestively.

'You have only just ended your *affaire* with Camille.'

'Ah…but this lady will be far less demanding of either my time or my commitment, you see. So she is the ideal solution.'

'She is married, then?'

Max hid his disapproval. Many men did conduct discreet liaisons with bored married ladies—an inevitable consequence of so many convenient marriages—but the practice left a nasty taste in his mouth after his own parents' loveless marriage. He left Simon and sought his host and hostess to thank them and take his leave. He could not stay. He had not enough strength to restrain himself if he saw Aurelia act the flirt with other men. It had been hard enough before. Now, though…

He rubbed his forehead as he waited for his coat and hat and wondered how this charade would end.

The following evening Max waited in Sir Benedict and Lady Poole's salon for Aurelia to appear. The hands on the ornate ormolu mantel clock counted off the seconds as he chatted with other guests. Seconds, minutes and, eventually, hours passed and still she did not come. His mood lurched from impatience to anger to pain and, finally, as he registered that not one member of her family was present either, to worry.

'Why so gloomy, Maximilian?' Simon sauntered up to him and thrust a glass of champagne into his hand. 'Should you not be courting the debutantes we selected as your top targets? There are several here this evening, even though Miss Newton is not among them. You will end up a monk at this rate.'

Max gulped back the champagne. Something was wrong. He could feel it in his bones. Perhaps she was ill? It must be serious if even the Dolphinstones were not here, for they did not live at Tregowan House, but at Dolphinstone's family residence.

'Max? Are you all right?'

'It is nothing.' He had told Simon nothing of his second encounter with Aurelia the night before…he had not dared, for Simon's offer to use his house for a tryst still dangled in his thoughts, tempting him.

We could dine together. Nothing more, just eat and talk, and spend time with one another without the worry of being seen.

He knew it would not take much persuasion for him to succumb. And after last night he was convinced Aurelia would leap at the chance if he told her of Simon's suggestion. And then what? It did not take much imagination to see where it all would lead.

'Lord Tregowan?'

Max turned. 'Yes?'

A footman bowed and handed him a folded sheet of paper with his name written on it. 'A maid brought this to the staff entrance, milord. For delivery direct to you.'

A faint trace of Aurelia's perfume teased his nostrils as he opened the note, aware of Simon watching him with interest. The message was brief, discreet and to the point.

> *M.*
> *There has been an incident tonight that forced a change to our plans. Everyone is safe and well. Do not worry.*
> *A.*

'Is the maid waiting for a reply?'

'No, milord.'

'Thank you.' The footman walked away.

'A.?' Simon stroked his chin while managing to look the picture of innocence, but he soon abandoned the pretence. 'That argument between you and Miss Croome last night! You made up afterwards, didn't you?' He frowned then. 'Seriously, I hope you know what you are doing, Max.'

He didn't have a clue what he was doing, but he wasn't about to admit that to Simon. Max folded the note and tucked it in the hidden pocket inside the tail of his evening coat. 'I must go.'

'I shall come with you.' Max glared at Simon, who raised his brows. 'I recognise the signs, old chap. You are about to act with impetuosity and I intend to take you to my club first and talk about what has happened to set you on fire *before* you do something you might later regret.' He grinned. 'No need to thank me.' He clapped Max on the back. 'That is what friends are for. Come...let us go and, after we've had a chat over a glass of brandy, if you still have the urge to do whatever you were thinking of doing, I promise I shall not stand in your way.'

Simon was right. Of course he was right. What could Max possibly say if he had followed his first impulse to charge around to Tregowan House and bang on the door? All that would do would be to draw attention to him and Aurelia and that was the last thing either of them wanted.

But he would see her tomorrow. Somehow. Because not knowing what had happened...not knowing she was truly safe...was killing him.

Chapter Twenty-Three

'You are sure that footman will have delivered my note to His Lordship, Bet?'

'I'm sure, miss.' Bet smiled as she assisted Aurelia out of her new bronze silk gown. 'He promised faithfully. Why would he lie?'

'You are right. I am being silly.'

'He will forgive you when he hears about what happened, miss.' Bet folded the gown carefully. 'Such a pity he did not get to see you in your new gown...you really did look beautiful tonight.'

'It couldn't be helped—I could never have enjoyed myself, knowing what Beatrice has been through.'

She, Mrs Butterby, Leah and Dolph had been en route to Lady Poole's soirée earlier that evening when they had met Jack, also on his way there. Beatrice had felt unwell and remained at Tregowan House. A chance remark by Jack and a sighting by Leah, however, alerted them to possible danger for Beatrice. They had rushed back home just in time to thwart Sir Percy Fothergill and Sir Walter Belling in their plan to abduct her and force her into marriage.

'But it has all turned out for the best, has it not?'

The shock of realising he had almost lost Beatrice had

brought Jack to his senses and he and Beatrice were now betrothed. Jack would obtain a marriage licence the next day, and they hoped to be wed on Saturday, just two days' time.

Aurelia quashed the selfish little voice in her head that whined it wasn't fair. She was delighted Leah and Beatrice had both found happiness and contentment with men they loved and she would not allow self-pity to sour her mood. But it did cast a shadow over her own future. How on earth was she to find a suitable man to wed when her head and her heart were full of Max? The thought of a loveless marriage when her beloved sisters were both so happy and content would be a constant reminder of what she could not have.

She had pictured her future as one of close friendships between their three families, but now she couldn't help wondering if she was generous enough to put aside her own dissatisfaction to celebrate their happiness. Her own life looked as though it would be empty by comparison although the alternative—remaining unwed and living in a cottage as a pensioner of her sisters—held little appeal either. Both Leah and Beatrice would be part of the aristocracy and wealthy. They would lead lives that reflected that status. Aurelia could not believe either of her half-sisters would deliberately exclude her, but their lives would inevitably drift apart. Especially when they had families and Aurelia remained childless. Another incentive, surely, to get married and claim her inheritance and remain her sisters' equal.

'Everyone downstairs is so happy for Miss Fothergill and Lord Jack, miss. Especially the news that they are to live here with us. It would have been a shame to lose Miss Fothergill so soon after she arrived.'

'It would indeed. And did you hear that Mrs Butterby

plans to move into Miss Thame's old bedchamber, next to mine, so the newly-weds can have the back two rooms? We will move her belongings tomorrow, to prepare for Lord Jack moving in.'

They all slept late the following morning after the excitement of the night before and, over breakfast, Mrs Butterby surprised Aurelia and Beatrice by asking them if they would call her Prue. Looking back over the weeks since her own arrival, Aurelia could see how the chaperon had relaxed into her role, especially since Leah had arrived. She was less overbearing and had become more of a friend and a confidante to all three of the sisters. Even Aurelia. How Prue must have worried over the responsibility of guiding three young women who had been utterly green about the ways of society and yet were already adults and therefore not as biddable as girls fresh from the schoolroom, but she had taken on that burden for the love of her former employer and friend.

They began the work of moving Prue's belongings at noon with both Beatrice and Aurelia helping with the extra work. As Aurelia listened to Beatrice's excited chatter about her wedding, however, she realised that meant she would not now see Max for several days. They were staying home tonight, the eve of the wedding, and they had no plans to go out tomorrow after the wedding. Then it would be Sunday, with church in the morning and they were already invited to Dolph and Leah's house to dine that evening so—unless the weather was dry and they met by chance in the Park one afternoon, when it was always crowded with walkers, riders and carriages—Monday would be the earliest possible day she could see Max to explain her absence last night.

Three whole days.

She sighed as she deposited an armful of clothes on the bed in Prue's new bedchamber. Before heading back to fetch another, she slipped into her own bedchamber next door, closing the door behind her. She wandered around the room, wondering how she might see Max earlier. She paused by the window and leaned her forehead against the cool, soothing windowpane, gazing unseeingly across the street. At least it had stopped raining. The day before, the sky had emptied down all day until Dolph had joked they would soon need to build an ark.

She frowned as something in her line of vision grabbed her attention and she focused her eyes. She snapped upright, her heart pounding in her chest, as she saw Max, standing across the street and staring up at her. How long had she been looking at him and yet not seeing him? His expression revealed his confusion and he gestured at himself and then at the front door. Aurelia shook her head at him, pointed at herself and then at him. She spun around and ran for the door.

'Bet!'

Her maid, on her way to fetch more of Prue's belongings, stopped and looked around. Beatrice was heading towards Aurelia, a pile of shawls and cloaks in her arms, and she stopped, too, looking her enquiry.

'Bea. My dear, I am sorry. I have remembered an urgent matter I must attend to. Bet, I shall need you to come with me. We are nearly done now, though, aren't we? I don't want to let you down, but this…it is most important.'

'There is very little left to move now,' said Beatrice cheerfully. 'Janet will help Prue put her clothes away and I shall clean out the cupboards and drawers ready for Jack's belongings. I really do not need any help with it…' Her smile beamed joy and contentment. 'I shall enjoy the task.'

'Thank you, Bea.' Aurelia couldn't resist giving her

younger sister a swift hug. 'Come, Bet. I must change my gown and then you must hurry and get ready to accompany me.'

Ten minutes later, dressed in a peacock-blue walking dress, Aurelia exited Tregowan House with Bet by her side. She looked up and down the road and spied Max on the corner in much the same spot he had stood all those weeks ago when she had first arrived in London. So much had happened since then. She headed down the street towards him, her pulse quickening.

'Not a word about this, mind, Bet. Not to anyone.'

'Of course not, miss. I am on your side. You know that.'

Max's stormy expression grabbed her attention as soon as she was close enough to interpret it. His eyes were almost black in their intensity under his lowered brow and a muscle ticked in his jaw. She longed to soothe him…to stroke her fingers through his hair and pepper his tightly compressed lips with tiny kisses until they relaxed.

'Why are you cross?'

'I am scowling at you in case anyone sees us,' he said. 'But now you mention it, it took you long enough to notice me.'

'When? Oh…' She recalled snapping out of her thoughts as she stared out of the window and finally noticing him on the opposite pavement. 'I am sorry. My thoughts were miles away…' She frowned. 'With you, actually. Wondering how I might contrive to see you before Monday. My head was so full of you, my eyes did not realise you were there in front of me. Silly, is it not? But it is true.'

He gestured behind him at a hackney carriage waiting further down the street. 'I thought it would be more discreet if we talk in private about last night.'

'Of course. And I shall keep frowning at you even

though I am delighted to see you. Just to continue our subterfuge.'

'That is wise. Now, if you and... Bet, is it not?' Bet turned pink with pleasure as she nodded. 'If you and Bet walk along the street and get into the coach, I shall follow in a few minutes. Hopefully no one will be paying enough attention to notice what we are up to.'

'You are not planning to abduct us, are you, Max?' Although her voice was light and teasing, she maintained her disgruntled expression.

'Do not tempt me,' he growled, before tipping his hat at her.

Aurelia stuck her nose in the air and flounced away, along the street. At the carriage she paused, glanced around to ensure no one was watching and she and Bet climbed inside. Max soon joined them.

He sat opposite Aurelia and leant forward to clasp her hands. 'What happened last night? I have been worried about you.'

She returned the pressure of his hands. 'There was no need for concern. I was never in any danger—'

'*Danger?*'

She told him about Beatrice and the kidnap plot. 'And now she and Jack are betrothed. They hope to marry tomorrow—he is obtaining the marriage licence today—and that is why I feared I would not see you to explain everything until Monday.' Her eyes searched his face in the dim interior of the carriage. 'I knew you would be worried, but I did not want to write anything in my note that would point to me being the author.'

'I understood that, even last night, but I still—' He glanced at Bet. And then bit his lip. 'I cannot speak freely here, but Simon is out tonight. Will you...can you devise a way to join me for supper at his house? I can send the carriage for you.'

A thrill of excitement chased up her spine. A real lady should, surely, be horrified at such a suggestion. But she trusted Max to respect any boundary she set and she, too, longed for the chance to speak freely with him. The myriad emotions swirling inside her head were creating such confusion she barely knew what to think any more. There seemed to be no answer to their conundrum other than to cast aside all she had ever believed and take Max as her lover. If they were careful…if they were discreet…why should she not sample at least some of the joy her two half-sisters would experience with the husbands they loved? Who would it hurt?

'I will find a way,' she promised even though she was still torn by doubts.

He raised her hand to his mouth. 'Tonight is about the pleasure of your company, Aurelia. That is all. I promise.'

His words reassured her that he had no expectations of their tryst and yet she remained torn, this time between disappointment and relief. She pressed her mouth to his in a loving kiss. He cupped her chin, but made no attempt to take her into his arms or to deepen the kiss. As their lips parted, she saw the fire banked in his eyes and the same longing she was certain was mirrored in her own.

'Until tonight,' she whispered. 'I shall be ready at nine. Tell the coachman to wait at the end of the street until he sees me leave the house.'

Chapter Twenty-Four

Max's heart kicked up a pace as he heard the carriage halt in front of the house. Guilt hovered in the background—guilt because he knew, without any shadow of doubt, that the only person to suffer if this should become known was Aurelia—but he was not strong enough to resist this chance to spend time together. Just the two of them. And it might prove to only be this one time because his honour would never allow him to continue in such a deception once either one of them were betrothed and he, at least, did not have time on his side.

He scanned the room…the cold supper laid for two on a small table by the window. The decanter and glasses on a silver salver set on a side table. The fire burning merrily in the grate, with the scuttle full of coal by its side. Simon—taken into Max's confidence—had impressed upon his staff the need for discretion and secrecy, upon threat of instant dismissal, and they had been ordered not to come above stairs for any reason this evening.

The only exceptions were Parkinson, the butler, who was to open the front door for Aurelia, plus the coachman, who would collect her from South Street this evening. *He* would surely know her identity, but Simon had assured Max he would never betray Simon's trust.

He has been with me for years. I trust him implicitly.

And Max had been convinced.

The salon door opened, and a cloaked, hooded and masked figure entered. The door closed again and they were alone.

Aurelia pushed her hood back to reveal her golden tresses, simply pinned back to spill down her back in looser, more casual waves than the ringlets she often wore. As she raised her hands to untie her mask, Max stayed her.

'Allow me.'

Even to his own ears, his voice sounded husky and he saw her eyes widen and darken behind the blue velvet mask. Her arms lowered.

'Thank you.'

He reached behind her head, feeling for the ends of the ribbons to untie the bow. He did not remove the mask, however, but held it in place as he gazed down at her—the long blonde lashes visible through the eyeholes. The tip of her delicate nose, below the lower edge of the mask. The perfect bow of her slightly parted lips. The enticing curve of her neck as she tilted her face to meet his scrutiny. The glistening tip of her tongue as it darted out to moisten those lips…

His blood heated and thickened, but he reined in his desire and gently brushed her mouth with his, rather than seizing her in a crushing, passionate embrace as he longed to do. He might be impetuous at times but, tonight, he would give her no cause to regret that she had agreed to this tryst between them.

'You are welcome,' he whispered as he finally lifted the mask away from her face and lowered his mouth to hers again, wrapping his arms around her and kissing her tenderly. Worshipfully. That was what this evening would be about. Showing her how much he loved her. Proving she could trust him.

As she tried to deepen the kiss, he eased away from her and indicated the laid table. 'Let us eat.'

'I do not have much appetite, having dined as normal, at home. But, by all means, let us eat. I am sure there will be some delicacies to tempt me.'

Her mouth quirked at the corners as though she smiled at a secret. She wandered around the room, looking at the paintings on the wall—mainly landscapes—and admiring the small number of decorative vases and figurines set on side tables and windowsills.

'Did you have any trouble leaving the house?'

She crossed to the table, where he held her chair for her to sit. 'No. Everyone is exhausted with all the excitement, and with the anticipation of tomorrow. They have retired early, and they believe I, too, am in bed.'

Max's pulse leapt at the thought of her in his bed... sprawling naked and wanton, pink with the afterglow of lovemaking. He pushed that image from his brain, telling himself that was not the reason for tonight. He wanted to talk with her and spend time with her without fear of discovery. Was that so very wrong?

He poured two glasses of wine, then sat opposite her. 'Help yourself to anything you wish to eat.' He uncovered the dishes, revealing cold meats and cheese, bread and pickles, sweetmeats and pastries, dried fruit and nuts. 'You will not want a late night, either, I presume?'

He caught her flash of relief, although it was quickly masked. So, despite his promise to her, she had not fully believed his motive in arranging this evening. But she had still come, even with that doubt. He was more determined

than ever to prove he asked no more than the mere pleasure of her company.

'I would prefer not to appear at Bea's wedding with
black shadows under my eyes, it is true. Even though everyone's attention will be on the bride, quite rightly, I
should not like to be too tired to enjoy the occasion.'

'I have asked the coachman to bring the carriage to the
door at eleven.' A mere hour and a half from now. It was
not enough. He feared a year and a half with her would
not be enough. But they must snatch what time they could,
while they could.

Aurelia gave him a direct look. 'I confess to being
somewhat surprised. I did wonder...' Her cheeks glowed,
but her chin lifted with resolve. 'I did appreciate your
promise, but I still wondered if you might try to persuade
me to remain longer. I *thought* you might have seduction
on your mind after our more recent encounters.'

She selected a pastry and bit into it. Her direct manner was one of the many things he admired about her. He
would pay her the respect of being honest with her in return.

'Seduction,' he said, 'has been on my mind since the
very first time we met.'

She arched her brow at that. 'The very first time?' She
cocked her head, a smile playing around her mouth. 'Had
you been deprived of female company so very long, my
lord, that you would immediately think of seduction upon
bumping into such a raggedy, hungry soul on the street?'

He laughed, shaking his head at her. 'Of course not!'
Although there had been something compelling about her,
even at that first, very brief, encounter. 'But...by the time
we reached London...' his voice deepened '...somehow,
you had worked some kind of magic upon me, and I could
not get you out of my thoughts.'

She blushed at that and lowered her gaze to her plate. Max raised his glass and drank. She was a contradiction, even now. At first, it had been the anomaly of a hungry-looking woman dressed in inadequate clothing who had somehow bought a ticket on the mail coach and purchased sufficient food for three or four people for the journey. Now, though, he noticed the more subtle contradictions, such as her direct way of speaking and her readiness to stand up to people, yet beneath that directness there were glimpses of a woman who was not always as sure of herself as she pretended to be. She portrayed herself as a woman of the world and yet he would lay odds she was still an innocent. She flirted outrageously with other men, firing his jealousy, and she spoke boldly of seduction, but when he called her bluff and *he* spoke genuinely of the effect she had upon him, she was swift to blush and break eye contact.

He knew the story of how his predecessor had seduced her mother and he had heard tales of the character of Augustus Croome, the man who had raised her as her father.

He leaned back. 'Seduction, however, is not the purpose of tonight. Will you tell me about your childhood?'

Her eyes narrowed. 'Ancient history,' she said, lightly. 'Why should we waste time talking about that?'

'I want to understand you. I want to know you better. How can I do that without understanding your childhood and what you went through?'

She visibly withdrew. He placed two slices of cold beef and a spoonful of pickles on his plate and changed tack.

'My boyhood…it was not all happy,' he said.

She met his gaze again, warily.

'My grandfather was a banker in Florence, and my parents met when my father travelled to Florence on his Grand Tour.' He shrugged. 'My mother was blessed—or cursed, possibly—with a large dowry and even then my father was in debt, although he hid it. You have heard about my father's gambling…it was one of the reasons the previous Earl left nothing more than he absolutely had to by law to my father's branch of the Penroses. Mama grew to hate my father—they were estranged before my father died and that was when Mama and Letty returned to Italy, ostensibly for Mama's health as well as to help my grandparents as they aged but, in reality, to enable my parents to live separate lives.'

'But you stayed?'

'I stayed. At first I was at university and then, when Father died shortly before the Third Earl, I inherited Tregowan and the title.' He sighed. 'That has been a double-edged sword.'

'Especially since Lady Tregowan left her fortune to me and my half-sisters?'

'You wouldn't believe me if I denied it, so I won't even try,' Max said. 'And, before you say it, I'm aware I have still had an easier life than you. You deserve your good fortune. I do not resent you for it. But,' and he captured her gaze 'I should like to understand how you came to be in such dire straits as you appeared to be when we met.'

Aurelia watched as Max cut a portion of cold beef and ate it. Although she had never denied the facts of her past, she had never spoken of her childhood, nor her own feelings about it. It was too painful. Too private. She had not even discussed it with her sisters or with Prue because she did not wish to be viewed as a victim or as someone to be pitied. Augustus Croome's relentless rejection of any attempt by her to garner his good opinion or to earn his love had left her feeling worthless. But Max…he said he wanted to understand her past. She did not think he would pity her or look at her differently. She hauled in a deep breath.

'There is little to tell. My father…my so-called father… married my mother when she was carrying the Third Earl's child. For money. *He* did not even have the excuse of gambling debts. He was self-indulgent and self-entitled and, once he had spent the money Lord Tregowan paid him, he ran up more debts rather than curb his desire for high living. I knew none of that when I was growing up. I only knew my father—the man I believed to be my father—despised me. When he died, he left us with nothing, but Mama had already been making hats to earn enough money to feed us, so she set up as a milliner in Bath. And I helped her.'

'When did she die?'

'Last year.' That aching lump took up residence in Aurelia's throat. 'She became sick and I did my best, but I was not as skilled as her at making hats and my time was limited because she was so ill, and the debts mounted up. Scarily fast.' The fear that had gripped her back then resurfaced to squeeze the air from her lungs. 'When Mama died, the landlord refused to rent me the shop on the same terms. He wanted more money…which I couldn't afford… and then…then…' She swallowed. But it would be good to get it off her chest. 'He offered to lower the rent if I…if I…'

Her show of boldness could only take her so far, but she saw from Max's black scowl that he understood exactly what role that scoundrel had attempted to force her into.

'Tell me his name,' he growled, 'and I shall happily pay him a visit.'

Aurelia smiled. 'Once, I would have thanked you for it, but now I simply want to get on with my life.'

'By getting married so you do not lose your inheritance.'

'Yes.' The fear of losing everything—including, now, the fear of drifting apart from her sisters—still stalked her dreams. 'Can you blame me?'

'How could I?'

His lightness of tone did not completely fool her. She searched his expression, seeing the fire in his dark eyes, feeling her body react to his suppressed passion—her pulse quickening and her stomach flickering with a nervous energy that made her want to leap to her feet and pace the room. She selected a few nuts and chewed them as she—yet again—mulled over their impossible situation.

'You need to marry for practical purposes, too,' she said after she had swallowed.

'I would rather not.'

He pushed his chair back abruptly and rose to pace the room. Aurelia knew precisely why—that same nervous energy she had kept suppressed was charging around his body and sitting still had become an impossibility. He paused behind her and laid his hand on her shoulder before stroking her neck.

'I would rather marry you.'

She stiffened, and brushed his hand aside so she could swivel in her chair and look him in the eyes. 'You know that is impossible.'

Oh, but how I wish it were not. Why can't I be like Leah and Beatrice? Why did I have to fall in love with the one man I cannot have?

A deep groove formed between his dark brows. 'Knowing it makes it no easier to bear.' He tugged her chair around and dropped to his knees, his hands on her thighs. 'You do know I would marry you in a heartbeat, Aurelia?'

She caressed his cheek and he leaned into her touch. 'We can neither of us afford the luxury of self-indulgence, Max. How long would it be before we began to blame one another under the strain? I have heard people say that money cannot make you happy and I am finding that is true. But it is also a fact that *not* having the money to provide a roof over your head and food on the table does not make you happy either.

'After Augustus died, Mama told me how the early months of their marriage had been good. But he changed as money grew scarce and their debts multiplied. Augustus blamed Mama for his misfortune even though it was he who frittered the money away on his own pleasures. Poverty made him bitter—poverty and the extra responsibility of a family. We were a millstone around his neck.'

'I would not do that.'

'I do not believe you would, but how long would it take before you buckled under the burden of a wife and family on top of your responsibilities to your workers and to your mother and sister? No. I cannot put you through that. And I...' She sighed. The hunger...the desperation of those weeks before she had received the letter that had changed her life so spectacularly...the loneliness of being alone in the world...they haunted her still. '*I* cannot go back to such a precarious existence.'

Max leapt to his feet. 'I know. Of course. I am being selfish. Forgive me... I know it is a foolish fantasy.' He swept his hand through his hair and then smiled ruefully. 'Come.' He held out his hand and she took it without hesitation. 'Let us make the most of this time together. Will you dance with me, Aurelia?'

She laughed, pleased to see his good humour restored, but still bruised inside at having to crush his passionate nature and pretend that she was able to dismiss her own wants and needs without effort.

'We have no music.'

He held her gaze, his dark eyes still stormy, and he

began to hum. His voice—of course—was a deep baritone that sent shivers of desire chasing across her skin. She rose to her feet and he tugged her closer, one arm around her waist, the other holding her hand, and they began to waltz. Aurelia—having only recently learned the steps—had to concentrate at first, but very soon she forgot about her feet and her eyes closed as she followed Max's lead through the turns and the twirls of the sensual dance.

By the time Max fell silent and their steps slowed, Aurelia would almost have agreed to anything, even marriage. Almost. But the spectre of her past—hunger and the dread of what was to become of her—could not be entirely banished. And Max…he was being impulsive. She loved that about him, but he needed to be practical, for the sake of the many people who relied upon him.

'It is close to eleven,' Max whispered, nudging her chin up with his forefinger. 'May we do this again?'

'Yes. Please.' She would make the most of him while she could, for who knew when they might meet again after this Season was over. Or how easy it would be to meet after one or both of them were married.

Their lips met, hungrily, as she clung to him, her legs turning to jelly as he deepened the kiss with deep thrusts of his tongue His hands caressed her bottom, pulling her hard against him so she could feel his thick arousal against her belly. Oh, how she ached for this man. Could she ever feel the same about another? She combed her fingers through his soft, dark hair, curving them around the back of his head as she pressed closer to him to ease the ache in her swollen breasts.

Too soon, a discreet knock at the door announced the arrival of the carriage to convey Aurelia home. Neither of them spoke as Max wrapped her cloak around her and retied her mask before pulling the hood up over her head, tucking her hair back out of sight. Aurelia understood. There were no words to say, because there was no solution and they both knew they must accept the inevitable.

'Goodnight, my darling,' Max whispered into her hair as he embraced her.

She had come here tonight despite half believing he would try to seduce her, but her need to be with him had been impossible to resist. Now, at the moment of leaving, she wished he had been less honourable and that he *had* seduced her. Regret surged through her. So much regret. When in her whole life might she know how it felt to lie with the man she loved if she did not take a chance?

'Goodnight.' She leaned back against his arms and put her fingertips to his lips, gazing up at him through the eye-holes of her mask. 'I want to do this again, Max, but...next time...' She could feel the heat building in her cheeks, but she would not deny herself the experience she craved because of missish embarrassment. 'I want all of you. I want to know what you will feel like.' She pressed a hasty kiss to his lips, her legs quivering at the audacity of what she was saying. 'I want you to be my first.'

She pivoted on her heel, opened the door and hurried from the room.

Chapter Twenty-Five

Max stared after Aurelia, her final words echoing
through his head. *'I want you to be my first.'* His head
tilted back and his eyes closed as he hauled in a deep
breath, his hands fisting at his sides. She would be the
death of him. How was he supposed to resist? He fought
the compulsion to go after her...to take her upstairs...to—

The door opened and he opened his eyes to see her
standing there, her eyes glinting through the eyeholes of
her mask, her lower lip caught between her teeth.

'Max?'

He looked beyond her. The hall was empty. She stepped
into the room.

'I sent the carriage away,' she whispered. 'I told the
driver he wouldn't be needed. Not tonight.'

Lust surged through his body, his blood thickening and
settling in his groin. He could no longer fight his need for
her. He strode forward and hauled her into his arms, seizing her lips in a crushing kiss. She responded instantly,
opening her mouth and stroking his tongue with hers and,
more by instinct than rational thought, he swept her up
into his arms and strode for the stairs.

Once the door of his bedchamber was closed behind

them, however, he released her, cupping her upper arms tenderly as he bent his knees to look straight into her stunning blue eyes, now dark with desire.

'Are you sure, my darling? Once we do this, there is no going back. What about the man you marry?'

'Shush.' She feathered his lips with hers. 'He will never know, but *I* know that if I do not lie with you, I will spend my entire life in regret. I must know... I need to experience what it feels like to lie with the man—'

She spun away from him without finishing her sentence, leaving him in limbo...leaving him to wonder...

He moved to stand behind her and lowered her hood before slipping her cloak from her shoulders.

'With the man...?' He could not resist pressing her. He yearned to hear the words from her lips. *With the man I love.* What else could it be?

'With you.'

She untied her mask, dropping it to the floor, then turned and slid her arms around his neck. She tiptoed up to kiss him as she moulded her body to his, firing his blood again, driving all thought of words and meanings from his head as pure need roared through him. His hips moved to grind his length against her and a mewl of pleasure...of need...sounded in her throat as she pushed his jacket off his shoulders.

'I want to see you,' she whispered against his lips.

He shrugged out of his coat, and untied his neckcloth, unwinding it from around his neck. She tugged his shirt loose and he pulled it over his head. Her eyes widened in obvious appreciation as she curved her hands over the twin muscles of his chest, smoothing them up to his shoulders and then out and down to caress his biceps. He forced himself to remain still. It was agonising and yet unbearably erotic to just stand there, his erection straining against the fabric of his trousers, as she explored his upper body with her eyes and hands.

Only when she moved closer to mould her body into his, pressing open-mouthed kisses to his chest, did he touch her, freeing her hair from the few pins holding it back to bury his hands in the heavy mass. He tightened his fists in her tresses and tugged, pulling her head back, tilting her face to his. Her lips were already open and he plundered her hot, sweet mouth, stroking deep with his tongue, her moans urging him on.

He felt for the buttons that secured her gown and made short work of freeing them. Her gown slipped from her shoulders and then pooled to the floor. Her corset followed in a matter of seconds, leaving her in her shift and stockings. He ran his hands along her arms, caressing her silken, scented skin, until he reached her wrists. He encircled them with thumb and forefinger. So dainty. So fragile.

He inhaled. And slowed down.

'Let me look at you,' he breathed.

Glorious. Utterly irresistible, with her hair a cloud of golden curls framing her face, standing there in a simple shift, the twin tips of her breasts outlined by the fabric. Watching her reaction, he reached out to touch one nipple. She gasped. When he lightly pinched, she released her breath in a soft moan and when he cupped her breast she pushed into his touch, moaning again as he kneaded the soft mound.

He dropped to his knees and turned her, before rolling her stockings and garters down her legs, one at time, then he held her hips, steadying her, as he kissed the sensitive skin behind each of her knees before lightly scraping with his teeth. He turned her again before rising to his feet. Her eyes were dazed. Filled with longing.

He reached for her hem. 'May I?'

She nodded, and Max raised her shift over her head, baring her to him.

Aurelia trembled at the heat and longing in Max's heavy-lidded gaze, aware of her body softening, opening, ripening. Their mouths met again in another hot, passionate kiss and she clung to his strong, muscled shoulders as her knees turned to water. He walked her backwards to the bed and followed her down, his hand on her breast, squeezing gently. Too gently. She wanted…more. He seemed to understand, though, because his fingers were again on her nipple, rolling, lightly pinching, sending a dart of pleasure to her core. Then his mouth was on her breast, tugging at the tip, and her body arched involuntarily as she felt an indefinable need build within her.

She could not lie still. She dug her fingers into his hair as her legs opened of their own accord.

'Lie still,' he whispered. 'Let me love you', and his hand stroked down her thigh and then up again to brush against her curls.

Everything inside her seemed to tighten and clench as one finger delved between the lips of that most feminine part of her, touching her, bringing forth a gasp as he pressed lightly, sending a shard of unfamiliar pleasure through her. His mouth was on her breast again, while his hand…his hand… Her hips arched without volition as the tip of his finger dipped inside her. Her eyes were closed. She ceased to think…the only reality was his mouth on her breast and his hand on her sex as one long finger pushed up and in with a mildly burning discomfort that paled into nothingness next to the sheer need welling inside her. The slow push and pull of that finger, in and out, spoke to some instinctual knowledge deep within her and her hips began to move in rhythm as her thighs spread wider, the heel of his hand pressing against her swollen, sensitive flesh.

A second finger joined the first, stretching her. His mouth left her breast to take her lips again in a searing kiss, his tongue moving to the same tempo as his fingers. Small mewls of impatience sounded in her throat as she clutched his shoulders, feeling the muscles bunch and flex beneath his smooth, warm skin. He kissed and nibbled her ear…throat…breast…and then as he sucked her nipple deep into his mouth, grazing it with his teeth, he pressed against the sensitive nub between her legs and she cried out as wave after wave of ecstasy broke over her and through her.

Aurelia came back to herself, slowly becoming aware she was being held tenderly in Max's arms, her head pillowed on that fascinating chest of his, with its sprinkling of dark hairs over defined muscles. She was aware, too, of his thick, hard shaft as it pressed against her thigh. She wriggled free and sat up.

'You…we…'

That fascinating mouth of his quirked up in a half-smile. 'We…?'

She narrowed her eyes at him. Her mother had told her what was meant to happen between a man and a woman and she was pretty sure she would have noticed *that* happen. She reached down and slid her hand between them until she could wrap her fingers around his erection.

His eyes closed as he groaned.

'I want all of you,' she whispered, pressing kisses over his chest and then following that light covering of hair as it narrowed and disappeared into his waistband. 'Every…' kiss 'last…' kiss '…inch.'

With a visceral growl, he grabbed her, rolled her on to her back and leaned over her. He kissed her, hard, and then stood up to strip off his trousers. Her eyes drank in his dark, spectacular virility as his staff sprang free—his strong shoulders, chest and arms; those fascinating muscles that roped his abdomen; his strong, straight legs—before he joined her on the bed.

Their lips met. The kiss at first tender, turned urgent as their hands stroked and caressed and then, as desire erupted and need drove them on, it turned frantic. Max settled between her wide-open thighs, the tip of his shaft nudging at her opening. Slowly, steadily, he filled her and then, just as she felt she could not take any more, he thrust. The sharp, burning pain made her gasp and he stilled, feathering kisses over her face and throat while he cradled her head with his hands.

'That is the last pain. I promise. I won't hurt you again. And I will take care. I will not get you with child.'

She smiled up at him. 'It feels…so good…to have you inside me.'

His eyes closed, almost as though he were the one in pain. He moved then, sliding out, and then pressing forward again. 'And now?'

'You feel wonderful.'

As he began to move steadily inside her, she shut her eyes to concentrate on the feelings that soared and swooped, committing them to memory. Her hands roamed the planes of his back and shoulders as his muscles shifted and bunched beneath his smooth, warm skin. She heard his breathing quicken, his murmured groans, the quiet, almost rasping endearments in language that, in the cold light of day, might have shocked her but—right here, right now—served only to heighten her own pleasure as her body moved with his and those wonderful, irresistible, indescribable sensations once more held her in their sway as they built to a crescendo.

He reached between them to find that same sensitive place as before and, when she at last cried out her joy and clenched around him, he thrust fiercely once more, and then withdrew the split second before reaching his own fulfilment.

Her love for him burned brighter that he had honoured his word and for his strength in doing what was right to protect her, but she still could not quite quell the feeling of loss and of somehow being cheated.

When he turned to take her in his arms, she instantly snuggled close, draping her leg across his thighs and wrapping her arm around his torso as if trying to absorb him that way into her own body.

As if, that way, she need never let him go.

She slept in his arms, feeling safe. Secure. But her heart could not be fooled. *It* knew the truth as soon as she awoke from her slumber. She lay half across him, her fingers playing among his crisp chest hair. He, too, was awake.

'I do not want to go,' she whispered. 'I never want to leave you.'

His arm tightened around her. 'Then don't. Stay.'

It was too tempting. But she would regret it. And he... *he* was saying it in the heat of the moment. She adored his passion and his impulsiveness, but she must stay practical. If they followed their hearts, they would both regret it.

'You know I cannot.'

She pulled away from him and sat up, the sheet falling away from her upper body. Max's eyes dropped to her nipples, and they tightened in an instant. His gaze moved upwards to hers and they shared a smile. He reached with one finger to circle the bud and then flick it gently, and a dart of desire shot to her core. But she could not stay. It was...

'Good heavens!' She leapt from the bed and snatched up her clothes. 'Help me. Please. It is Beatrice's wedding day!'

Chapter Twenty-Six

Max leaned back against the squabs of the hackney carriage as it carried him back to Portman Square after escorting Aurelia to Tregowan House. She had entered without being seen, thank God, her maid having been tasked with unbolting the front door after the butler and the rest of the staff had retired for the night.

Dawn would soon break; the sky to the east was already lightening. Another day and, somehow, he must get through it without seeing her, for her family would remain together to celebrate her sister's marriage. And tomorrow was Sunday. He might see her at church. Or he might catch sight of her in the Park. But they had agreed to a pretence. Agreed to keep everyone fooled and to make everyone believe that what they felt for one another was hatred. He could not even hold an innocuous conversation with her without calling that narrative into question. At least, though, he would be spared the agony of helping her to find a husband, as they had once agreed.

He sighed. He had only just left her and already he was counting the hours until he could see her again. And what, then, when she married, as she must? His sense of honour would never allow him to come between husband

and wife. Nor would he betray his own wife. He had always believed the vows taken on marriage should be inviolable. He had seen the pain his father's philandering ways had caused his mother and Max, from a young age, had sworn not to be like his sire.

Back in Portman Square, he climbed the stairs to his bedchamber, his head still reeling with questions to which he had no answers. He stripped off and climbed into his bed, breathing in her sweet scent. He fell asleep with his heart and his head full of Aurelia.

'Maximilian?' It was mid-afternoon when Simon poked his head into the library, where Max was trying to distract himself in the pages of a book. 'There you are. No time to waste. We are off to the Park. Miss Newton will be there with her family this afternoon and we, my dear fellow, are to walk with them. It is all arranged.'

Max scowled at his friend. 'What do you mean, all arranged? What have you done?'

'Me?' Simon's eyebrows shot up. 'Nothing. I have merely agreed with Mr Newton for the two of you to meet and for him to introduce you to his daughter. I *told* you. He is determined on a title for her and he's prepared to offer a huge dowry to get one. You need to stake your claim quick before someone else gets in there.'

'But—'

Simon shook his head. 'No time for "buts". No one is asking you to propose to her today. You are meeting her, that is all.'

He knew it was the sensible thing to do. He still had debts. Mama and Letty would soon be here. But his heart felt hollow as he set his book aside and his feet were leaden as he joined Simon.

* * *

Later, as they strolled through the Park among the other walkers, riders and carriages, Simon said, 'What ails you, Maximilian? I thought your spirits would be soaring after last night, but you look like the weight of the world is on your shoulders.'

'Nothing ails me. I dislike treating my search for a wife as though it were a business transaction.'

'As I have said before, you have no choice. Do you?'

The memory of Aurelia—beneath him, all warm and willing, her sighs, the way she breathed his name, her scent—flooded his brain. Frustrated, Max thrust that image aside.

'No. I have no choice. You are right. This needs to be done.'

'At last! Practicality. And in the nick of time, for there they are.'

Max looked ahead, but could not discern who 'they' might be among the several groups on the footpath. But every muscle in his body tensed as he recognised one of those groups and he slammed to a halt. For there she was. Aurelia. On the arm of Lord Quantock, damn his eyes, and in a large happy, smiling, family group consisting of Lord and Lady Dolphinstone, together with a massive dog, three children and what looked like a governess; Mrs Butterby, looking as happy as could be as she held the children's hands; Beatrice, now presumably Lady Jack Kingswood, clinging to the arm of her new husband, both their faces bright with joy.

Quantock, of course, was Lord Jack Kingswood's twin brother and would naturally have attended the wedding, but that did not stop jealousy spiralling through Max with almost dizzying speed.

'Keep walking, for God's sake,' Simon muttered, *sotto*

voce. 'You are giving off signals a blind man could interpret.'

Max glared at him, but put one foot in front of the other as ordered.

When they reached a couple walking in company with a young lady, Simon halted, and raised his hat. 'Good day, Mr Newton. My friend, Lord Tregowan, has begged an introduction, if you will permit?'

His last words came just as Aurelia's party drew abreast of them. Max kept his attention firmly on the Newtons, the muscles in his neck straining to keep from turning and looking at Aurelia. She would not thank him. They had an agreement.

'Lord Tregowan, may I present Mr Newton, Mrs Newton and Miss Newton?'

Max raised his hat and bowed. As he did so, he slipped a swift sideways glance at Aurelia. She was facing forward, but he saw the tight, bunched muscle of her jaw and a swell of relief tamped down that surge of jealousy at this sign she felt it as keenly as he.

He forced his attention back to the Newtons, as the father bowed and his womenfolk curtsied, Miss Newton's cheeks flushing pink. She was attractive…tall and slim, with brown curls peeping from beneath the brim of her bonnet and soft, docile-looking brown eyes. But Max wanted petite curves. Golden hair. Brilliant blue eyes. However, that was not Miss Newton's fault and he set himself to getting to know both her and her parents as they walked together. He thought he put on a good show even though half his mind was with Aurelia—longing to be the one with her on his arm. To be the one walking with her. Talking with her. And longing to send that damned Quantock to Hades.

He kept all of that bottled up inside as they chatted and

he genuinely found the Newtons an interesting and pleasant couple and Miss Newton a well-brought-up girl, if a bit dull. Although that could be shyness. What he could not escape, though, was the guilt. The Newtons did not deserve his deception. And Miss Newton, in particular, did not deserve a husband who would be forever hankering after another woman.

'Well? What do you think?' Simon asked after they took their leave of the Newtons.

Max shrugged. 'She seems a nice enough girl.'

Simon halted, his expression a picture of exasperation. 'I don't know why I bother. What is *your* solution, then?'

That question lit a fuse within Max. His solution? There was only one.

Simon nudged Max. 'Max? You have a peculiar look on your face.'

'It is called an epiphany. I cannot marry anyone while I love another woman, so I am going to ask Aurelia to marry me.'

'What?' Simon's voice was close to a shout and those closest to them turned their heads to look in curiosity.

Max grabbed Simon's arm and began to walk again. 'You heard me. I cannot marry another woman while I feel like this about Aurelia. So, the only answer is to wed her. If she will have me.'

'But...the money...your debts...'

'We will manage. Somehow.'

He was willing to take the chance. To live in the gatekeeper's lodge for the rest of their days if Aurelia was by his side. But although he spoke with confidence, he was not so certain Aurelia would be easily persuaded, so he made a bargain with himself. If she accepted him, they would manage somehow. If she refused, however, he would not—*could* not—continue to see her while they each searched for a spouse, for it had dawned on him that each meeting would be increasingly painful and so he would stay away, however much strength and resolve it took.

Aurelia had succeeded in sneaking back into Tregowan House without being seen, climbing into her cold bed and, despite believing she would never be able to sleep, had dropped off almost immediately. From the moment Bet awoke her with a cup of chocolate and the promise of a most welcome bath Aurelia had pushed her night with Max to the back of her mind, determined to thoroughly enjoy Beatrice's day.

Beatrice and Jack's wedding day had followed a similar pattern to that of Leah and Dolph. After the ceremony, the family—which had now expanded to include not only Jack but also his brother, Kit, Lord Quantock—had returned to Tregowan House to celebrate the marriage with a lavish wedding breakfast and Aurelia had gazed at the happy faces around the table and blessed her good fortune. A short time ago she had been alone and in despair. Now, she need never be alone again, although she could not quite shake her doubts about the future if she failed to marry, too.

In the afternoon, just as they had after Leah's wedding, the entire family set off for a walk through the Park. Kit offered Aurelia his arm and—with Prue happily helping Miss Pike, Dolph's governess, with the children—Aurelia accepted. It was a struggle to keep her self-pity at bay, however, as she watched her sisters, both radiating that unmistakable newlywed glow, with their new husbands. She was happy for them, but she wanted what they had and it was impossible.

She had swallowed past the lump that formed in her

throat—castigating herself for her selfish thoughts—and directed her gaze ahead, only to see Max and Mr Effingham approach a couple and an attractive young lady who was clearly their daughter. Aurelia steadfastly trained her eyes on the path ahead but, once they had passed the other group, she could not resist a quick glance over her shoulder, only to see Max offer his arm to the girl. A tide of jealousy swamped her that this stranger could take his arm in public, but that she would never have that right. She must have hidden her distress well, however, because Kit appeared not to notice anything was amiss as he told her stories about his and Jack's childhood.

Upon arrival back at Tregowan House they all trooped into the drawing room, but they had barely settled before Vardy came in.

'Miss Croome? A gentleman has called and wishes to speak with you.'

Oh, no! Surely not Sampford. Or Runcorn. Not today.

'Tell him I am with my family and therefore unavailable.'

'He insists on waiting until you *are* available, miss.'

Jack stood up. 'Allow me to send him on his way, Aurelia.'

'Thank you, Jack.'

She would not normally hesitate to deal with an unwelcome caller herself but, today, she felt too raw. Jack left the room and they heard male voices filter up the stairs from the hall. Jack soon returned, a peculiar look on his face as he beckoned to Aurelia to join him, away from the others. Aurelia's stomach began to churn and, glancing back, she could see concern on her family's faces.

'It is Tregowan,' Jack said quietly.

Chapter Twenty-Seven

Aurelia's heart skipped a beat and then her pulse raced. *What on earth...?*

'He said that if I tell you it is he, and if you still refuse to speak to him, he will leave without further ado.' His blue eyes were filled with concern. 'Bea told me about your argument and that you hate the man. Do not feel obliged to speak to him, but...'

He paused, his brow wrinkling.

She needed time to gather her thoughts, so she prompted him, 'But...?'

Jack smiled, not his usual, easy grin, but a rueful, slightly embarrassed smile. 'But... I thought, maybe, that I recognised the signs of a desperate man. The signs of a man who has lost his heart.'

Then his visit can mean only one thing.

Her passionate, impulsive lover. But nothing had changed. Their love was still impossible. Her throat constricted, aching unbearably.

'I will speak to him. Thank you, Jack.'

He tipped his head to one side. 'Would you like me to come with you? Or perhaps Bea? For moral support?'

Aurelia laid her hand on his arm and smiled at him, sorrow and regret weighing heavy on her soul. 'Thank you, but no. I know what I must do.'

The slenderest of threads held her emotions in check as she left the drawing room. Her breathing was too fast. Too shallow. She paused out of sight of the hall downstairs as she braced herself to face him. Nothing in her life would ever be as hard as this. She hauled in a deep breath and then headed downstairs.

Max was pacing the hall while Vardy kept a stern eye on him. On hearing Aurelia's descent, he came to the foot of the stairs, his stormy brown eyes brimming with a determination that squeezed her lungs until she could barely breathe.

He bowed. 'Thank you for seeing me, Miss Croome. I regret the interruption to your family celebration.'

They could not talk in the entrance hall where anyone might hear.

'I can spare you a few minutes only, my lord. Please follow me.'

She led the way to the morning parlour, her head high, and her mind skipped back to the very first day of her arrival at Tregowan House and following Prue along this very passageway. She marvelled at how her life had changed, distracting herself from what was to come. Once inside the parlour, however, she whirled to face Max.

'What are you doing? What happened to our agreement to behave as enemies in public?'

Max thrust his hand through his hair and paced the room. Her heart went out to him, but she stopped herself from reaching out to him. Soothing him. Why give him false hope?

'I cannot honour our agreement. Not…not while…'

A sense of foreboding filled her. 'Not…?'

He stopped before her and stared down at her, a frown

stitched between his brows. 'I love you, Aurelia. So very much.' His frown deepened. 'You are part of me.' He placed his hand over his heart. 'You are in here. Every minute of every day. You are the very air that I breathe.'

His dark brown eyes shone with sincerity. And with hope. And with dread.

Aurelia took his other hand in both of hers. 'And I love you, too, Max.' She caressed his knuckles with her thumbs. Her attempt at a smile wobbled. It felt like a *sad* smile. A smile of hopelessness. Of resignation.

'I shall never love anyone as much as I love you.' She was way past playing coy games with this man. Their love…their predicament…demanded nothing but brutal honesty. She had recognised him as her all-time love almost from their first meeting. Felt that tug of recognition deep inside her. They were bound together by an invisible, unbreakable thread—slender, but strong as silk.

'We cannot go on like this. *I* cannot go on like this. When I saw you in the Park…on his arm… I…' He shook his head, his eyes burning into her.

Aurelia's sense of foreboding intensified. Deep down, she'd known this moment would come, although she'd hoped it would be delayed. This would be no passing *Marry me* or *Stay with me* that she could brush off. This was to be formal. A serious proposal that would demand a serious, formal reply. And she already knew her answer.

Max grabbed her other hand and sank to his knees before her. His fingers firmed around hers.

'Aurelia. Marry me. We will manage. I promise you. We will manage *somehow*.'

Every single fibre of her being tensed as that inner tussle that had never been far from her thoughts intensified. Her heart and soul cried out for her to accept.

But the fear…those memories…the dark times…they

were the eddies and the deep, swift currents that lay hidden beneath the bright simple surface of *we will manage*. She had vowed never to be that vulnerable again. To never again find herself teetering on that knife edge of poverty and hunger and sheer desperation. And how could she risk Max's love for her slowly turning to resentment as the financial pressures grew?

She must stay strong, for his sake as much as hers.

'We will manage,' he said. 'We will be together. Surely that is all that matters?'

He knew. She could see it as hope turned to hopelessness in his eyes. She could hear it in his voice.

'I cannot, Max,' she said gently. There was no need to elaborate—he knew the reason why. 'I am sorry.'

He surged to his feet and released her hands to frame her face, his intense gaze searching her eyes.

'You can! Anything is possible. We will be together...' He seized her lips with fierce passion. 'That is all that matters.'

But that was not all that would matter. She had lived it. Max *thought* he was poor, but he had no idea how low it was possible to sink. Aurelia was still shaken by the knowledge of how close she had come to the ultimate degradation—selling her body just to have enough to eat.

But, oh, how she longed to throw caution to the wind and to accept him, and to share his trust that—somehow—everything would turn out all right in the end. But she was terrified to take that risk. That was the truth.

She gave a helpless shrug.

'I cannot. But, Max...we can still see—'

'No!' He almost flung her from him. 'No. Do *not* fool yourself with that.' He paced the room.

His words shook her as she absorbed their meaning. She had not truly thought this through. Somehow, she realised, she had clung to the belief they would still see each other, even after marriage. Now she examined that belief fully, she realised it could never have been. Not for either of them.

'No. You are right, of course.' Her throat thick with suppressed emotion, Aurelia watched him, drinking in his stark, beautiful masculinity, committing every inch of him to memory. 'You need say no more.'

How could she bear to hear him say this was the end?

He ignored her. He halted in front of her and scrubbed his hand through his hair.

'I must say it. Total honesty between us. Remember? No matter how painful.'

She nodded.

'If you will not have me, Aurelia, then neither of our situations has changed. I need a rich wife. You need a husband to save your share of the inheritance that means so much to you. And I—' he slapped his hand to his chest '—will neither cuckold another man nor will I break my marriage vows.'

She covered his hand with hers. 'And I love you all the more for your integrity.' Tears prickled her eyes.

'Then marry me. It is my last time of asking. *Please*.'

Misery swamped her. Everything hurt. But how could she? She must stay strong, for both their sakes. She shook her head. 'I cannot.'

He snatched his hands from hers and strode to the window, where he stood, rigid.

'Max…?'

He ignored her.

'Don't be angry with me. Please,' she whispered, going to him and wrapping her arms around his waist from behind as she pressed her body to his. She flattened her palms to his chest and lay her cheek against his back. His heartbeat thumped in her ear.

'Please,' she whispered again, even as she realised this was the end. *Had* to be the end. For both their sakes. 'Let us not part in anger.'

His back expanded then, as he heaved a sigh. His hands came up to cover hers and—gently but firmly—he moved them so he could step away.

'Anger is all I have to sustain me right now.'

She had to strain to hear him and a knife twisted in her heart at the desperation in those muttered words. She did not dare press herself to him again—she had given up that right when she had refused his proposal. Refused *him*.

But she reached to grab the hand hanging limply by his side and tugged at it, at him, asking him without words to turn to face her. He did not resist, but his hand folded itself into a fist, making it hard for her to keep hold of it. Desperate not to sever that last connection between them—not yet—Aurelia wrapped both her hands around his fist and, her heart breaking, she raised it as she lowered her head to caress his knuckles with her lips, her eyes brimming over.

Max released a ragged sigh. 'Don't cry, sweetheart. I do not agree with you, but I do understand.' His arms came around her, then, and he gathered her close. Finally, but too soon, he released her.

'I will go.' He caught her hands and raised them to his mouth to kiss first one then the other. 'Goodbye. I wish you happiness. If we meet, then let it be as polite strangers. For the sake of our sanity,' and he strode from the room.

She had no idea how long she sat on her own after Max left. Although her throat was still thick with pain, tears no longer fell. It would be hypocritical when her misery was all her own doing. She tortured herself with images of him with that girl in the Park. Imagined them marrying. Having children. A burst of laughter from upstairs interrupted her thoughts—her family in the drawing room above having fun. Laughing together.

She tried to picture herself with her family. Married, like them. With…and her imagination was blank. There was no one there. It was a dark empty space and, try as she might, she could not even fill it with the faceless figure of a man. *No one* could fill that void. Only Max.

She stood abruptly to pace the room. She must stop torturing herself. She had done the right thing…the only thing…she *must* marry, or she would lose… And that spurt of energy left her as abruptly as it had arrived. She sank back down on to the chair as Bet's words from weeks before floated through her head.

And if it doesn't make you happy, miss?

Was Bet right? They would always have that two hundred pounds a year regardless of what happened to the mine. She had forgotten about that safety net, almost dismissing it as an irrelevance because, until now, it had been a choice between wealth and marriage to a stranger or the two hundred pounds and a solitary life.

Maybe you should compare the life you would have then with your life of a few weeks ago, rather than with this life of luxury. Then, you would feel yourself rich indeed.

Aurelia's hands twisted in her lap as she questioned her long-held determination to fulfil the conditions of her inheritance come what may.

What if she could never be happy without Max? What had she said last night? '*I have heard people say that money cannot make you happy and I am finding that is true.*'

Max had been willing to take that risk, even though he still needed funds for the Tregowan estate and to support his mother and sister. He had shown courage. And belief. In her and in their love. Would Aurelia Croome really allow fear of what *might* happen to stand in the way of her own happiness? Her and Max...they might never be rich in monetary terms, but they would have enough to put food on their table. Many people had far less.

And they would be rich in love. In that, she would be her sisters' equals.

She jumped to her feet, ran to the door and out into the empty hall.

Chapter Twenty-Eight

Max could barely think straight through his pain as he left Tregowan House, suppressed tears choking his throat as his heart shattered. Part of him understood. She was the one with the strength. She was the one being practical for the both of them. She knew the reality of the future that would face them. She had lived such a life.

But he was nowhere near the point where he was able to admit that with any sense of calm.

He'd known it was likely to be a futile proposal, but he'd had to try. He'd never have forgiven himself for not at least trying.

'Tregowan!'

He stifled a groan at the sound of that voice. William Austerly. He would know it anywhere. He tamped down his impatience to be alone and to hide away until he could accept the reality of a future with no hope. Not only could he not afford to offend the Austerlys, neither would he wish to because he liked the couple, and he enjoyed their company. Only…not right now.

He stretched his mouth in a smile and wiped any hint of impatience from his features before looking around to see the man himself, with Mrs Austerly on his arm, walking towards him from the Park Lane end of the street. He bowed.

'Good afternoon, sir, ma'am.'

'I saw it was you! Been to visit Miss Coombe, eh?' Austerly winked as those words pierced Max's heart like a dagger. 'Mother and I went for a stroll in the Park,' he went on cheerily. 'Came out of the wrong gate—'

'I *told* him it was the wrong one, but he wouldn't listen,' said Mrs Austerly, with a fond look at her husband. 'How *is* dear Miss Croome, my lord? Father and I said right from the start—didn't we, Father?—what a lovely couple you would make.'

That dagger pushed deeper, and twisted, as Max clung desperately to his attempt at a nonchalant expression.

'There now!' Mrs Austerly released her husband's arm and stepped closer to Max, reaching out and patting his hand as she scanned his face anxiously. 'Take no notice of us, my lord. It was only a bit of harmless funning. I am sure all will be well directly. We suffered plenty of ups and downs during our courtship, isn't that right, Father?'

'Eh... Mother's right. Take no notice of us, lad,' said Mr Austerly. 'Just our bit of fun.'

Their sympathy was agonising. 'I must go. I am late.'

'Don't go, Max.'

His heart leapt at that soft voice from behind him. He turned, slowly, scarcely daring to hope. Her blue eyes shone in her beloved face. Her lips trembled. Her hands gripped one another until the knuckles turned white. He barely registered the sound of Mrs Austerly's gasp. Every one of his senses came alive to centre on Aurelia as he waited for what she might say next. Their surroundings were but a muted blur.

'That question you asked me.' Her blue eyes searched

her face as she moved towards her. Her scent filled him and his own ragged breathing sounded deafening to his ears as he waited for her to continue. 'Am I too late to change my mind?'

That dark agony moved aside, to bring a burst of light and hope into his life. Max snatched Aurelia up into his arms and spun her around.

'It would never be too late, my darling.' He allowed her body to slide down his until her feet touched the ground. 'Never.'

'Then I say yes, Max. Yes, yes, yes. I will marry you.'

A stifled sob reached Max's ears and he looked around to see Mrs Austerly with her handkerchief to her face. Mr Austerly noisily cleared his throat.

'Yes. Well. Indeed.' His cheeks bloomed a dull red and his eyes were suspiciously shiny. 'We won't intrude, but do allow us to be the first to congratulate you both.' He thrust out his hand and Max shook it and Aurelia hugged and kissed both the Austerlys.

'Thank you.' Max, full of love for everyone and everything now that he would have his heart's desire, kissed Mrs Austerly's cheek. 'We shall see you soon. At our wedding, I hope!'

As the couple walked away, Max said, 'Thank you for changing your mind, my darling.' His arm was around her and he felt as though he might never find the strength to release her. Ever again. 'Why *did* you change your mind?'

'I realised you were right. We would manage...*will* manage. And I realised I could never marry any other man but you. I would rather be happy and poor with you than wealthy and miserable with another man.'

His heart expanded in his chest until it felt like it might burst.

'What do you think your sisters will make of this?'

She drew in a deep breath. 'There is only one way to find out.'

Aurelia and Max walked up the stairs to the drawing room, pausing in front of the closed door beyond which they could hear the murmur of voices.

Their eyes met and they shared a smile. Aurelia's heart felt as though it was brimming over with all the love she could finally allow herself to feel for this man, without reservation. Never again did she want to see the pain that had clouded his eyes when she had turned down his proposal. There was nothing she wanted more than to banish those doubts and that pain for ever and she would spend her life striving to do just that.

'Are you ready?' she asked.

He nodded. Aurelia opened the door, took Max's hand in hers and they walked into a sudden silence. Every face turned to look at them with varying expressions of surprise and shock. Dolph was the first to speak.

'Miss Pike,' he said in his deep voice. 'Would you take the children downstairs, please?'

The governess shepherded the children, and Wolf, from the room. 'Tell Vardy to show you to the parlour and that I said for Cook to send refreshments up for you,' Aurelia said, as they passed.

The door closed.

'Everyone?' Ridiculously, her stomach roiled with nerves and her mouth felt dry now the time had come. 'This is Max, Lord Tregowan. Max, meet my family— my sisters, Leah and Beatrice; their husbands Lord Dolphinstone and Lord Jack Kingswood; Jack's brother, Lord Quantock; and Prue, you already know.'

Beatrice leapt to her feet. 'Aurelia?' Her voice was strained and Aurelia could see her concern. She couldn't blame her after witnessing that argument at the Smethwicks' ball. 'Are you all right? I wanted to come to you, but Leah said… Leah thought you needed to…um…you are holding his hand,' she ended, lamely.

'I am. And he is holding my hand, too, Bea. And everything is fine. We did need to…*um*, as you put it.'

Aurelia really did try to hold back her laugh, but she could not, she was so happy. It must have been contagious for, of a sudden, everyone else was laughing too, although their laughter was a touch strained. As soon as there was a lull, Max's fingers tightened their grip on Aurelia's hand.

'I have asked Aurelia to be my wife and she has agreed.' She beamed up at him, so thrilled that her dream was to come true. She felt as though they could face anything, as long as they were together. 'And in order that there is no awkwardness over the matter,' he went on, 'yes, I am aware she will forfeit her share of Lady Tregowan's inheritance. That is a consequence we are both fully prepared to accept.'

Everyone came to their feet at that. They crowded around, voicing their congratulations.

'You are sure about this, Aurelia?' Leah said quietly to Aurelia. 'You were always so adamant you would never risk your share.'

'I am certain.' Aurelia could tell that Max had heard Leah's comment and her reply. She raised her voice, catching Max's eye, and grinned at him. 'A woman,' she said, 'is entitled to change her mind. And, if you recall, I also always swore I would not wed an aristocrat but, well, here we are.' She hugged Max and kissed his cheek, breathing in his scent, feeling a flutter of desire awaken deep in her belly. 'And I could not be happier.'

'And neither could I,' Max said, hugging her back.

'At least you will still have the two hundred pounds,' said Leah. 'That is better than nothing.'

'Two hundred pounds?' Max gave Aurelia a puzzled look. 'What two hundred pounds?'

She bit her lip and then smiled, ruefully. 'I never did tell you—I was too cross when you asked what would happen to my share of the inheritance if I didn't meet all the conditions and then, somehow, I forgot all about it because it seemed irrelevant. So, yes, my share will be divided between Leah and Beatrice, but I won't have nothing. I will still get an annual allowance of two hundred pounds, plus a cottage on the Falconfield estate if I need it.'

Max laughed, lifted her high and swung her in a circle once again. 'Then we are rich indeed.' He kissed her full on the lips as he lowered her to the floor, seemingly oblivious to their audience. Or simply not caring who might witness his display of affection. 'So...what on earth took you so long to say yes, you little minx?'

Aurelia flicked her brows high. 'I was merely making sure you were not marrying me for my money, my lord,' she said haughtily.

She couldn't keep up the pretence, though, and she soon dissolved into laughter, flinging her arms around Max's neck and kissing him again.

'I love you, Max,' she whispered.

'And I...' he kissed her again '...love you, too.'

'Oh! This is the best wedding present *ever*,' declared a beaming Beatrice, her blue-grey eyes misted with tears.

Epilogue

August 1816

Falconfield Hall came into view as the carriage that had been sent to convey Max and Aurelia from Bristol bowled along the driveway that led from the huge wrought-iron entrance gates in a straight line to the house itself. It revealed an Elizabethan three-storeyed mansion of honey-coloured stone, with gable-roofed wings projecting forward at either end of the main body of the house and a profusion of stone-mullioned windows.

It was Aurelia's first visit to the country estate that could have belonged to her—one-third of it, anyway—and she and Max had been invited to a house party, together with Leah and Dolph and their family. 'Is the Hall how you remember it, Max?'

Max leaned forward to peer past her at the Hall.

'It is,' he said. 'The façade is largely the same as when it was originally built, but the interior was extensively modernised by the Third Earl.'

'Using money that could have been used on Tregowan.'

'Yes.' His finger on her cheek nudged her to face him and her heart twitched at the poorly concealed concern in his dark brown eyes. 'I hope coming here won't lead you to regret all that you gave up to marry me, my sweet.'

'I would have given up Carlton House itself to wed you, my darling Max.'

She snuggled against him, slipping one hand beneath his jacket as she feathered kisses along his strong jawline. She knew he'd been worrying about this visit, although he had tried to hide his increasing anxiety, and she knew he would not fully let go of that worry until the visit was over.

This first visit would be the hardest, yet she was fizzing with joy at the prospect of seeing her sisters again. Beatrice and Jack had taken at residence in Falconfield Hall, which lay midway between Bristol and Bath, while Leah and Dolph, of course, lived at Dolph's family seat, Dolphinstone Court, situated on the north Somerset coast. Briefly, her thoughts rested on Tregowan Place. The roof was now weathertight and, soon, work would begin on refurbishing the main body of the house. The wings could wait until a later date but, at least—she laid her hand on her still-flat belly—their baby would be born in the main house and not in the gatekeeper's lodge where they currently lived.

Max stroked her cheek and smiled at her. 'As would I, sweetheart. I would marry you again in a heartbeat.'

The carriage rocked to a halt. The front door flew open and three small figures tumbled out on to the forecourt.

'Aunt 'relia! Uncle Max!'

Max jumped to the ground and lifted Aurelia down, not waiting for the steps, and they greeted Stevie, Nicky and Tilly, who was now walking with more confidence. Then Wolf joined them, bouncing around with excited little grunts, demanding his share of the attention.

'Children!' Miss Pike hurried from the house. 'Where are your manners? Do not mob your fellow guests the moment they arrive. You will have ample time to spend together this week.'

'But this is a splendid welcome, Miss Pike.' Max ruffled Stevie's hair. 'Just what was needed to make us feel right at home.'

The governess began to shepherd her charges away and it was only then Aurelia noticed Beatrice and Jack had joined them.

She breathed in sharply to quell the surge of emotion that thickened her throat at the sight of her sister. She could not speak but, it seemed, neither could Beatrice, for she simply shook her head and opened her arms. The two hugged one another, their feelings clear without the need for words.

'Welcome to Falconfield Hall.' Jack—his familiar, easy smile in place—shook hands with Max and then kissed Aurelia on the cheek. 'Come on in. The others arrived an hour ago.'

By unspoken mutual agreement—or so it seemed— Aurelia and Beatrice hung behind as the two men strode to the house.

'You look so happy, Bea. So content.' Aurelia's younger sister had certainly bloomed in the months since they had last met.

'I am, Aurelia. So very happy.' Beatrice sighed. 'As do you.' She halted, and grabbed Aurelia's hand. 'Is...? How is it at Tregowan Place?' She waved an arm, encompassing the Hall. 'I cannot help but feel—'

Aurelia gave her a fierce hug. 'No! Say no more. I chose Max and I would do so again. I want you to feel nothing but happiness for me, for that is what I feel every day when I awake. Happiness. Contentment. Joy at life. *Our* life.'

'May I join you?'

Leah stood framed in the open doorway. Tall and elegant as usual, her red hair bright in the afternoon sunshine. Elegant, but…

Aurelia ran to her. 'Leah!' Those tears she had held in her throat had somehow reached her eyes and now burned there. She hugged her older sister, but gently. Not the fierce hug she had given Beatrice. 'You…you are…?' She indicated the pronounced swell of Leah's belly.

Leah laughed and tightened the hug. 'I am. And I promise you a proper hug will do me no harm.'

'I have not had the chance to ask when the baby will be born, Leah,' said Beatrice, as they lingered on the doorstep as though they each realised they needed this time together, just the three of them, before joining the others.

'At the turn of the year,' Leah said.

Beatrice beamed. 'I, too, am with child. It will be born some time in February, we think.'

'How perfect…' Aurelia's voice came strangled from her throat '…for my baby is due in early March.'

They exchanged delighted smiles. 'What wonderful family gatherings we have to look forward to,' said Leah. 'And yet, just eight months ago, none of us knew of the others' existence.'

'Or that we would all find true love in such unexpected ways,' added Aurelia.

'And so swiftly.' Beatrice laughed. 'We fell in love one after the other and our weddings followed suit, so it seems fitting our babies will follow that pattern, too.'

'And Letty—Max's sister—is also *enceinte*,' said Aurelia. 'It must be catching!'

'Max's mother must be delighted,' said Leah.

They had all met Max's mother and sister—plus Letty's surprise new fiancé, Alfred Casbourne—when they had finally arrived in London just after Eastertide. Max and Aurelia had delayed their nuptials until his family could attend and then there was yet another wedding when Letty and Alfie got married, to everyone's delight. Max's mother had made no secret of her desire to become a grandmama.

'She is thrilled,' said Aurelia. 'We shall go on to visit them when we leave here.'

The Casbournes lived in Wiltshire and Max's mother had made her home with them, easing yet more of the financial pressures on Max.

She looked around, surprised and a touch hurt that Prue had not come outside to greet her. 'Where is Prue?'

Aurelia had missed their former chaperon more than she had thought possible after the Season had ended and they had all gone their separate ways, to build new lives in their new homes. Any one of the sisters would have offered Prue a home, but Leah and Aurelia had agreed between themselves to leave Beatrice to make the first offer—firstly because Beatrice and Jack were to make Falconfield Hall their home and Prue had lived there as Sarah Tregowan's companion for many years, and, secondly, because they were both aware that Beatrice viewed Prue as a second mother and they agreed she deserved all the love and security she could get after her life at the hands of the Fothergills.

'Oh, she is in her element with the children here. Do not expect to get much of her attention while they are around,' said Leah with a wink.

'Oh!' Beatrice halted just outside the open doorway to which they had been heading and her voice hushed to a whisper. 'I have something to tell you both. You know how we plan to set Falconfield up as a place for soldiers disabled by the war to come here to learn new trades?'

'Of course.' Beatrice and Jack had spent time during the Season gaining subscribers to the Kingswood Foundation and raising funds, and both Leah and Aurelia had helped.

'Well, Jack met up with a fellow officer, Captain Irving, who is helping with our endeavour. He has visited Falconfield a few times and we are *convinced* there is a spark between him and Prue, although they are both trying very hard to pretend it does not exist. Is that not wonderful?'

'That *is* wonderful!' Aurelia was so happy for Prue and she hoped Beatrice was right.

'I shall look forward to seeing them together.' Leah's beautiful bluey-green eyes twinkled.

'Unfortunately, the Captain is not here this week because he is looking for suitable veterans to benefit from the Kingswood Foundation. But, once we are all set up, he is to live in a cottage here on the estate. So he will be here on a permanent basis.'

'Beatrice, you must swear to keep us fully posted,' said Aurelia.

'I will.'

At that precise moment, a tall, powerfully built figure darkened the doorway.

'Sharing secrets, ladies?' Dolph's ruggedly handsome face creased into a smile. 'Greetings, Aurelia.' He bent to kiss her cheek. 'It is good to see you again. Now, come on in. I am sure we all wish to hear the gossip that is keeping you three skulking out here in the hall.'

In the salon, Aurelia crossed immediately to embrace Prue, who was sitting on a sofa with Tilly on her lap and that huge, black, motheaten cat, Spartacus, curled up by her side. She looked… Blissful was the word that came into Aurelia's head. So very happy and content.

'Aurelia! My dear. You look radiant. But then, you always did once we got a few decent meals inside you.'

'It is lovely to see you again, Prue. Have you settled in well?'

'Oh, yes.' She sighed contentedly, rubbed her cheek

against little Tilly's fair curls and stroked Spartacus, who responded with a rumbling purr. 'I always did love it here. Please forgive me for not coming outside to greet you, but I met Miss Pike with the children on their way in and they were so excited I thought I should stay and help to calm them down.'

'Well, you have certainly done that.' Stevie and Nicky were sitting at the far side of the room with Miss Pike, who was reading to them. Wolf was sprawled across the governess's feet. Aurelia sat on the sofa, with Spartacus between them. 'And soon you will have a new baby to help Beatrice with, too.'

'Yes. Is it not wonderful? And Leah, too.' She eyed Aurelia, her gaze drifting downwards.

Aurelia laughed. 'You will be too polite to ask,' she said, leaning close so her voice didn't carry, 'but, yes. We, too, are to be blessed.'

Dinner that evening was a lively affair—the conversation ranged over so many diverse topics it was hard to keep up at times—but Max enjoyed the chance to catch up with all the family's latest news. And, especially, he enjoyed watching Aurelia with her sisters, a feeling of deep contentment settling over him at her utter joy in being with them again.

He had fretted about this visit in case it reminded her of all she had given up by marrying him, but she had assured him she had no regrets and then she had demonstrated as much earlier, when they had retired to their bedchamber to rest before dinner. He just managed to bite back a wolf-ish smile at that particular erotic memory.

After dinner, Prue retired, leaving the rest of them to return to the drawing room. As they moved into the room, however, Max sensed a sudden change in atmosphere, almost as though there was an air of expectancy about rest of the family that he could not fathom. His gut stirred uneasily and he saw his puzzlement reflected in the slight crease between Aurelia's golden brows as they all sat down. All except Dolph, who remained on his feet, standing in front of the unlit fireplace.

Silence fell. A tense silence. Max caught a look of significance pass between Leah and Dolph that he could not decipher and he was aware of Jack and Beatrice both watching Dolph as though waiting for him to speak.

He frowned, narrowing his eyes at his brother-in-law. 'There is clearly something here I...we...don't understand. So, come on. Let us have it out in the open.'

Dolph raised his brows and then smiled. 'Apologies,' he said. 'I...we...did not mean to be mysterious.'

'We? You speak for...?'

'I speak for the four of us. Me and Leah. Jack and Bea. We are all in agreement. It concerns the inheritance.'

He felt Aurelia reach for his hand and he wrapped his fingers around hers. 'Go on.'

'We wish to offer you—both of you—Aurelia's share of the inheritance.'

Aurelia gave a soft gasp. 'But...you cannot!' she said. 'The terms of the will...'

'The legal side has been completed and the property is in our names. So we can, if we choose to and if you are happy to accept. Leah and Beatrice have both been unhappy about you only getting two hundred pounds a year, Aurelia. And, to be frank, all of us are uncomfortable about the way Max was cut out of the will on what was a misunderstanding.'

Max felt the weight of Aurelia's gaze as she looked at him. He inhaled, his thoughts in a whirl as his pride reared its head and urged him to refuse point blank. He was aware such pride was probably stupid. It was definitely stubborn. But…it was hard to dismiss the feeling he was being treated as a charity case. He met Dolph's calm, grey gaze—the gaze of a diplomat and a negotiator, for Dolph had been an intrinsic part of the negotiations for a long-term peace plan in Europe after the end of the Napoleonic Wars.

'You would be a fool to turn us down, Max. For Aurelia's sake. For your children's sakes.'

He had a point. This was not just about him. Max was still coming to terms with the idea of becoming a father—the idea was daunting and yet hugely exciting, and he could not wait to welcome the little one to the world.

Jack stirred, leaning forward to prop his elbows on his thighs. 'How is your mine faring now, after Austerly's investment?'

'Well enough.'

'Have you found more copper?'

'Yes.'

And a lifeline it had proved, allowing them to continue the refurbishment of Tregowan Place, albeit slowly, as their finances improved. It had also helped when Letty had married Casbourne, relieving Max of the need to both fund a Season for his sister and to provide a suitable home for his mother.

All of that, though…it rankled that he had not provided it himself.

But there was still so much left to do. He would be a fool to cavil when there was a desperate need to repair and modernise his tenanted farms, especially since the price of wool had dropped so drastically after the war. And now… this summer's weather had been an utter disaster so far. Nobody could explain just why the temperature had stayed so low and the sun had barely shown its face all year, but the harvest nationwide would be poor, and the talk was of hunger stalking the land next winter.

'The weather will harm this year's harvest,' said Jack, as though he had read Max's mind. 'It will put everyone under strain.'

'But...this is your home, Jack,' said Aurelia. 'And you have the Foundation to think of. It would not be right to take even a part of that from you.'

'You would not have to if you choose not to,' said Bea. 'You could choose to do as Dolph and Leah have done.'

'Yes,' said Leah. 'We have transferred our share of Falconfield Hall to the Kingswood Foundation. That way it is under Jack and Bea's control. You would still have the income from the investments, and a one-third share of the house in London.'

'I see.' Aurelia tightened her hold on Max's hand, and he turned his head to meet her eyes. 'What do you think, Max?'

'The idea to make this offer was unanimous,' said Dolph. 'If it had not been, it would not have been made.'

The income from that investment. Five thousand pounds a year. Max stared into Aurelia's beloved face. What could they do with that money? Suddenly, a life filled with possibilities stretched before them instead of a life spent making compromises.

'Then, thank you for your generosity. And we accept. We are delighted to accept!'

'And that,' said Jack, leaping to his feet and tugging on a bell pull, 'calls for a celebration.'

The door opened and Vardy—who, along with all the London staff, had moved to Somerset with Jack and Beatrice—entered almost immediately, carrying a tray with two bottles of champagne and six glasses. When each of them was holding a glass of the sparkling liquid and the door had closed behind Vardy, Max raised his glass.

'I have no words.' Well, he did, but they seemed to be lodged somewhere in his throat. 'Thank you.'

'Thank you all from the bottom of our hearts,' added Aurelia. 'And here is to us—the Dolphinstones, the Kingswoods and the Tregowans. To my wonderful, beautiful sisters. To my beloved Max. And, most of all, here is to Sarah, Lady Tregowan, without whom we would never have met and life would be…'

She stopped and gasped. Shook her head. 'I cannot even bear to imagine what life would have been.'

Looking around, Max saw her emotion mirrored in the others' faces.

'To us!' Six voices sounded as one. 'And to Lady Tregowan!'

* * * * *

*If you enjoyed this story, be sure to read
the first two books in Janice Preston's
Lady Tregowan's Will miniseries*

The Rags-to-Riches Governess
The Cinderella Heiress

And why not check out her other great reads

Lady Olivia and the Infamous Rake
His Convenient Highland Wedding
Daring to Love the Duke's Heir
Christmas with His Wallflower Wife
The Earl with the Secret Past